I'd like to dedicate this book to my best friend Reid, long may he live, and to my father, may he rest in peace.

I'd also like to thank the people who've read my books and my short stories on the way to getting to finishing the Mostly Human story. And I would like to thank all the people who have participated in Poetry Club over the years.

Thank you all, I hope you enjoy it.

Tinpot Publishing

MOSTLY HUMAN²

D.I. JOLLY

Mostly Human 2

Published by Tinpot Publishing

Cover illustration: Tom Kyffin

Copyright of text and characters © D. I. Jolly

Back Page Photograph by Ted Titus

www.tinpotbooks.com   First published Electronically 2020

Second Print edition 2020   ISBN: 9798563399921

Contents

Prologue

Well, I spent two weeks on that ship before it docked again in Bergen on the west coast of Norway – turns out that's where Syn gets most of its milk. It was the longest I'd spent as Mork in one go and I'd started to forget what it was like being human. But I still had brief flashes, and I remembered Danny telling me about a wolf sanctuary in Norway he'd read about and had always wanted to visit. Set up by two women in the Børgefjell, a small mountain range in the middle of the country, and far away from any kind of civilisation. The idea was that people volunteered there for a few months, mostly students doing environmental or veterinary studies or something like that. They'd work for a pittance, certainly by Norwegian standards. There was a small bar-cum-coffee shop; accommodation was somewhere between a bed-and-breakfast and a backpackers; then there was the sanctuary and the mountain – and that was it, for kilometres. I didn't actually know where it was, but I didn't care – once I was in Norway, that was where I was heading. I didn't know if anyone was chasing me, but I was running. I wasn't really sure what I was going to do, but I knew I needed to do something ... to somehow get a handle on my situation. I'd been brushing it aside for too long and a wolf sanctuary seemed as good a place as any to learn about being a wolf.

Chapter 1

Six months had slipped by since Alex had arrived at The Sanctuary, and winter had set in with a vengeance. He had quickly endeared himself to Aina and Kristin, who owned and operated the place, and installed himself behind the bar. Thanks to a thick black beard and a small dose of denial, he was – for the first time in his life – just another guy. Not a rock star, not a werewolf. Just a charming and disarming barman, a little lost, but smart, polite and friendly. He would occasionally go out on solitary camping trips into the mountains and liked to help out wherever he could. Along with Kristin and Aina, The Sanctuary had two other permanent residents: Fredrik and Ella, forest guards who were there to oversee activities in the wildness and make sure people were safe. They were also responsible for transporting the quarterly influx of volunteers back and forth from Trondheim. In the six months Alex had been there he'd seen two batches come and go, and both times it had been a party, three intense months of working hard and, thanks to Alex, playing hard. Then the volunteers were returned to their normal lives, with some experience under their belts and a nice shiny letter of recommendation to include in their CVs.

Fredrik and Ella had been there pretty much from the start but they had it easier; every two weeks one would return home to see family and have a week to unwind, but Kristin and Aina stayed on full time. The Sanctuary was their entire lives and they inevitably grew very attached to their volunteers. So they relied on Alex, Fredrik and Ella for stability, and considered them family and they, in turn, were everyone's moms. Ella and Fredrik were charmed by it, but still had other lives beyond the wilderness; Ella had a husband back in Oslo and Fredrik took each day as it came. Alex, on the other hand, loved every minute of it. It was the simplest his life had ever been. It was also, however, the longest he'd gone without sex since he was sixteen, and Kristin had decided that it was her personal mission to find him a nice woman before he moved on.

Alex stood behind the bar and checked the clock, waiting for the sound of Fredrik's truck so that he could start making coffee and lay out the food for the next batch of volunteers. For the first time since he'd arrived, he was slightly nervous. Not because he thought something might go wrong, but because in the two-week build-up, Kristin had not stopped talking about one of the new girls she'd hired.

"Oh, I can't wait for you to meet her – she's perfect for you!"

All of this filled him with a weird mix of embarrassment, dread and maternal love – it reminded him of his mother and what she might have been like now that he was older. Alex's ears twitched and he let out a short snort, trying to hide his smile as the door burst open and Kristin and Ella came bounding in.

"They're here! They're here, quick, get the coffee ready ... and don't forget to smile!" Then, looking at his beard added, "Well, with your eyes."

He frowned, and then let his smile shine through.

"Calm down, will you ... I'm sticking to my original statement though. I'd rather be with no one than with the wrong one."

Ella smiled and joined in.

"Bullshit!'

She slapped him on the shoulder. "You'd rather maintain that whole dark-and-mysterious thing you've got going on than open yourself up to connecting with someone on an emotional level. Typical man!"

She then stuck out her tongue. Alex kept his smile, and shook his head, while Kristin went into the back room to fetch the sandwiches and snacks they had prepared for the volunteers. The bar wasn't huge; along one wall were four built-in booths that seated four, six stools sat in front of the bar and there were three tables with chairs – which, considering they only ever had to accommodate nine people, plus the occasional tourist or two – was more than enough.

Alex had been fighting off the urge to ask about the girl since he first heard about her, but now that she was just beyond the doors his curiosity was piqued. What would she look like? What about her had made Kristin so excited? The questions played on his mind but he pushed them back, insisting to himself that it didn't matter now anyway, especially as he was about to meet her. Fredrik opened the door and invited the four well-wrapped bundles in.

"This is the bar ... where you'll be spending most of your time when you're not working, whether that was your original plan or not."

The volunteers began to peel off their layers of coats and hang them on the hooks at the door. Then, as one shivering creature, they headed straight to the coffee and food. Alex allowed himself a second to glance over them but quickly felt a little stupid, taken up by Kristin's game. He blushed under his beard, relieved that no one could tell. Then he turned and walked a little too determinedly to the back room. Of the four new volunteers, only one was a girl, but he was so annoyed with himself that he hadn't realised. Cassandra, on the other hand, had noticed the stark contrast between Alex's jet-black hair and pale blue eyes the moment she walked in. She was American, about five foot seven, with a slightly curly mess of black hair and bright green eyes currently hidden behind black-rimmed glasses. She was in her last year of veterinary school and had come to The Sanctuary for her final practical training. Alex, a little calmer, and less rattled, reappeared a minute later holding a second tray of sandwiches, which he placed near the others and made an attempt to smile at the four new faces.

"Howdy, folks, I'm Mork and I'll be your barman for the rest of your stay here."

He had switched names the moment he arrived. Mork was the only one he knew he'd respond to automatically. They all mumbled greetings through mouthfuls of food.

"And that," he said, raising a hand and pointing at Kristin, "is your boss."

They all turned to Kristin who was beaming at them from the doorway.

"Hello, and welcome to The Sanctuary. It's so nice to finally have real faces to go along with the pictures and the phone calls. Once you've all warmed up a bit and finished eating, we'll start the tour. This is obviously the bar and where we do breakfasts if you'd like. Each of your rooms here, though, has a small kitchen attached and we get supplies delivered once a month, so if you'd prefer to sort out your own food just let us know and we can make a plan. Fredrik will be taking your things to your rooms; everyone gets their own. If you'd like to swap around, that's perfectly okay, but each room is the same. We usually put boys on one side and girls on the other, but since that's a little unbalanced this time it's girl and staff on one side and boys on the other."

She smiled at Cassandra.

"Don't worry, though, you'll have Ella between you and the other two and she's far tougher than they are so if you scream in the night she'll come save you."

Fredrik and Ella nodded in agreement and everyone laughed.

"Just a word of warning to the guys," Fredrik piped up. "If any of you scream in the night you're on your own."

His smile grew broader and he winked at the crowd. Ella rolled her eyes, punched him in the arm, and Kristin continued.

"No, we all look after each other here. Between the bar, the house and the sanctuary, we're going to be spending a lot of time together, and with winter here we're going to be indoors a lot of the time.

It's not always easy but you can always come to the bar for a drink with Mork or stay in your room if you want to be alone. We have lots of books and games … We know what it's like to live here, and we love it. You'll meet my partner Aina a little later today as she's currently asleep. Any questions?"

The room fell silent while everyone hurried to chew and swallow their food. Then one of the guys, an Englishman by the name of Greg, put up his hand.

"Uuhmmm, so when do we start working?"

"Technically, tomorrow, but should we be alerted about something in the night we have to react. None of you are on call tonight, but we always have someone who stays sober and well rested just in case. Tonight, that's me, so I'm sorry I won't be able to celebrate your arrival with you, but I promise we'll have plenty of time to get to know each other. Tomorrow we'll start with lectures and explain what exactly we do here and why we do it, but we'll only get to that in the afternoon. We had to abandon morning lectures when Mork started here."

They all turned to look at Mork, who bowed.

"I do what I can."

Cassandra shot her hand up, her eyes fixed on Mork, who turned then to Kristin who beamed back at him and then back to Cassandra.

"Yes?"

"This isn't really relevant but do you have anything other than coffee? Tea maybe?"

Mork took stock of the girl for a moment; she seemed different somehow.

"Yeah," he volunteered, "we have tea if you'd like."

"Great. Can I come by later?"

And before he could stop himself, he said, "It's a date."

Kristin almost squeaked with excitement but checked herself and pushed on.

"All right, if there are no further questions then let's start the tour."

The volunteers grabbed their coats as they shuffled out into the cold behind Kristin and Ella. Fredrik waited for everyone to leave and then took up the barstool closest to Mork and poured himself some coffee.

"Well, that was quick ... Must be the beard. You know, she barely spoke to anyone on the drive here."

"Huh?" Mork shook himself out of the daze he'd drifted into.

"Yeah, she mostly just slept."

"Who?"

"Your date?" Fredrik laughed.

"Oh come on," Mork frowned. "You know that's just a turn of phrase. It's not a real date."

Fredrik leaned over the bar and patted him on the shoulder.

"It's as real as they get out here, man. Whether you like it or not, my friend, you have a date with the only single girl we're going to see for the rest of the winter."

He leaned back in his chair and took a sip of coffee.

"I'd be jealous, but you know back home I have to fend girls off with a stick. It's why I took this job, to get away from it all. Too many girls in one place just makes life complicated. I prefer the simple life."

Mork laughed. "Yeah? I wouldn't know."

He raised his cup at Fredrik.

"Lucky you," said Fredrik, clinking his against Mork's. "I tell you, it's a real burden being this pretty."

"Oh, I can only imagine, must be like being a rock star."

"Not far off actually ... I keep telling you, man, you need to come with me to Oslo when I go down. You'll have the time of your life. Well, it would have been, but now that you're practically married."

"Now that I'm what?"

"Please, I saw the way she manipulated you into asking her out so quickly ... She'll have you proposing by tomorrow morning, just you wait and see."

Mork dipped a finger into his coffee and flicked it at Fredrik who flinched and then replied in kind.

"Don't get angry at me, just because you can't handle the truth. But maybe getting some pussy will be good for you, get you out of your head and back into the real world for a change. Or at least keep you warm in winter. I don't know what it's like where you're from, but here it gets cold. Really cold, if you know what I mean ..."

"Oh, it gets pretty cold in Canada, don't you worry."

"Oh yeah? I still don't think you sound Canadian."

"Too much television as a child."

Fredrik laughed. "So, you going to help me unload the truck or what?"

"Yeah, go on then."

They quickly finished what was left in their cups and headed out into the cold.

"I'll take your girlfriend's stuff; that way, you won't appear too needy."

"If you keep this up, I'm going to start locking away my beers."

Fredrik laughed a little, pulled the room assignment list out of his pocket, tore it in half and handed a piece to Mork.

"Ouch, man, too far."

Chuckling, they went about splitting the luggage between them before carrying it off to the rooms.

The house was essentially a collection of ten single flats, five on either side of a narrow courtyard. Each room had a reasonable-sized front room with built-in cupboards, and a small passage leading to a bathroom on one side and kitchenette on the other. Mork was handsome and broad shouldered, and still a lot stronger than he looked, whereas Fredrik was well practised and efficient, so it didn't take them long to get everything moved in and sorted. Fredrik, with his typical Nordic features – blond hair, blue eyes and high cheekbones, was six foot when his hair was combed back, which it always was. He wasn't especially well built, but not thin either. His muscles were hard and wiry, built up by hard work rather than hours in the gym.

Once they'd moved someone into a room, they wrote the new occupant's name on a small white board on the door and left the key in the lock. No one in the house really locked their doors but newcomers often took a few weeks to get out of the habit. Fredrik stayed in the first room on the right, then Mork, then Ella. The next two rooms would generally be the guys, with the girls staying in the two opposite, leaving three for any tourists who may come through.

Kristin and Aina tried to keep it an even split between girls and boys, but as it was winter and coming up to Christmas the majority of applications had been men, and the only stand-out female applicant had been Cassandra. It hadn't been until Kristin had wrapped up her telephone interview that she decided that she and Mork were made for each other. It hadn't been something Cassandra had actually said, rather the way she answered. Her calm confidence reminded Kristin so much of him.

Fredrik and Mork returned to the truck and quickly whipped through it to make sure they hadn't missed anything.

"Oh, hey, I've got good news and bad news."

"Yes?"

"Your girlfriend brought a guitar."

"She's not …" But he gave up before he could even finish, then sighed and said, "So's that the good news or the bad news?"

"It's both."

Fredrik grinned and Mork rolled his eyes, but Fredrik continued: "One thing I don't understand, though … I've seen you dodge a few women now. What on earth made you say something as stupid as 'It's a date' this time round?"

Mork stopped for a moment and thought about it.

"Absolutely no idea … It was just the first thing that found its way out of my mouth."

Fredrik shook his head.

"See? That's what I was talking about. If you can't get that under control, before you know it you'll be asking her to marry you. Not because you want to, but because you can't think of anything else to say."

Mork stared at him for a few moments before saying, "You know man, sometimes I really don't know if you're joking or not."

Fredrik threw back his head and laughed.

"That's the trick. Always keep them guessing."

Mork shook his head.

"Let's just get inside. If we stay out here any longer, I'm going to lose the parts she's most interested in."

Fredrik nodded.

"If that's the part she's most interested in, she's going to be seriously disappointed."

The two laughed together as they made their way back to the bar. They needed to clean up and get everything ready for the welcome party. Fredrik then went to his office in The Sanctuary and

Mork headed to his room to shower, meditate and nap.

He had just drifted off to sleep when he heard a gentle knock at the door; blurrily, he crawled out of bed, grabbed a towel, wrapped it around his waist and opened the door. Cassandra gasped in surprise to be greeted by a mostly naked man, and promptly blushed crimson. Mork was over six feet tall, with the body of a deity. Like Fredrik, he wasn't massive, but without a shirt Cassandra couldn't help but notice that his muscles were lean and extremely well defined. She just stood there gaping, which gave him just enough time to realise he was standing near naked in front of a stranger and couldn't help but laugh.

"Sorry, just give me a second."

He quickly closed the door and scrambled around for some clothes. He pulled on the trousers and shirt he'd been wearing earlier then reopened to door, to see her rubbing her cheeks with her hands and taking a few deep breaths.

"Hello?"

She quickly looked up at him again.

"Hi."

There was another awkward silent moment before he remembered.

"Tea! That's why you're here! I totally forgot, I'm so sorry. Let me just grab some shoes and we can head down to the bar."

Cassandra nodded as he turned in a few small circles looking for his boots, then dropped down onto his bed to pull them on. She didn't walk in but leaned in a little to take a look around. His room was a boy's room. Immediately left of the door was the bed, next to which was a small table covered in a dozen books, empty beer cans and a small lamp. The rest of the room was fairly tidy, except for a mound of clothes that looked like it could be the laundry pile. And, finally, there was a desk littered with papers and pens and a chair against the wall directly in line with the door, with a small fridge sitting discreetly under it. The wall in front of the desk seemed to have things stuck on it but from where she was standing she couldn't really tell what they were. Mork sprang back to his feet, grabbed his coat from its hook and made his way over to Cassandra.

"Right, let's go get you that tea," he smiled a little sheepishly.

She smiled wickedly, then crossed her arms and raised her eyebrows.

"Are you always so blasé on first dates?"

It was his turn to blush, and for the second time that day, be grateful for his beard. To cover his tracks, he came back with a dramatic false sincerity.

"Oh please, my lady, do accept my sincerest of apologies."

With a flourish, he cocked his elbow and bowed his head slightly.

"If you can find it in your heart to forgive me, and allow me a second chance, though I dare say I don't deserve it ..."

She covered her face with her hands and tried to stifle her laughter but the sheer ridiculousness of the performance got to her.

"You're insane."

He smiled and for a moment was entirely taken by her charm, and by how much she was loving his little joke.

"Is that a yes then? You forgive me?"

She slipped her arm through his and nodded politely.

"Indeed, you may escort me for tea this afternoon, good sir."

"Splendid."

With that, they walked merrily arm in arm to the bar, just a few minutes away in the snow. Mork tried to ignore the faint but distinct smell of attraction coming off Cassandra and focused instead on the disappointment on the faces of the other three volunteers as the pair walked passed. It wasn't that he liked one-upping people, but he did find it funny and the smile on his face broadened. In the back of his mind there was a low growl, reminding him that he needed to be careful around this woman. It had been a long time since he'd interacted with anyone that way and he needed to remember to maintain control. Since fleeing Syn Island, the one thought that had never left his mind was the fear of losing control, and now it rang just a little louder in his head than usual. They stopped at the bar and Mork quickly unhooked his arm and held open the door. Cassandra gave a mock curtsey and walked in. He took a deep breath before following her and told himself that he was, in fact, being stupid. This was tea with a volunteer, nothing more. In reality, he'd done it loads of times with many of them, of both genders, and it was always fine. He had to admit, though, that it felt a little different with Cassandra, and he wasn't exactly sure how or why she'd gotten under his skin so quickly.

"If you wanna grab a table, I'll make the tea and join you in a minute."

"Great, thanks ... And just anywhere?"

"As long as it doesn't have decorations on it."

She looked around and realised that the tables had been shifted together and had tablecloths. They were covered in glasses and platters and various party accoutrements.

"Uhmmm ..." Cassandra frowned nervously, "are we even allowed in here?"

Mork had already disappeared into the little back room but called out.

"Yes of course, it's my bar after all. Don't worry. Also, it's not like the welcoming party was a surprise."

She bit her lower lip and made her way over to one of the booths. Suddenly the awkwardness of the situation struck her and she flushed a little, shifting nervously in her seat. Who was this man and why was she acting so strange and so out of character? She didn't do this kind of thing, she was a career girl. She was going to be a vet and help endangered animals. That was the plan; that was why she was in the middle of the frozen Nordics in the first place. Not so she could hook up with some hairy barman, as charming as he may be. Besides, he probably did this with the prettiest girl of every batch of volunteers. For a moment, she thought about bolting, but as she turned to look at the door, she saw him reappear holding a tray with two cups, a sugar bowl, milk jug and tea pot.

"Tadaaah! I give you ... tea."

He quickly made his way to the table and set the tray down. He then straightened slightly and Cassandra noticed his nose twitch a few times.

"Are... you all right?"

"Yeah ... Just, uhmmm, trying not to sneeze."

He frowned.

"I guess the real question is, are you all right?"

"Why? What do you mean by that?"

Her reply came fast and with the faintest hint of defensiveness. Mork took a deep breath in through his nose. It was a smell he recognised; not exactly fear but a clear waver in confidence. It reminded him of Waterdogs standing backstage, waiting to do their first big stage show. She smelt of stage fright. The moment when you suddenly lose confidence in something you were absolutely sure about just a moment before.

He dropped his head to one side then to the other, she allowing mild annoyance to brew at being judged by said hairy barman. He smiled and started pouring the tea.

"I get it, you know ... I really do."

"Get what, exactly?"

"Out in the middle of nowhere, on a big brave new adventure and, just hours in, you're sitting down on your own with one of the locals. It's all really fast and really ... intimate? In an already really intimate situation. It can rattle one's cage a bit."

"Excuse me?" She frowned at him.

"Not intimate as in candles and rose petals, but if you take a step back and look again, you'll see that we already basically live together and no matter what happens now we're going to see each other practically every day for the next three months."

She stared at him blankly for a moment before coming to her senses.

"That's quite a line, does it work?"

She had meant it to sound casual, but she was forcing it and it came out a little harsh. He winced without meaning to, but managed to hold back a low growl as he stopped stirring his tea and locked eyes with her, and she stifled a breath.

"Ma'am, nothing about me changed between walking in here and fetching you a pot of tea. Now something has clearly shaken your confidence."

He leaned back in his chair smiling and took a long sip of his tea, pinkie extended.

"So, my dearest of dears, I cannot tell you how grateful I am that you've granted me the pleasure of your company. I do just wish you would relax a little, and I'd love to know more about you."

She hesitated for a second, realising what he was trying to do, and that, when she thought about it, she did feel safe with him. He was being over confident, piggish, and she didn't like that he was basically telling her to calm down, but she really did want to get back to the playful repartee of a few minutes before.

"Well, what would you like to know?"

He could see her shoulders shift ever so slightly as she eased back into the situation.

"Well, for starters, I see you've brought a guitar. Do you play?"

She let out a little uncomfortable laugh.

"No, no … I mean, I've had a few lessons, but not really. I brought it along in the hope that I'd have time to practise and learn a bit more. I've got some of those Guitar for Dummies books with me as well. What about you?"

A cold shiver rippled from between his shoulder blades and quickly ran over his whole body, but he managed to keep it from showing on his face.

"Me? Naah, never been very musical. I mean, I like listening to it but that's about as far as it goes."

As he spoke he couldn't help but think, lie number one.

"Never wanted to learn?"

"Who hasn't really thought about it? But I don't know, not really my thing."

"Fair enough." There was a brief pause. "So, what do you want to be when you grow up?"

A mocking laugh slipped from his lips: "When I grow up?"

"Yeah, well …" Cassandra gestured around them. "You're a barman in the middle of nowhere. Is this really all you want from life?"

"I don't know," he shrugged. "I'm happy here, I meet new and interesting people, and sometimes I get to help animals in need. What's so bad about that?"

She genuinely hadn't thought about it like that.

"Okay, yeah, I get that, but is there no big dream?"

"Sure there is. I mean, who doesn't want to be Batman? But then again, maybe this is all part of my secret training? Just do me a favour, if you hear about a mysterious hero saving the people of

Gothenburg, don't tell anyone about me?"

She laughed and rolled her eyes.

"You really are a little strange, aren't you?"

"That's the second time you've said something like that and it's only the first day. Imagine how it's going to be after three months."

He took another sip of his tea and smiled. Her shoulders relaxed a little more and laughter returned.

"I think, Mr Mork, I'm looking forward to finding out."

"I'll drink to that."

He held up his cup and they clinked – "Cheers!" – before both taking another sip.

"Now your turn. What brings you to this frozen wasteland I call home?"

"Oh well, you know, final year of veterinary school … This is a great learning opportunity, and it's supposed to be an awesome experience. It'll look great on the CV. Plus, I wanted to get away for a bit, get out of the US and see some more of the world. I like dogs and want to feel like what I do in my life makes a difference. I mean, my other options were to take an intern job on a farm in the same state I grew up in and went to school in. I wanted a bit of adventure."

"Groovy, most people in that situation take the easy road and never go on a single adventure in their lives."

Cassandra frowned.

"Groovy? Really? That's the word we're going with?"

"Don't hate the groovy, it's a great word and I will bring it back."

"Aah, okay, sure, good luck with that one. But I think you have to be somewhere where people might actually hear you use it, to bring it back, and or possibly be famous?"

"I could be famous … one day, maybe."

She let out a sharp burst of laughter then pulled herself together as he dropped his jaw in mock offence.

"And just what are you insinuating?"

She blushed and held up her hands, fighting back more laugher.

"Nothing. Nothing, I promise … I have total faith in your campaign to become famous for bringing back the word 'groovy'."

He pulled himself up and putting on a voice of a movie general, said, "That's good to hear, that's the kind of dedication we here at Groovy need! Now, if you are as committed as you say you are, I expect to hear you say 'groovy' at least twice a day, as a replacement for more trendy words like 'cool' or 'awesome'."

She wanted to bark, 'Sir! Yes, sir!' but couldn't hold back the laughter long enough to get it out, at which point he too lost the plot a little and the two collapsed in helpless hysterics. Which cleared away any remnants of the awkwardness from before and connected them far more than their conversation had. When they had composed themselves, Mork glanced up at the bar clock.

"You, ma'am, need to go get ready."

"For what?"

"The party. Aina will start knocking on doors in about forty-five minutes or so and everyone will head over there for dinner at The Sanctuary, then back here for the getting-to-know-you part of the evening. It's a good time."

"Oh shit, yeah, okay, that sounds like a plan then."

They stood, and she smiled at the idea that he had risen because she had, but quickly shook it off as silly. He stepped past her and opened the door as she slipped into her coat. She frowned, noticing that he hadn't reached for his.

"Not going to escort a girl home?"

"Wish I could, but I've got to finish tidying this place up first, and sort out a few things in the back before work."

The sudden switch back into reality took her a little off guard and burst her bubble a little, bringing her sharply back down to earth. She started fiddling with the hair behind her ear.

"Ah, right, of course, I … uhmmm, yeah. Will you be there? At dinner I mean."

Another familiar smell reached his nostrils and he was tempted to smile, but held it together.

"No, that's just for the volunteers. But I'll be here waiting for you all afterwards, as will Fredrik and Ella. It gives you guys a chance to really get to know the friendly neighbourhood forest rangers."

"Cool, okay then, I guess I'll see you later."

"Yes, ma'am, you will."

She smiled at him for a moment.

"I'm glad you work here. I was worried that there wouldn't be anyone I'd click with and I'd spend months away from everything I know and have no one to talk to."

His wasn't sure what to say, and she stepped closer to give him a hug. Mork wrapped his free arm around her and brought his head down to lean on her shoulder. It was no more than a few seconds and she was off into the cold. He stood watching her for a moment before letting the door close.

Chapter 2

By the time Aina and the volunteers arrived at the bar, they had shared three bottles of wine and were all ready for a good night. Mork, Ella and Fredrik had been waiting, intentionally not drinking so that they wouldn't be too far ahead of the pack by the time the actual party started. Mork enjoyed the luxury of drinking at work as long as he was still able to do his job and didn't get too drunk, which, given his physiology and lifestyle, was practically impossible. It wasn't that he couldn't get drunk, it was just that it took a lot to get him past a point of being able to think.

Sobriety hadn't stopped them dancing, though, so when the others arrived, they were greeted by loud energised music and Mork, Fredrik and Ella all waving their hands in the air. Without missing a beat, Aina joined in. Greg, the youngest of the group and the only Englishman, was next, and soon everyone else piled onto the makeshift dance floor.

Mork waited until the song ended before taking up his position behind the bar.

"Welcome, welcome. I'm almost ready for you, just one more thing to do. So please bear with me."

The volunteers all crowded around the bar while the staff tried not to roll their eyes. Mork ducked down to reach into a fridge and pulled out one of his beers, which he opened and downed half.

"Right, now that that's done, what can I get everyone else?"

The volunteers all laughed and shook their heads, as Mork started handing out drinks. Under usual circumstances, Norway is one the most expensive places in the world to drink, but as it was the volunteers' first night, an allowance was made to ensure everyone would have a good night. For most part, this was the drunkest anyone would get until the leaving party, when they would do it all over again.

The eldest of the volunteers was Sagi, who had trained as a para-medic while in the Israeli military then decided to pursue veteri-nary science when he enrolled at university. He was also the first to approach the bar and, smiling, extend his hand.

"Hey, man. I'm Sagi. Nice to meet you properly."

Mork smiled back and they shook hands.

"Good to meet you too. What can I get you?"

"Oh, uhmmm, just a beer for now. But I've been wondering, how long have you lived here?"

Mork lifted a glass to the beer tap and started filling it.

"Just six months."

"So this is your first winter up here?"

"Yeah, but I'm from Canada so I know about cold. What about you?"

"Israel. I mean, it gets cold in the mountains, but not like this. This, this is terrible."

Mork chuckled quietly and placed the beer on the bar.

"So, man, how'd you end up working in a bar in the middle of no-where?"

"On a journey of self-discovery and suddenly found myself here, got to know Aina and Kristin, who offered me a place to stay in exchange for my services as a barman, and here I still am."

"Nice one ... So, do you speak the language?"

"Norwegian? A little. Fredrik over there has a tendency to forget how to speak English once he's had a few, but generally with all the international volunteers, we just stick to English."

Mork picked up his own beer and raised it.

"Cheers."

They clinked drinks and Sagi laughed, "I think I'm going to like it here."

A tall gangly man with a cheerful smile threw his arm around Sagi's shoulder and held out a hand.

"Ken McGinty."

The voice was cheerful, with a charming Irish lilt. Mork shook the hand of the final volunteer.

"Mork. Nice to meet you. Drink?"

"Sounds grand, what do you have?"

"Beer, wine, some spirits?"

Ken's smiled broadened.

"I'll have whatever my man Sagi here is having."

"Good choice. So, Irish, I gather."

Sagi patted Ken on the back and slipped out from under his arm to go introduce himself to Ella and Fredrik.

"Yes, and yourself?"

"Canadian."

"Ahhh, I have family in Canada. Where about you from?"

"Edmonton."

"That's sort of middle, right?"

"Middle-ish. Where does your family live?"

"Toronto, so east side."

"Fair enough. So, what brings you to The Sanctuary?"

"I love wolves, always have, in fact in school I did my final art project on them. Everything from medical drawings to fantasy-style oil paintings. I called it the Lupus to Lycanthrope: A study of wolves."

Mork blinked at him for a moment, almost spilling the beer.

"We don't get many art students here. In fact, I think you might be the first."

Ken laughed, "Oh no, I'm taking veterinary science like the others, although I'm focusing predominantly on research. The aim is to get into conservation and protection. I'm doing my minor in Politics; I think hunting and killing these animals to the point of near extinction is the worst crime humans have committed against nature and I want to help stop it."

Mork handed Ken his beer.

"Well, you've got my vote."

Ken laughed again.

"I'll hold you to that."

"So, you still draw?"

"Oh yeah, all the time. Art is my other great passion. My back-up plan for if I can't save the world from poachers is to draw comic books. Sometimes I just wish I had superpowers so I could chase down poachers that way."

Mork dropped his head to one side quizzically; Ken reminded him more and more of his friend Brandon, the bassist for Waterdogs.

"Well, happy to meet you, Ken. Good to come across people who are so passionate about the conservation of these beautiful creatures. It's also nice to see new faces; you can go a little stir crazy around here during the two-week changeover, and we do end up like a happy little family for the three months we're here, you'll see."

Ken took a long drink and turned to watch the others. He had missed what Mork had said. Mork, on the other hand, drifted into a kind of melancholy as he thought back to his friends, his band and his family. A cold prickle of goose bumps danced over his body as he zoned out, staring past the crowd and into the night. He felt a stirring behind his eyes. Full moon was coming, he could feel it.

Cassandra clapped her hands in front of his face, snapping him back to life. Startled, he jumped and spotted her staring at him with wide eyes, biting her bottom lip trying not to laugh.

"Sorry! I didn't realise you were that far gone," she chuckled.

"Oh don't worry, I was just thinking about how I plan to lead you four innocent souls into ill repute over the next three months."

She pulled a face.

"So that's what you do here."

"Everyone needs a hobby. Some people write, some people paint, I lead people into temptation."

She laughed and shook her head.

"God, that's so cheesy!"

"I know. Great, isn't it? That said, it's probably more accurate to say my hobby is trying to sound clever."

"Emphasis on the trying."

He let his jaw drop open.

"Ouch! Too mean."

But he couldn't stop himself from laughing.

"So, a drink?"

Cassandra shook her head. This guy is crazy, she thought, and charming and drinking with him could be very, very dangerous.

"Sure, what do you have in the way of spirits?"

"Vodka, gin, a couple of whiskeys left over from the last lot of volunteers who decided it was a good idea, and Jäger."

"Do you have tonic?"

"No, we keep the gin around to tease people."

She frowned and he stuck out his tongue.

"Sorry, I come from a very sarcastic family. Gin and tonic? I don't have lime but there's plenty of ice and I do have bitters so I can make it pink?"

"Pink? Really?"

"You don't like pink?"

"It's not that I don't like it, I've just never heard of a pink gin-and-tonic before."

A childish excitement spread across his face and he had to take a deep breath to compose himself before saying, "Groovy."

Cassandra laughed and rolled her eyes, then pulled up a barstool. Which is where she stayed for most of the rest of the night, laughing and chatting as Mork served drinks. Occasionally, a voice in the back of his mind would remind him that this was a bad idea, that he couldn't, or at least shouldn't, get involved, and that this was not why he was there. While in her mind she kept telling herself that she wasn't here to meet cute and charming barmen with big blue eyes. She had a goal and a plan, and he had none of those things. No dreams, no direction, there simply because that was where he'd ended up. But still they flirted and smiled and joked the night away.

Sagi rescued them from Ken a few times. The Irishman was apparently far too smart for his own good, and a little socially unaware, and the drunker he became the more enthusiastic he got about conservation and saving wolves, at one point even attempting to form a mob to start hunting down poachers. Greg, on the other hand, just got amorous and tried in vain to hit on Ella who didn't have the heart to tell him she was married. Eventually Greg got the hint that Ella was just being polite and fell into a long deep conversation with Ken about Batman, with Mork occasionally making a brief appearance to top up their glasses and add his opinion.

Aina stepped back from the crowd, and just observed her new batch of family. This, she mused, might be the best batch yet. Already everyone seemed to be getting along, and getting so close. It reminded her to have faith in people, that not everyone was a poacher and a bastard.

As the night drew on the music grew more and more relaxed, and eventually, as it had done on every other party night in the bar, everyone gathered around a single table with an ashtray and a few bottles of whatever Mork could grab from the bar. Those who could still stand and stomach the sight of alcohol lingered on, laughing and chatting. Surprisingly, other than Cassandra the only other surviving volunteer was Greg, who'd been cornered by Fredrik, who was determined to teach the Englishman the art of wooing a woman. Fredrik took a long drag of his cigarette, a sure sign to Mork that he was fast approaching the point at which Norwiglish would become the language of the room. Fredrik was shaking his head at Greg.

"Well, a friend of mine said that, you know, if you buy her some nice soaps and bath oils and things like that, that'll encourage her to use them."

Fredrik turned to Cassandra and gestured at Greg as if to say, "Can you believe this?"

"No, no, no." He turned back to Greg. "For starters, what self-respecting man actually knows what stuff to buy? Women have spent eternity trying to find the perfect products to suit their skin, smell, hair type. No, you're just opening yourself to being wrong. Trust me, that's an argument just waiting to happen."

He took a long swig from his beer and leaned a little closer to the boy.

"Besides, you've clearly misunderstood the whole situation. If you really want to get her to make herself beautiful, you've got to take her somewhere she'll be seen. She no longer has to impress you – you're the one dumb enough to move in and tell her you love her for her. So, she's relaxed, she no longer needs to impress you."

He leaned back and took another pull on the cigarette before stumping it out. "Honestly, hairy legs is the best compliment a woman can give a man. It means she's happy spending the rest of her life with you. If she suddenly shaved them, she's cheating on you. But if you want her to shave them for you, and make herself all pretty, here's what you do ... Friday, around 10 o'clock in the morning, you call and make a reservation at a really nice fancy restaurant for Saturday night. Then at eleven, before she takes her lunch break at work, you call her and say you've decided you want to treat her and you've booked a table for just the two of you at this nice restaurant for Saturday, because you think it'll be nice to do something different and get all dressed up. Maybe even say something like, 'Wear that dress I love you in.' But only do this if you know she thinks it still fits. Otherwise, you're fucked. Now she has enough time to go buy her own nice oils and things during lunch and has all of Saturday to make herself beautiful for the people at the restaurant who are going to notice her. And if you play your cards right, you get to take advantage of her freshly oiled and shaved body when you get home."

Greg looked up at Fredrik in wonder. He wanted to write it down so that he'd remember it in the morning. Fredrik pulled out another cigarette and lit it before finishing his beer.

Cassandra, who was watching open mouthed, managed to pull herself together to lean close to Mork: "He's not wrong, you know, but I kind of hate him now."

Mork closed his eyes, let out a sigh and whispered back,

"Whatever you do, don't tell him."

Greg, on the other hand, was gushing.

"How do you know all of this?"

"I just understand women, my friend. I know how they think ... I've been inside their minds and, let me tell you, it was fucking beautiful."

Cassandra chuckled.

"You have sisters, don't you?"

Fredrik smiled and tapped his nose with one finger.

"Only boy and youngest of five."

At which point Mork let out a laugh, wanting to say, "And I thought one was bad," but thought better of it, stopping himself just in time. The thought lingered for a moment and quickly turned cold, stripping him of his enthusiasm. He took a long breath in and quickly stood up.

"All right, folks, I think we've done ourselves a great honour in surviving this long. Now, I think, it's time for bed."

"Oh God, hear-hear," Cassandra chimed in, prompting Fredrik to offer a naughty grin at Mork. Greg yawned and stretched out his arms.

"What time is it anyway?"

Mork turned to look up at the bar.

"Four."

"Shit, what time do things start tomorrow?"

"Breakfast starts at twelve."

Fredrik put his hand on Greg's shoulder.

"Don't worry ... We've adopted a more fluid system since Mork moved in."

The end of the evening was in sight and everyone started gathering their things together to get going. Mork picked up the bottles that hadn't been emptied and took them back to the bar, then started shutting the place down. Fredrik pulled Greg, grabbed their coats and dragged him out the door as quickly as he could, leaving only Cassandra behind. Mork walked out from the back room where he'd turned off the music and put away some stock and looked out into the empty bar. Cassandra stood alone in the middle of the room, quietly waiting. A part of him both loved and hated Fredrik.

"Hi," she said calmly, and his heart rate shot up.

The entire night had been heading steadily towards this point and he'd known it; he'd known and done nothing to stop it. Now that it was time, the voice of protest had somehow found new strength in the reminder of his sister and he felt his resolve harden. He stared at Cassandra for a moment and decided that she was beautiful, not only for the way she looked, but how she held herself, her confidence, her sense of humour, the way she was fidgeting nervously. She smelt beautiful, in a way that no other woman ever had, and that terrified him. He stalked across the bar with long bold strides and wrapped himself around her and they kissed. Her body moved against his and it all felt so natural. The hair on the back of his neck stood up and pressure started to build in his mind.

Cassandra, on that other hand, found her mind empty of thought, of logic and sanity. It all seemed to evaporate in the heat of the moment; no plan could possibly have made more sense than what was happening right now. Then suddenly he pulled himself up with a long sharp in-breath, and looked down at her. She blinked up at him, biting her bottom lip. The pressure in his mind urged him towards her, so much so that his breath grew quick and he had to close his eyes for a moment to focus on staying human. When he opened them again Cassandra was still smiling and pulled herself slightly harder against him, letting out a staggered sigh. He leaned down and kissed her again, but just the once and then whispered, "I have a few quick things I have to do to shut this place down, I mean; then we can get out of here. Grab your coat."

"Okay."

He quickly untangled his arms and started to close the blinds and shut things down, while she slipped into her coat and zipped herself up. The weather outside had only gotten worse as the night had worn on and was fast approaching risky. He ran through his usual routine with the skill and precision of practice, before he finally appeared in a flurry of coat and movement next to Cassandra, who smiled.

"Ready?" she asked.

"Yeah. The door will lock when I close it."

She slipped her hand into his, and leaned her head against his shoulder. He squeezed her hand in reply. It had been a long time since he'd even kissed a girl and far longer since he was both nervous and excited about it. Likewise, throughout high school and university she had only a number of semi-serious boyfriends, none ever overlapping but none ever lasting more than a few months. They all seemed to get in the way of her studies. Not that Mork was her boyfriend. They'd only just met, and she'd never picked up a boy in a bar before. She took a long breath and mentally repeated her mantra. Don't overthink it, just do it. This was what her best friend had tried to teach her. The bracing cold wasn't helping though, and by the time they reached her door she felt a little too sober and her courage was waning. She stopped and turned to face him, reaching up for another kiss. Then she pulled away and stared into his eyes, which now seemed to have little green flecks that almost sparkled. A naughty smile spread across her face and she reached a hand behind her to open the door, then put her free hand on his chest and took a couple of steps backwards over the threshold ?. She closed her eyes and took a deep breath.

"Goodnight," she said.

A shocked giggle bubbled up from inside Mork and he stared at her blankly.

"This has been a wonderful first date, but we have three months for all of … this, and I don't think we should, or need to, rush into anything."

His blank look turned into a tantalising smile and he shook his head.

"Yes, I ... agree."

Her smile turned a little brighter as she said, "Thank you."

She stepped forward for a goodnight kiss. He placed a hand on the side of her neck and gently ran his thumb over her cheek. A gentle groan slipped from her lips, then he gave her a big kiss on the cheek, making a 'mwah' sound for emphasis.

"Sweet dreams."

He winked, and headed off towards his room.

She stood at her door feeling slightly dissatisfied. Then it was her turn to shake her head and giggle as she shut the door. As soon as the door closed her giggle grew into a happy laugh. It didn't matter who it was, she always seemed to have a laughing fit after kissing a boy for the first time. As she got older, it had seemed to come later and later, which was good, as the first few times she had ended up laughing in the poor boy's face, which led to a lot of really rushed explanations and some hurt feelings.

She didn't even bother switching the lights on; instead she let her coat slip to the floor and stepped out of her trousers on her way to bed. After some wriggling around she got her bra off, and finally climbed in under the covers. It was late, and she was fairly drunk, but happy to be closing her eyes to sleep. It had been a better start to her adventure than she could have imagined. Even if he was only a barman.

Three doors down, Mork wandered back from the kitchenette to his desk with a couple of glasses of water. It had been far too long since he'd gotten that close to a girl and he was a lot more awake than he wanted to be at four in the morning.

Since arriving at The Sanctuary, he'd been trying to find out as much about local and European werewolf myths as possible. But living in hiding in the middle of nowhere had made things a lot harder than they needed to be. It helped that it was a wolf sanctuary, so people weren't really suspicious when he ordered books about wolves and werewolves, but it took such a long time for them to arrive and it was hard to do research with an internet connection that seemed to have a life of its own. So, finding out which books to buy and read was a battle in itself. He drunkenly flipped through a book of physiological case studies on people raised by wild animals, but he'd read it before and wasn't really paying attention. Cassandra was taking up an awful lot of space in his mind, and it both worried and excited him. It had been a long time since there had been someone to think about, but was it really such a good idea? Had that ever stopped him before? He took a deep breath and quickly downed one of the glasses of water and made a dent in the second one. Then he decided he could think about these things with his eyes closed, and took himself to bed. He stripped as he went, leaving a trail of clothes across his floor, and was asleep a few moments later.

Chapter 3

He closed his eyes in his small room in Norway and opened them in a snow-covered forest. Sword in one hand, he was hacking his way through dense bush, thrashing branches with a purpose. He wasn't sure how, but he knew where he was going, and it didn't take him long to get there. He stepped out of the forest into a clearing. A winding stone-cobbled path leading to a castle in the distance. Familiar yet strange and confusing. He looked down at his hands, his body, and realised he was wearing a tunic. He dropped the sword and rubbed his face as he looked up at the castle. He could swear he knew it, that he belonged there. Then from somewhere inside he heard the piercing cry of a wolf's howl, but not any wolf. Somewhere up in that castle was another werewolf. Without thinking, he took off at a run, stopping only when he saw the full moon start to rise up and sit at the very top of the sky. Suddenly, as hard as he tried, he couldn't make his body do what he wanted. It seemed to sap everything from him to take only one step closer before he dropped to his knees.

He could feel the transformation stirring, it was coming. Slowly, his body twisted and writhed, his bones cracking and stretching, hair sprouting from every pore. He thrashed about, trying to fight it off, but then something caught his eye. He flicked his head to the side and came face to face with the biggest, blackest pack of wolves he'd ever seen, and the irrational fear that nightmares bring reached into him and grabbed hold of his soul. A blood-curdling scream escaped from his throat and he turned to flee ... only to find himself back in his room in Norway, heart racing and sweat running off him in sheets.

Mork took a deep breath, then swore and put his face in his hands. He'd had some pretty intense dreams since being bitten, but nothing as vivid, as real as this. He glanced over at his clock; he'd been asleep for about four hours. No one else would be awake for hours. He turned his attention to his lunar calendar and realised that full moon would be starting that night. He grabbed his jeans and pulled on a shirt flung over the back of the chair. He opened a drawer in the desk and pulled out a sign that read 'Dratt på telttur' – essentially 'Gone camping' in Norwegian.

Bundled up in a coat and boots, he stepped out into the snow, a much icier world than he'd expected. He hung the sign on the door and headed off in the direction of the cave he'd claimed deep in the woods.

The journey wasn't long, but it wasn't easy either; most people would naturally avoid the path he took, which is precisely why he took it. Once there he ran through his ritual of building a fire with the sticks he had collected along the way, snacking on the rations he kept in a small locked box inside the cave. Then he stripped naked, wrapped himself in a blanket and settled down to meditate by the fire until the transformation. As he sat, his mind rested and calmed, an old childhood memory drifted through his mind: how he had always hated the cold. But now, even in the intense cold of Norway or Canada, it no longer had much of an effect on him. It was hardly that he relished being naked in the snow, but he didn't suffer nearly as much as other people would have. The cave wasn't massive, but it was deep enough that he could not be seen if he didn't want to be, and could move around in it just fine as a wolf. He'd come across it only a few days after arriving at The Sanctuary and almost immediately took up residence. Over the course of a couple of weeks, he'd moved things up there; nothing major, just a couple of blankets to sleep on, some non-perishable foods for when he needed it and some supplies to make a fire.

Unlike in his dream, with the full moon imminent, the transformation came quickly and easily. He had been feeling the wolf leaning on his mind more and more as he approached the cave. Then all he had to do was let go and let his human side melt away to reveal the wolf inside.

He knew that he probably wouldn't be able to return to his human form for a few days, at least until the moon began to wane, but he didn't care. He had learned to let things go; once he knew that there was no going back he could let the inevitable take its course. He sniffed around the cave for a while before heading out into the snow. As usual, he lifted his leg around the front of the cave to remind everything else in those woods whose cave it was, then took off at a full sprint. The woods were thick enough to shelter him from much of the falling snow, but there was a lot of it everywhere, and more still falling.

***

Fredrik groaned and cursed Mork under his breath when the buzzing from broadcast radio broke the early-morning silence of his room. He dragged himself out of bed and staggered over to it.

"Hello?" he answered gruffly in Norwegian. "I mean, Fredrik at The Sanctuary checking in."

A voice on the other side laughed politely and then turned more serious.

"This is Thomas at the weather station reporting the potential of pending emergency conditions. There is a blizzard heading your way. It might hit further north but we doubt it. You need to lock down your people until further notice."

Fredrik blinked a few times in the hope that it would clear his head.

"Please repeat."

"Incoming blizzard. You're on lockdown until further notice."

Fredrik took another moment to allow the information to sink in. He dug around in a drawer, pulled out some painkillers and took two without water.

"Understood. Thank you, weather station. I'll start getting every-thing moving and report back from The Sanctuary proper. How long do we have?"

"Approximately five hours."

Fredrik looked at his clock, just past nine o'clock.

"Short notice?"

"It only just changed direction. Last I looked it seemed it was go-ing to miss you."

Fredrik cracked his neck and willed himself to feel better.

"All right, I'll put someone on the radio ASAP. Keep us informed."

"Will do, Sanctuary."

The radio went silent. Fredrik replaced the receiver and glanced around the room looking for his clothes while running through the lockdown procedure in his head. Then, as quick as he could, he pulled on his gear and headed out the door to alert Ella. He was halfway to her room when he stopped suddenly, the blood in his veins turning to ice. He prayed that the sign on Mork's door meant no more than that he and Cassandra didn't want to be disturbed. He knocked, gently, then more urgently, and finally opened the door to peer in. Empty.

Fredrik shot over to Ella's and, without hesitating, walked right in. Ella snatched at the towel she'd just let drop and frantically covered herself up.

"What's wrong with you?"

Her instinct was to reach over and slap him, but the look on his face stopped her.

"We have a problem."

She stiffened.

"Shut the door. What's going on?"

Fredrik flicked the door closed behind him with one hand and sat down on the bed. Ella, in turn, went back to getting dressed. It wasn't the first time he'd seen her change and it probably wouldn't be the last.

"The weather station just called in. There's a blizzard on its way and we're on lockdown until instructed otherwise."

She raised an eyebrow.

"And how does that justify you walking in on me?"

"We have only five hours to get everything set up ... and Mork is not in his room, with the 'Gone camping' sign on his door."

Ella ran over a few things in her head.

"And he's not just in the girl's room?"

It wasn't a thought that had occurred to Fredrik.

"Don't know, but I don't think he'd hang the sign just to sleep in someone else's bed."

They stared blankly at each other for a moment, both furiously thinking. Then Ella tightened her jaw.

"All right, you start getting the volunteers ready. I'll go check the bar, and alert Kristin and Aina."

"If he has gone camping, I don't think we have enough time to secure the others and go find him."

They were both very aware of the potential seriousness of the situation and neither was particularly happy, but they had to do things in order of priority.

"Right now we have to deal with the problems we can solve; we still don't actually know that he's not here."

Fredrik nodded, then got up and headed back out into the cold.

Step one was to get the volunteers up and into The Sanctuary, but first he took the sign off Mork's door. The last thing they needed was people coming to the same conclusion he had, and panicking.

To his surprise, he found Sagi awake when he knocked on his door, and after a short explanation the ex-soldier offered to get Ken and Greg up while he fetched Cassandra. Lockdown meant getting everyone into The Sanctuary so that they could be brought up to speed on the situation, and then be split into teams and allocated tasks.

Cassandra groaned when she rolled over and squinted at the time, for a second she thought she'd dreamt the knocking on the door and closed her eyes again, hoping to fall back into her dreams. Remembering only vaguely that they seemed intense. Then the knock came again and, groaning, she slid out of bed, wrapped herself in one of the blankets and went to the door. Fredrik couldn't be sure whether the look on her face was just hangover or disappointment that it wasn't Mork standing there.

"Morning, sorry to wake you but we've been informed of an incoming blizzard. You need to get dressed quickly, and we need to get to The Sanctuary building."

She stared at him for a few seconds before she realised what he was saying.

"Oh, okay, just give me a few minutes."

"Sure, but time is short. You don't have to gather your things right away; we'll get all of that done later. Right now, I just need everyone in one place."

She blinked at him a few times and nodded, shut the door and scanned the room for her clothes, not quite sure she knew what she was doing. She pulled on what she'd been wearing the night before and immediately headed out.

Since the party had ended a lot more snow had fallen. Across the little yard she could see Sagi and Ken waiting patiently for Greg to appear. Fredrik gestured for her to join them while he ducked back into his room to grab his list of emergency codes. A pale, slightly confused Greg had joined the group by the time Fredrik re-emerged and the five started off towards The Sanctuary, all the while Fredrik quietly praying that Mork would be there when they arrived.

At the entrance they found Aina, Kristin and Ella staring impatiently at each other. All glad none of the volunteers understood Norwegian, Fredrik raised an eyebrow as if to say, "Well?" but Ella simply shook her head, then said, "I did a quick check in the bar, and nothing. I take it he wasn't in anyone's room." She shot a glance at Cassandra.

"No, in fact I'd bet she was disappointed I wasn't him when I knocked. Makes me think he definitely slept in his own bed."

"Shit, why would he just leave like this in the middle of a snow storm?"

"He's done this before, you know. Just decided in the middle of the night that he couldn't sleep and left. Of course, it wasn't the middle of winter."

Aina sighed and joined the conversation.

"We don't have the time to play guessing games. We need to get the volunteers organised and just pray that Mork knows what he's doing. Once we're secure, then we can either make a plan to try look for him or just hope he comes home. But first things first."

Ella and Fredrick looked at each other, then at the volunteers, and Fredrik launched into action, and back into English.

"All right, everyone, we've been alerted of an incoming blizzard and have been ordered into lockdown. We only have a little more than four hours from now to get everything organised. So, here's what you're going to do. You will split into two groups and go back to your rooms and collect the things you desperately need. Warm clothes, blankets, pillows, two towels, and soap. Just because we're going to be cold doesn't mean we need to smell funny. Nothing else! Then make sure all the windows are closed and secured and lock the doors when you leave. Help each other pack and come straight back here. Ella will be with you to double check everything is secure and to make sure the extra rooms are locked up. Kristin and Aina, you two need to get the food supplies from the bar. I will be here maintaining radio contact with the weather station to get the latest details on the storm, what sort of temperature we can expect and how long it might last. I will also be brewing coffee and hot water so when you get back we can look at getting something warm into you. Weather here isn't a joke ... This isn't a drill; this is an emergency situation and we have very little time to get everything done. If you have questions, save them for later, go now."

As soon as he finished, Ella, Kristin and Aina leapt up, which prompted everyone else into action. Greg, Ken and Cassandra were simply too tired and a little panicked to argue, but Sagi had been in the army and his calm allowed him a thought. He turned back to Fredrik.

"Where is Mork?"

It was the question Fredrik didn't want to hear and didn't have a good answer for. He looked up at Ella, who took a breath in and said, "Truth is we don't know. He sometimes likes to take himself off into the wilderness for a few days, and it looks like he did that this morning."

"But if this is an emergency situation, shouldn't we go looking for him?"

Ella looked back at Fredrik, who took back the reins of the conversation.

"Honestly, yes, we should, but right now we don't have enough time. Our first priority is to make sure you're all safe, and have faith that he is an experienced camper and knows what to do in these situations."

Sagi looked back at the other volunteers; he could tell that they were just as unsatisfied with that answer as he was. But before he could argue, Fredrik took control.

"Look, we don't have the time to debate this right now. The sooner we get everything that has to be done, the more time we will have to try to resolve other problems. Move with a purpose and move now!"

His voice was direct, his point made, and everyone immediately started towards their given tasks, with no more questions asked. Ella couldn't help but admire him for a moment, then followed the others. Fredrik waited until everyone else had left before he allowed himself a moment of anger and frustration that he was going to let Mork tackle the blizzard alone and not go looking for him. Then he got onto the radio for updates.

By the time everyone had returned to The Sanctuary, the snow had started falling again, and this time it looked like it wasn't going to stop for a long time.

***

Mork eventually ran out all his pent-up energy and found his way back to the cave to crash in a heap and sleep. When he finally stirred, a strange smell twitched at his nose. He opened his eyes and looked out at a world covered in white, with more fresh falling snow. A shiver ran down his back. As his senses awoke, he could smell the approaching storm and knew he was in trouble. First he wondered whether he could stay in his cave and wait it out, but quickly realised that if he got snowed in, he might suffocate. Second he considered looking for the wolf pack he had spotted in the area and see whether they'd take him in. He paced up and down, weighing up the options and decided that if the Alpha took offence he may end up in an unnecessary fight. Which left only one choice. He needed to get back to The Sanctuary and try to find shelter there. The problem with that was if he went too early, he'd run the risk of being spotted, and if he waited too long, he could end up trapped out in the snow. As he continued to pace, the scent of the storm grew and he could feel himself growing more restless and wild. Instinct was pushing to take control, and the urge to run tickled the back of his mind. He thought about his options again, about the consequences, about his sister, who always worried about him. Her face flashed into his mind, a still image of the last time he'd seen her, desperate and terrified for her son.

Mork took off out into the snow. Aiming for his room back at The Sanctuary, feeling his humanity slip away with every step, and the instinct to survive taking over. Back at the compound the window in his bathroom was just large enough for him to break and crawl through, and he could close the door once inside. He had some food and enough blankets and clothes to keep warm as he waited out the storm. Even with all the snow, he still moved faster as a wolf than as a human, so it didn't take nearly as long to get back to as it had to get to the cave. He slowed to a cautious trot once he was close enough to be able to make it to his room no matter what.

Most of the volunteers were busy in the main building, helping to set up; only Sagi and Ella were outside moving supplies. Once the people and food had been sorted, blankets and bedding had been next on the list of priories. As he watched from the woods, careful not to move or be seen, he could pick up the scent of nervous fear that enveloped the place. He would have to wait until the right moment, when everyone would head inside The Sanctuary, and he could make a break for his room. He didn't have to wait long before the final loads were carried in and the main doors locked and secured. For a moment as he watched the shadows move across the windows a familiar feeling of isolation washed over him, and the urge to bolt prickled the back of his mind. Until now, he'd managed to stay connected to the others at The Sanctuary, bonded in a way, but as reality settled in it began to feel like the bubble had popped. He knew he'd be fine, but he also knew that they didn't know that and would be worried and confused, and that at the end of the day all he'd have to offer them would be another lie.

Suddenly, a movement caught his eye. He noticed that one of the shadows in one of the windows seemed to be staring at him. He wasn't sure whether it was instinct or imagination that told him it was Cassandra and that she could see him; either way it snapped him back into reality. The moment the figure turned away, he made a dash for his room. He was both pleased and slightly annoyed to find that someone had closed all his windows and locked his door. It was nice that they cared, but it was also something of an inconvenience. He lined himself up, took a short run up and dived through the bathroom window. The shattering glass seemed to ring out against the stillness the snow had brought. A shard of glass nicked his hind leg as he crashed through but not enough to be a danger to even a normal wolf. However, landing half in the toilet and half in the bath left him a bit wet and embarrassed. Snow now also poured in through the broken window bringing with it the cold.

It wasn't easy, but he managed between paws and teeth to stuff sheets and towels under the bathroom doorframes, blocking out the incoming cold. Then he grabbed his blanket in his mouth and crawled in under the bed to wait out the storm.

***

Snow continued to fall. At points, the wind would pick up and the snowfall would get heavier and the people in The Sanctuary would huddle together and quietly worry. As they were all together and had all the time in the world as they sat tight and waited, Kristin and Aina decided to launch right into the theoretical elements of the training as a way to pass the time and keep the volunteers and themselves distracted. Ken, mindlessly pushing food around his plate with his fork, stared out the window watching the snow get heavier. A thought came to him.

"Why is he called Mork?"

No one had really been speaking much during the meals and his voice made a crack in the silences. At once everyone realised what had been occupying all their minds, the nagging worry they shared for their barman friend. Fredrik swallowed a mouthful and forced a smile.

"It's short for G'mork. As he tells it, he started growing facial hair quite young and had a big black beard when he was like twelve or something. One of his friends said he looked like the G'mork and it stuck."

Ken nodded thoughtfully.

"What's a G'mork?" Greg added his voice to the conversation.

Everyone turned to look at him in slight shock and Fredrik narrowed his eyes, waiting to see if he was joking.

"Have you never seen The NeverEnding Story?"

"N ... No?"

"How?"

"I, uhmmm, didn't watch a lot of TV as a child."

Fredrik turned to Kristin, who smiled.

"We have it in the DVD library, why don't we all watch it now after dinner?"

Everyone made excited and positive noises.

"I actually have the book with me," Sagi spoke up. "If anyone wants to read it, I have an English translation."

Cassandra waited to see if anyone else was going to accept the offer and then raised her hand.

"I love that book, I mean, I love the movie too. And just so everyone knows, I will cry."

Everyone laughed, and then hurried to finish their food quicker so that movie night could start.

Chapter 4

Mork had bundled himself up in his blankets under his bed, intent on just hibernating until the storm passed. His thoughts wandered to Cassandra and the others at The Sanctuary, on his time spent in Norway and what his future plans might be, anything to avoid thinking about his family. He knew he should contact them, but he just couldn't, not without finding some kind of answer first. He wanted to know more about his condition and not from books or fairy tales, but to actually go and find answers. He was proof that there had to be some truth in some of the stories and he was going to find out more, or never go home. *Never go home* ... The words circled in his mind, pulling him down into a melancholy sleep. Over the years, he'd gotten used to the type of dreams that invaded his mind during full moon. He always had strong wolf-based dreams but at full moon they were more intense, more real.

This time, however, they were different. He opened his eyes to find he was human, dressed in layer upon layer of thick clothes and marching along a cobbled street through a forest. As he walked, people stepped out of the darkness and began to hand him things, bread or meat, an extra layer of clothing; some just shook his hand and would then step back into the shadows and disappear. Eventually, after what felt like days, he found himself approaching a clearing and a castle – the same one he'd dreamt of before, and once again he heard the werewolf inside howl. This time his body didn't freeze and he was able to run up to the door and try to open it. But then there were more howls, but not from inside the castle and not just one wolf. He spun around to scan the woods behind him, and there, emerging from the dark of the trees, were hundreds of werewolves. Panic tightened his muscles and they all howled as one. The pitch of the wolves rose like a wall and hit him square on, but instead of fear he felt a strange comfort, a sense of belonging, of family. He ventured a few steps towards them and in a single moment transformed. The pack circled around him and they all howled again, the sound once again hitting like a wave, only this time he threw his head back and joined them. Then came the reply from inside the castle, a ferocious and violent reply that sent the hundreds of others fleeing back into the woods and Mork standing alone in the clearing.

The great castle door swung open and out padded the same massive black creature as before, teeth bared and snarling. Mork dug his paws in and tensed his muscles, howling with all his might. The slow stalking stride of the skulking menace immediately changed to a full-paced charge and Mork launched himself forward in reply, only to bounce off the wall of his room in Norway. Still filled with the fury and fear of his dream, he once again threw his head back and let out an almighty howl. He then headed straight for the bathroom window and slipped out into the night.

***

Everyone at The Sanctuary woke with a start as the howl echoed through the building. Immediately, both Fredrik and Ella dashed from window to window to see if they could spot where it was coming from, knowing that anything that loud couldn't be far away. The volunteers, too, rushed to the windows, staring out into the darkness beyond trying to spot the source of the eerie call.

Suddenly Ken turned ghostly white and took a few steps back, pointing. The others all turned to him, then looked out the window. And then, for just an instant, they saw it, the massive black beast that was Mork at full moon, his eyes glowing bright green with fury, as he loped through the snow. Without a word or thought, Fredrik went to the safe and collected his and Ella's rifles. He had no intention of going after the creature, but if it came at them, they needed to be ready. Greg swallowed and finally broke the silence. "Well, I don't know about the rest of you, but I'm going to be having G'Mork nightmares for the rest of my life."

While he was trying to lighten the mood, it did occur to him that he might not be joking. Kristin and Aina had also spotted the beast from their bedroom window and hurried down the stairs to join the others. They frowned when they encountered Fredrik and Ella holding a gun.

"Put those away," Aina hissed. "That's not what we're about here. This is a wolf sanctuary."

Fredrik nodded. "I know," he said, "I'm just not so sure that that was a wolf."

A shaken Kristin turned to address the room.

"People, we don't know exactly what just happened but it does seem as though whatever that was has run off. It's not uncommon for extreme weather like this to cause animals to act strangely. I assure you we're very safe in here. It's very late, I know, but perhaps we could all do with some tea or hot chocolate to calm the nerves before getting some more sleep?"

Everyone agreed, but that didn't stop them from unpacking what they had just seen, theorising about what it might or might not be.

"Can a wolf get that big?"

"Was it a wolf, though?"

"What else could it be?"

It took a while, but eventually the conversations ran their course and one by one people made their way back to bed, to try and sleep and once again think over what they'd seen.

***

Mork continued to sprint across the whitened landscape until he stepped into snow much deeper and softer than it looked and sank in over his head. The loss of balance, the fall and sudden shock of the icy cold woke him back to his senses. He clambered out of the hole he'd fallen into and, calmer, started to make his way back to his room. By the time he arrived, he was cold and wet and tired, so leapt up and through his broken window and did his best to shake off the wetness before crawling back into his bed nest and retreating into sleep.

Over the days that followed, he continued to dream about the wolf pack and the castle, but the black wolf did not make another appearance. Finally, after a long restless slumber, he woke to a dim sunshine casting a beam across the floor at his head.

He was human, naked and rather stuck under his bed. He quickly, albeit gracelessly, clawed himself out and scrounged around for some clothes. Not even he was that immune to the cold. His next thought was whether there was a way to get to The Sanctuary or not, and if he could let them know he was all right. He thought briefly about trying to make it to Ella or Fredrik's room to use their radios but decided against it. He knew the rooms would be locked, and he'd either have to break a door or a window to get in. Which wasn't ideal. The Sanctuary, while well stocked, wasn't equipped for that much maintenance. Especially during a storm. As more snow fell and he realised he was stuck, his mind went to the castle and what to do about it. It all seemed too intense, too specific to be just another dream; it had to be, he was sure, some kind of transferred memory, but it wasn't clear what he could do with that idea. He boiled the kettle and poured a mug of coffee, pulled back his chair, sat down at the desk and started to sketch. The image was clear in his head. It helped that even as a human every time he went back to sleep he would dream about the place.

By the time the snow had stopped falling, he had run out of paper and was sketching on the covers of books and any other blank page he could find. He had also run out of food waiting for everything to settle, so was even more happy to venture out to the others.

***

Back at The Sanctuary everyone had fallen into the quiet routine of academia and pleasant conversation while waiting out the weather. There was still the constant underlying worry about Mork, but it had gone unspoken for so long that no one now dared bring it up. Except for Fredrik. He was desperately counting the days until he could get out and start looking for him.

When a full day passed with no further snowfall, he started mentally preparing himself, which Ella immediately recognised. She took her time, conscious not to have the conversation where the others might hear. They were all worried and she didn't need more people wanting to go adventuring in the snow. Unfortunately, there wasn't a lot of private time in such a confined quarter, so at the first opportunity she followed him into the bathroom.

"And just what do you think you're doing?"

He turned to look at her, his trousers open.

"Funny" he said smiling, "that's what I was going to ask you."

"I know you, and I know what you're planning."

"What?" Fredrik shrugged. "Take a piss? Everyone knows what I'm planning to do right now."

She raised her eyebrows at him.

"The weather is settling down," he surrendered, "and it has to be done. We can't just leave him out there. And the sooner I can do something the greater the chance he has at … at still being alive."

"Fredrik."

"What? It's our job, and he's our friend."

"Fine, but you're not going out there alone – that'd be just as stupid as Mork going out there in the first place."

"We don't have a choice, Ella. We can't leave The Sanctuary unmanned during a blizzard."

There was a gentle knock. Sagi peered around the door, looking severe.

"I believe I can help you there. I was a sergeant in the Israeli army; I think that makes me qualified to go with you."

They both stared at Sagi for a moment, then Fredrik frowned: "Can we talk you out of it?"

Ella looked at him firmly: "Question is, can I talk you out of it?"

"That's settled then ... We leave at first light tomorrow. Provided it doesn't snow again during the night."

Ella's eyes flitted back and forth between the two men, desperately trying to find an argument against their plans, but she wanted to find Mork as much as they did. A sudden flash of insight hit her and she put her hand on Fredrik's shoulder.

"You know the radio systems better than me. I'll go out tomorrow and start the search."

Fredrik's jaw tightened as a prickle of anger and frustration ran up the back of his neck. Not because he wanted to be the hero, but because in his mind he was trying to save her as much as anyone else. Sagi saw the look on his face, nodded and closed the door. Fredrik breathed a sigh and folded his arms.

"And what if I'm actually going out there to find a body? What then?"

The room fell silent.

Fredrik would be the first to admit that Ella was more of a man then most men. She could handle herself in any situation and God help you if you're in a fight with her. But she was also still a person with feelings. Tears welled up in her eyes and she looked up at him.

"And what about you? Are you just okay with that?"

"No, of course not, but I've been preparing myself for days. Just let me go, let me be the one who finds him and brings him back. Regardless of what condition he's in."

Ella stood silent for a moment, then simply nodded. They both stood there for a moment before Fredrik broke out into his usual smile.

"Now," he said with a grin, "I really do need to pee."

"I know," Ella laughed. "This is your punishment."

"Suit yourself."

He turned back towards the toilet and reached into his trousers to pull himself free, at which point Ella squealed and hurriedly backed out of the room.

The rest of the night passed by as it had every other night since the storm had hit. The volunteers continued their theory studies before settling down to watch a movie and finally heading to bed, while Fredrik and Ella took turns manning the radios for updates on the weather. Fredrik knew he had to get approval from the weather station before he could head out, but once that came through, he and Sagi quietly made plans for the following morning. Although still not happy about being left behind, Ella helped where she could, and made them promise to keep her informed.

***

Mork sifted through his wardrobe and realised that he really only had one winter coat and that was back in the cave. Desperate, he pulled on as much as he could and after a few frustrating minutes of struggling to get the door open, headed for the bathroom window. As he trudged through the snow towards The Sanctuary building it dawned on him that although he knew he wasn't in any danger, no one else knew that. Guilt suddenly welled up in him; he really should have made more of an effort to get back to them sooner.

There were two entrances to The Sanctuary: the front door, which was completely snowed under, and a private door into Aina and Kristin's apartment, which was atop a flight of stairs. It took much longer than usual, but eventually he made it to the second door and stood staring at it. Guilt washed over him and a childish sensation to hide from his problems whispered in the back of his mind. A small scared voice that urged him to run, leave, escape. He thought about how he'd felt when he left the Island and the world around him grew very quiet – to the point that every move he made seemed to disturb the silence. Then all at once he heard voices from inside, voices he recognised, talking about mounting a rescue to find him. He blinked a few times as he snapped out of his downward spiral and it reminded him that the people here cared about him. His confidence bubbled back up to the surface as he said casually but loudly.

"Sounds like fun! Can I come too?"

He knew how to make his voice carry and, as it rang through the door, all conversation on the other side fell dead. Mork waited and listened for a few moment, then heard hurried footsteps and the sound of locks and keys. The door swung open and standing in front of him were Sagi, Fredrik, Ella and Aina, all staring at him in disbelief. He smiled his normal charming smile.

"Best. Party. Ever."

They all gawked until Ella, frowning, stepped forward and slapped him, hard, before wrapping her arms around him. The others quickly joined in, even Sagi. A warm, safe feeling washed over Mork and tears welled up in his eyes. Hurriedly, the group unravelled and then dragged him in out of the cold. It was early morning, but since the storm had rolled in sleeping patterns had become a little erratic. They tended to go to bed early and wake up early. So while everyone was still in bed, they were also mostly awake when the excited party made their way down the stairs.

"And look what we found on our doorstep this morning!" announced Ella. "What do you guys think, shall we keep him?"

There was a moment of confusion as everyone looked at her blankly. It was only after they spotted Mork that the realisation set in and pandemonium broke out. Despite the excitement, everyone managed to settle down quickly to a large pot of coffee, an impromptu breakfast and explanations. Mork explained that when he realised he'd made a mistake going camping, he'd started heading home right away. The things is, he said, by the time he finally managed to get back the storm was so heavy and he was so cold that when he found his room, he took shelter there rather than trying to make his way to The Sanctuary. He apologised again, and then came the barrage of questions about the beast, and whether he'd spotted it and what he thought and did he think it may have been a wolf and was it likely it was still out there ... Mork skilfully dodged them all by claiming he'd heard the howl but had been asleep and in no position to see anything so wasn't sure if it was even real or just a nightmare. Then he turned it around and asked what everyone else had seen. Ken was the most vocal about the experience, to the point that everyone else looked as though they might laugh.

Throughout the conversation Cassandra sat in silence, not making much eye contact, despite Mork occasionally glancing in her direction to catch a reaction. He recognised the look; seeing him again had made her realise how worried she had really been and that bothered her. In a way, she felt as though she hadn't known him long enough or well enough to be as concerned as those who'd known him longer and the whole cocktail of thoughts and emotions was now spinning around in her mind. Even before Ken could round off his long, convoluted story, she quietly got up and slipped away back to her bunk in a huff, not sure if she was angry at Mork, herself or both. Mork had noticed, though, and bringing Ken's narrative to a swift end, he excused himself to follow her. He could smell the conflict from across the room, and worry aside, it wasn't pleasant or easy to ignore.

"I'm sorry."

She looked up at him with a slight start.

"What?"

"I said I'm sorry, for causing so much stress for everyone."

"Oh yeah, right, well ... me too."

"Oh? What for?"

"I don't know. I mean you seem really cool and nice and everything, but I came here to study and learn. I don't think we should pursue anything more between us. I mean, maybe we should stop at being friends."

It wasn't what he was hoping for, but it wasn't entirely unexpected.

"That's fair ... It's not like either of us is really in a position for something serious, and you don't strike me as the kind of girl who's a player, or someone who takes this sort of thing causally. That said, even though we're now friends, you still can't cancel your one-woman show at my bar at the Christmas dinner. I've been turning down some really big acts since booking you."

Her face turned slightly pale.

"What?"

"Well, you told me you want to learn to play guitar and have books and stuff, so as inspiration I thought you'd want to play at Christmas, in front of everyone."

"Oh lord, that's what I thought you meant ... Uuhmmm ... no?"

"Sorry, doesn't work like that. But don't worry, I'm going to help you."

"You? How? You said you aren't musical."

A prickle ran over his checks, as he heard his own lies being said back to him, but he managed to hold the smile.

"I'm not, but I make a great audience. Plus, I can order a songbook, if you don't actually have one. So you'll learn to play guitar and I'll make sure you keep it up. Besides, it's a good balance: you'll be doing a lot of intense academic stuff here, some very physically and mentally taxing and demanding things happen here ... It's good to have a side project that will take your mind away from that side of things for a while. Trust me."

"Balance, huh?"

"It's important. She stared at him for a second and realised that she did actually trust him. She still felt that she didn't know him at all, was still being silly, but she wanted to trust him. She also realised that he'd managed to take her little internal outburst on the chin, and turn the conversation in a way that stopped her head spinning.

"Right then, deal, and friends."

She held out her hand and smiled. He was tempted to take it and kiss it, but had to acknowledge that he too wasn't there for that kind of fun; he needed to focus on finding himself, and finding out about his dreams, so shook her hand instead.

The excitement of Mork's reappearance eventually wore off as day-to-day life settled back into the routine. The volunteers returned to classes and training, and Ella and Fredrik, now with the help of Mork, made sure the radio was monitored and that supplies were checked and counted, and that meals were being prepared. The weather continued to stay calm, if not entirely clear, and by the end of the week everyone could move back to their rooms.

Time slipped by quickly, the volunteers were given more practical exercises to complete, and Fredrik and Ella insisted on knowing well beforehand when Mork was planning another camping trip. Despite their best efforts to remain just friends, it wasn't uncommon for Mork and Cassandra to cuddle or hold hands, particularly after a drink or two at the bar. Somehow they managed to draw the line at any kind of real intimacy, but did make out a couple of times when their frustrations got the better of their resolve.

Which just irritated Fredrik who was both disappointed that they weren't having sex and slightly jealous that Mork spent so much of his free time with Cassandra, instead of him.

Chapter 5

Annabel Harris had taken to spending her nights reading over internet articles, blogs and trashy tabloid websites looking for anything that rang true about either her brother or wolf sightings. Desperately hoping to find one that spoke of both. Occasionally, she'd stumble across one that held promise and investigate further but had always come up short.

Her father walked in carrying mugs of coffee and sat down across from her. Since his attack and Bastian's kidnapping, Kyle had moved in with Annabel, which boasted a 24-hour police guard.

"Anything new?"

"Some student blogged in Norway about seeing a massive wolf during a blizzard, but he's volunteering at a wolf sanctuary so that's not at all surprising. Have been keeping an eye on the blog, but there hasn't been anything else in weeks." She closed her laptop and looked at her father. "Where could he have gone?"

Kyle shook his head and sighed.

"I wish I knew. I wish I knew a lot of things about what had happened that night."

Annabel shuddered.

"I still try not to think about it, the things he did. I mean, I guess I know why, but I just ... I just want him back."

"I ... if only there was a way we could let him know that he can come home, that we miss him." Tears welled up in the old man's eyes. "Somehow he's always managed to make me feel helpless when he was in trouble. Couldn't just scrape his knee like other kids, no, he had to go and get bitten by a werewolf."

Annabel reached out her hand and laid it over her father's.

"I'm sure he's not trying to hurt us … In fact, I'm almost certain he believes he is protecting us, which is … maybe worse."

The room fell silent for a while until there was a knock at the door and Josh let himself in.

"Hey, everybody." He smiled at Annabel. "You ready?"

"Almost. I just need to shower, change and put on make-up."

Josh laughed and sat down, as Annabel sprang up and trotted off to her room.

"Evening, sir."

"Evening, Josh. So … tell me again what's this thing you're going to?"

"Brandon's insane attempt at a baby shower, but really it's Stacy who wants to have a big fancy, lights-camera-action baby shower, event thing. And we all have to be there."

To her credit, it didn't take Annabel long to get ready and back down stairs.

"You sure you're going to be all right here with Bastian by yourself?" she turned to her father.

"Don't you worry about us. The police are outside, and besides, the boy hasn't had a nightmare for over a week now. You go and try to have fun at this … thing."

Josh and Annabel both rolled their eyes at the thought, then Annabel gave her father a hug and they headed out.

Danny met them at the door, which annoyed Josh a little. He had hoped to be seen arriving with Annabel. Since Alex's disappearance, they had become close but, much like her brother, Annabel was in no rush to make any public announcements – unlike Josh, who had been in love with her since he was sixteen and wanted to shout it from the rooftops.

They sought out their hosts Brandon and Stacy, exchanged pleasantries, and then took their seats at the main table. Speeches were made, presents handed out and, eventually, food served. As usual, the conversation turned to theories about Alex's disappearance, which Annabel listened to, but very rarely took part in. Josh often took up a defensive position to anyone who made any kind of negative comment, and Danny was never one for talking. Generally, Stacy always had the most to say and, with her parents sitting alongside her, seemed even more confident in her opinions than usual.

"I just think it's very selfish of him to leave without as much as a word to his friends and family, and in the middle of such a crisis. I'm sure he had his reasons but I can't fathom what they could be. You'll obviously never do anything like that to our little family, would you, Brandon?"

Brandon smiled nervously in response, aware of how awkward it was with Annabel sitting there.

"Well?" Stacy continued, oblivious.

"Oh yeah, no, never, my love. I'd never leave you or the baby."

"Good. Now, Joshie, what do you think of all of this?"

Josh hated when she called him that; he wished she'd just shut up, or go away.

"I think we've been over this topic a hundred times, and when he's ready he'll contact us. In the meantime, we can just love him and miss him, and hope that wherever he is he's doing just fine."

Stacy rolled her eyes. The rest of the table fell into the usual uncomfortable silence that was inevitable whenever Stacy was around, until she blithely confessed: "... I mean, we were going to name the baby Alex if it was a boy, but I just can't even imagine doing that now."

Annabel's eyes grew wide with fury, a sweat breaking out on her neck, and she was just about to turn to Josh to insist that they leave when Danny's voice rang out across the table, shocking everyone into silence.

"Okay, that's enough! You know what? None of us would be here if it wasn't for Alex. Yeah, we were a band when we met him, but he pushed us, provided that missing spark and turned us into something real. When he led us, I mean, I don't know about the other guys, but when he was with us I felt safer, like we could do anything, conquer the world – and we did. So, yeah, it's shit that he's left, but give the guy a break; he deserves it. He deserves to have a bit of peace and calm in his life, without ignorant stuck-up, gold-digging..." Annabel bit back the word she wanted to say, "gold-diggers like you sitting in judgement. Everyone fucking hates you, Stacy, and it's time you knew it. Don't you dare name your child Alex – you don't deserve that honour."

Danny was on his feet now, his cheeks flushed red with fury. Josh stood and put a hand on his shoulder to stop him from saying anything more.

"It's all right, man, it's all right." He then turned to Brandon, who had a wild, panicked look in his eyes, knowing the onslaught he was going to get from Stacy later. "We'll always be here for you too, man, don't forget us."

Annabel folded her napkin, pushed the chair back and got to her feet and, without another word, she, Josh and Danny walked out.

"Thank you, thank you!" As soon as they were out of earshot, Annabel threw her arms around Danny and kissed him on the cheek. "God, that was everything I've wanted to say to her for ever – thank you."

Danny blushed as the reality of what he'd done dawned on him.

"Oh man, Brandon is going to get it so badly ... Shit!"

"Yeah," Josh shrugged, "but it was about time someone said that shit to her. Fucking bitch ... How dare she speak like that and, I mean, right in front of us!" His hands were shaking. "And I know what you mean, man ... When Alex was around, I did feel safer, and he really did push us to succeed. He made it feel like all we had to do was play music and it would happen, like there was no way we could fail. I miss that ... I miss him. If not for him, I don't know what I'd be now – maybe a music teacher like my father, talking about the band I was in that could have made it, if only we had gotten a break."

Josh choked up a little and Annabel slipped her hand into his.

"I just ... I just really wish I knew he was okay."

Danny grew a little pale and shifted uneasily, then said quickly, "I ... I gotta go."

And without another word, he turned and left, leaving Josh and Annabel both a little worried, but they also knew that Danny was never one who was much for company or sharing his feelings, so they decided to let him go and headed home themselves.

Everyone was asleep by the time they got home and Josh stayed the night, an occurrence that was becoming more and more regular once he'd got used to the idea that Kyle was fine with it. Annabel lay awake for a few hours going over Stacy's comments in her head and listening to Bastian's baby monitor, which she'd started using again since the kidnapping.

The next morning started out like any other morning: coffee, breakfast and idle chitchat. Kyle had always liked Josh, and spotted very early on how he felt about Annabel. He also knew that he'd been a stable presence in Bastian's life, so there were no major ripples now that he was around more often. The morning routine was broken, however, by a rapid knocking at the door. Annabel found Danny standing on the doorstep, still in the clothes he'd been wearing the night before. It was clear he hadn't slept.

"Uhmmm, can I ... can I come in?"

"You all right?"

"Yeah, yeah, I'm fine. Can I just come in please?"

For a moment Annabel wondered if he'd been out all night taking drugs. It was a rock-star trope, but she also knew he wasn't like that. She led him into the kitchen. Josh immediately jumped to his feet when he saw him.

"Jesus, man, what happened?"

Danny winced.

"I ... I gotta tell you guys something, and I – I'm so sorry ... Fuck, I'm so sorry, but I can't keep it to myself anymore. Just ... just please don't hate me."

Annabel sat down weakly and looked up at him expectantly.

"I, uhmmm ... I ... saw Alex ... like ... a month ago."

Chapter 6

Mork woke with a start, once again under attack in his nightmare. His eyes shone green in the darkened room but he managed to cling to his humanity, for the time being anyway. Since the nightmares had begun he had kept trying to sketch the castle, so he moved swiftly to his desk and continued his latest drawing.

Hours must have slipped before a sharp knock at the door rang through the room. Mork quickly pulled some books over his drawings.

"Come in!"

Cassandra, rubbing her hands together, stepped into the room and closed the door behind her.

"God, it's cold out there."

"Well, it is winter."

"Wiseguy!" She stuck her tongue out. "Why are you up already?"

"Oh, I don't know, I just woke up early."

Her frown turned serious.

"Another nightmare?"

"It's fine. Honest."

"It's not fine. It's not normal for people to have constant nightmares like that."

Mork sighed; it wasn't the first time they'd had this argument. But now it was approaching full moon and he needed to stay calm.

"Did you come here to lecture me?"

Cassandra's eyes flashed red for a moment. She'd actually come over hoping to find him asleep and to jump into bed with him to wake him up and cuddle, because she had had a nightmare of her own.

Mork didn't need any special powers to detect her anger; he could tell by the look in her eyes and knew she was having a sense of humour failure. So he quickly got up and tried to wrap his arms around her.

"Nope." She pushed him away. "Not that easy."

He took a deep breath. He felt the wolf stirring, pushing him.

"Fine, then get out."

"What?"

"It's early, I didn't get much sleep and so far you've judged me, lectured me and now you're angry at me, and you don't want to tell me what's actually wrong. So either talk to me, or get out."

Cassandra realised she was a lot more hurt than she thought she'd be, so turned and stormed off, leaving Mork feeling angry and guilty – and with a glowing green eye. Perhaps, he thought, it was time to go camping again. He grabbed his bag and headed for the door. On the other side he found Fredrik, looking slightly confused, with one hand in the air about to knock.

"You all right, man?"

"Yeah, fine. I was about to come ask you about the weather. I want to head out for a few days."

"Yeah, weather's fine – Cassandra isn't, though. What happened?"

"What d'you mean?"

"I just saw her leave here fuming, angry tears in her eyes."

Mork's shoulders sank.

"Oh, for the love of— I'll go talk to her."

Fredrik was still confused.

"You sure you're okay?"

"Yeah, I'll be fine. I just need to get out for a few days, you know how it is."

Fredrik shrugged and nodded, and allowed Mork past.

At Cassandra's door, Mork knocked gently.

"Cassandra, look I'm sorry ... Can I—"

"Fuck off, Mork!" echoed through the door.

His face flushed red with embarrassment, and not a little anger. Part of him wanted to stay, to tell her how sorry he was, but the wolf was coming and he wasn't stopping. So he turned on his heel and, once he was sure no one could see him, broke into a sprint, forcing himself to focus on a mental image of him as a human. But the wolf was creeping steadily up on him, as if it were running just behind him, chasing him.

Cassandra sat on her bed, furious. Firstly, because Mork had kicked her out of his room when she'd come there for comfort and, secondly, that he had not given her time to calm down before trying to apologise. Her mind shot back to her internal argument. She was there to learn not be distracted by men, which only irritated her more. She tossed a pillow across the room and took herself off to shower.

It wasn't until late afternoon that she discovered Mork had left on a camping trip, and that promptly undid any guilt she felt for swearing at him. In fact, she was beginning to feel that he was just being petty and childish.

At that precise moment Mork was still on the run, the wolf having caught up with him, and it wasn't long before he was bursting from his clothes as he sprinted through the snowy wilderness. He wasn't angry but embarrassed and wanted to get as far away from all of that as possible, hoping that distance would somehow make it less. But the further he got the guiltier he felt, having to literally run from his problems. He leapt into the air to help him brake, pushing his paws deep into the snow, then threw back his head and let out a deafening howl that rang out so loud that Cassandra, Ken and Fredrik, who were making their way back to their rooms, stopped and pricked up their ears. Fredrik rubbed his eyes and turned to the other two.

"Make sure you check your doors and windows tonight."

He then turned and headed back to The Sanctuary to check in with other stations and report out-of-the-ordinary wolf activity. Cassandra locked her door and double-checked her windows, which had been snowed closed all winter. Then she settled into a book to make sure she absolutely was not going to worry about Mork. Ken, on the other hand, headed straight to his laptop to update his blog.

Mork's heaving slowly dwindled to a whimper as he turned and started back the way he'd come. He needed to find his bag and destroyed clothes before anyone else did. Then he was going to wait out the rest of the full moon and, when he got back to The Sanctuary, distance himself from Cassandra. Being that emotionally vulnerable with someone was clearly becoming dangerous.

The next few days passed slowly and by the time he returned to the compound it felt like a lot more time had passed. Fredrik said a little thank-you to whichever gods were listening when he spotted Mork passing by the bar to his room and trotted out into the snow to catch him.

"Hey, man, good trip?"

Mork turned and stopped, waiting for Fredrik to catch up,

"Yeah, not bad. Bit of peace and quiet. Miss anything interesting?"

"Nothing major. We did hear an unusual howl the day you left, but nothing since then. But look, man, I just want to warn you. Cassandra, she's still pretty pissed at you. I don't know what you did, and she's not actually said anything, but I can tell, you know. So just take it easy there."

Mork's jaw tightened.

"Thanks for the heads up."

"Yeah, man, I don't know what happened ... Maybe it was the full moon, you know how that can affect women sometimes. She's been a bit edgy since your little thing the other day. My advice, be cool, don't lock your door, and let her come to you."

That had, in fact, been Mork's original plan; hoping things in general would calm down and he'd have some more time and space for wolf research. Now, however, he was annoyed, not because Cassandra was angry with him, but because hearing about it hurt. He needed to draw a line. Fredrik was right, though, she also needed time to calm down. So Mork put his stuff away, and headed to the bar to set up for the night.

He needed to just be okay with her being angry, that was it. Only, for the next three days, she went out of her way to avoid him, to not talk to him, and when she had to, the words were short, sharp and even at times a little unkind. From her perspective, every day he had been away had made him appear more childish and more of a negative distraction from her studies. Compounded by how much time she wasted thinking about how angry she was with him, she managed to convince herself that she was furious with him. He, on the other hand, tried to rationalise it and not let it affect him. But it did. Every time she glanced over at him, spat a comment at him or just plain ignored him, he got angrier. Every time she scoffed when she found him in a room or rolled her eyes when he entered, it cut him deeper. By the end of the third day he gave up trying to be okay with her hating him. The trigger was when she arrived at the bar with the other volunteers and shook her head, obviously annoyed at seeing him. Instead of trying to ignore it, Mork narrowed his eyes.

"Get out."

She stiffened and suddenly everyone looked uncomfortable.

"I said get out ... This is my bar and if you don't even have the decency to be polite to me here, you can get out."

Her mouth dropped open but no words came out. He, however, was on a roll.

"Why are you so shocked? Did you think I would just take you being a complete bitch to me with a smile? Like I'm some servant? Are you that much of a snob? Or did you think because I'm just a barman I'd be too stupid to notice?"

He raised his eyebrows and waited. Cassandra's cheeks flushed red as the reality of how he felt hit her. Suddenly, the whole situation was out of her head and back in the real world and he was a real person and not the person she'd been imagining. All arguments she'd been having in her head ended abruptly and she was overcome by the guilt washing over. He, on the other hand, hadn't fully realised how angry he was until it was too late and his heart rate was not slowing down. And, for a moment, he didn't care – he wanted to be furious and he was. Then sense returned and he turned away, making his way into the back room to calm down. Deep breaths, deep breaths, he told himself until he managed to regain some semblance of control. He felt bad for calling Cassandra a bitch, but he also felt better for getting that noise out of his head. When he finally returned to the bar, he found it empty except for Cassandra.

"I ... uhmmm, I know I've been a bitch and ... and I want to say I'm sorry. I'm sorry." She bit her bottom lip. "We need to talk, I know, but maybe not right now? You're still angry – and I get it – but I just wanted to say that: that I'm sorry."

She turned and walked out, hoping Mork would say something to stop her, call out to her, but he didn't. He just watched her leave.

The next morning Mork awoke early and managed to finish his latest sketch of the castle from his dreams. He had been thinking a lot about Cassandra and what they would talk about, what he'd say, what he really wanted, and he still couldn't work it out. He knew that he needed to apologise for what he'd said in anger and frustration the night before. But he knew, too, that he needed to spend more time on his werewolf investigations as he originally planned. Finding The Sanctuary had turned out to be as much of a curse as it was a blessing. He loved it here and had learnt a lot about wolves; his time here had also given him the opportunity to centre himself more, to throw off the cloak of being a rock star. But, he had to admit, he was beginning to feel a little closed in here in the wilderness, stuck. He loved the team and really didn't want to ever let them down, but staying now meant restricting what he planned to do. And then there was Cassandra. During the night he had realised that them being so angry at each other probably meant something. Combining those thoughts with him living a lie made him feel isolated and lonely.

A knock at the door broke the spell and he found Cassandra standing out in the cold.

"Do you think we can we talk now?"

Mork's shoulders dropped in both relief and trepidation.

"Yes, but … I'm not sure what to say."

She thought for a moment.

"Have you at least been thinking about it?"

"I have."

"And?"

Mork snorted in frustration.

"I'm sorry for what I said yesterday, I really am, but can we not do this right now? Please?"

There was no anger in his voice, just fatigue and a little desperation.

"Okay, okay … I just … I don't know what to say or do either."

"Right now I'm going with, if I do nothing, then nothing will go wrong."

Despite herself, she let out a little laugh, and he smiled.

"Look, maybe we spend some time just taking it easy. You focus on your studies and the work you're doing with The Sanctuary, and I'll do my own thing and we just let some time pass?" His words reminded him of a conversation he'd had with a girl when he was seventeen and a cold shiver rippled down his spine.

Cassandra smiled softly; she understood what he was saying, but was still a little disappointed. Not in him exactly, but their situation. She had been telling herself that she needed to step back and focus more, but hearing it from him just made her sad. It told her that he didn't want to open up.

"Okay, sure ... I think we can manage that. So ... I guess, I guess I'll see you at breakfast?"

"Yeah, for sure."

It was the outcome they had both been convinced they wanted, but here they were, and neither of them satisfied. The rest of the team were relieved to see them at least being civil to each other, pleasant even. Aina and Kristin were especially happy, as they had started to wonder at what point they would need to get involved. Mork worked for them and Cassandra had paid to be here as a volunteer and gain knowledge and experience. They couldn't really allow a personal relationship between a volunteer and a member of staff be that distracting to the team.

Although on the surface all was well between her and Mork, Cassandra was still frustrated with their situation; she desperately wanted it to get back to the way it had been. She missed the closeness, missed the security that had offered her, and she continuously had to stop herself from cracking jokes with him or venturing to his room in the middle of the night. Their being apart all seemed so unnatural, and forced. Mork felt exactly the same, but kept telling himself that it was for the best and perhaps all of this meant that it was time to think about leaving The Sanctuary.

A week passed before Cassandra had had enough to drink to find the courage to try to talk it out. She made a conscious effort to look perfectly sober when she made her way over to the bar.

"Can we talk?"

For an instant Mork thought about responding with, "About what?" but he knew that that would set them back even further. At the same time, though, his instincts told him that this was neither the time nor the place.

"I'm not sure what I'd say," he ventured. "If we have a serious 'us' conversation, what would we aim it at? Are we talking about becoming a couple? How would that work? I'm a barman in the middle of nowhere and you're a vet back in the United States – one who's leaving in a month. Or are we going back to being 'almost a couple', where we're lying in bed together slowly getting angrier and angrier wondering whether or when we're going to get together or break up. Or do we break up ... which we kinda have already."

Cassandra opened and closed her mouth a few times, looking for words as she processed everything he had said.

"But you're such a smart guy, Mork. If you just applied yourself you can be anything you wanted. I don't understand why you're just a barman ... Okay, not just a barman. You're a lot more, I know."

Cassandra slumped down on a barstool, overwhelmed by a sense of helplessness. For a moment, Mork feared he would weaken and confess who he really was, but held himself back. Stepping from behind the bar to take her in his arms, he stopped dead and turned towards the door. An all-too-familiar scent. Cassandra looked up at him as he stared wide-eyed at the door, his breath coming in short, sharp gasps.

"What is it? Mork, what's the matter?"

He turned to look at her and she thought he might be about to cry.

"Oh my God, oh my God. Cassandra," he whispered. "I am so sorry.

I am so unbelievably sorry. I just – fuck! – I promise I wanted to tell you and ... and I understand if you never want to speak to me ever again."

A shiver ran over her whole body.

"What? What are you talking about?"

"You'll see."

The door to the bar swung open and in walked Annabel, with Aina, Kristin and Ella trailing behind her.

"And, finally, this is our bar, complete with charming barman. Everyone, if I can have your attention, this is Annabel Harris, a potential new sponsor, so be nice."

Everyone turned to look at her but she was looking at only one person. Tears started rolling down her face and Mork took a deep breath and a few steps forward.

"Hello, Annie."

The room fell silent.

"Oh my God, Alex, it is you."

She rushed forward and threw her arms around him and he closed his around her.

"How ... How'd you find me?"

"Danny ..." Annabel sniffed back tears. "Danny said he'd found you here on one of his pilgrimages, and I'd just found a blog by one of the volunteers here talking about a charming barman by the name of Mork. So, daring to hope, I followed my instinct and decided to come investigate."

Alex looked over her shoulder at everyone staring at them, mouths agape, every face mired in confusion.

Unwrapping themselves from each other, Alex took her hand.

"Come on, let's go somewhere we can talk." Nervously, he turned to the others. "If you'll please excuse us, my sister and I need some time."

He put his hand on Annabel's back and steered her towards the door as the room broke into excited chatter, only Cassandra retreating to her barstool alone.

Back in his room, Alex handed his sister a beer and sat down on his bed.

"So, how are things?"

Annabel let her shoulders drop.

"Things have been different without you. I mean, you've travelled for long periods before but no communication has been hard. Really hard. We've missed you, been worried about you and for a while I was really angry with you for disappearing."

He looked at the floor.

"You know what I did down at the docks that night?"

She nodded.

"Then ... then you know why."

"Yeah, I know, and I told myself that a lot, but nothing? Nothing, Alex. Not a word, no note or sign to say you were all right? Really? That sucked for us. For a while, I was terrified that you'd become the Hollywood monster and started waiting for reports of animal attacks in the city. How did you end up here?"

"For a few moments there ... I was that monster. That's why I ran. I had to get myself as far away from it as possible. I stowed away on a ship, and it turned out to be coming to Norway. I remembered Danny telling me about this place and reading up about it so headed here ... Been here the whole time."

"How did you get across Norway without clothes or money?"

"I was Mork. I didn't need any of that."

"Jesus, how long did it take?"

"A month, maybe, time sort of lost meaning."

"Wow ... wow ... That must have been difficult, different."

"I suppose it was, but it helped me realise that giving up on searching for answers about werewolves would be a mistake, had been a mistake. So I figured learning about wolves in general would be a good start, took the name Mork, and spent the last God-knows-how-long being no more than a barman, no one special, living in the middle of nowhere, desperately searching for a lead of some kind to follow. What about you? How are you? How's Dad, Bastian and everyone else?"

"Good, for the most part. Bastian has had nightmares since that night. They're getting less frequent these days, but for a while there it was pretty bad. Dad's okay ... I don't know how, but he managed to recover so quickly and stay strong for me, which I appreciate more than I really know how to put into words. And ... uhmmm ... Josh also helped a lot; he's really been there for us, and for me."

Alex raised an eyebrow.

"For you? Like for you for you? Like you and him?"

Annabel could feel the blush rise to her cheeks.

"Yeah, I mean, we've managed to keep it out of the press, so it still feels a bit like an affair sometimes but, yeah, it's been really good so far. I'm actually really happy. Really happy."

Alex ran his hands through his hair.

"Wow, good for you guys. He must be thrilled – although I bet he hates that he can't tell everyone."

"Why?"

"Oh come on, he's been into you since high school. I bet he wants to tell the whole world about you. Which reminds me, you don't happen to have my passport with you, do you?"

"Yeah, how else was I going to get you home if I found you? Why?"

Alex sniffed the air, sighed and got up to open the door. Cassandra stood nervously outside, still debating whether or not to knock and possibly interrupt something she really didn't want to think about. She looked up, shocked, when the door opened.

"Come on in," Alex gestured her inside. "I believe you deserve an explanation."

Cassandra took a few steps and smiled weakly over at Annabel.

"Annie, this is Cassandra. Cassandra, this is Annabel, my sister."

He knew he'd said it before, but wanted to repeat it and make it quite clear. Despite herself, Cassandra let out a sigh of relief before holding out her hand.

"Please to meet you, Annabel."

Annabel smiled.

"I think I will leave you two alone. Alex, I'll be in the first room across the way – come get me when you're free."

The two hugged and Annabel gently pulled the door closed on her way out. Cassandra sat in the only chair, and waited for Alex to settle down on the bed before she spoke.

"Look, I've known all along that Mork isn't your real name, but please tell me what's going on here?"

He ran his hands through his hair, pulling it back, then through his beard.

"My name ... I'm Alex Harris."

"Wait, wait … No … Alex Harris? The Alex Harris?"

"You'll be surprised how much of a difference the beard makes."

"But, but he went insane and disappeared?"

Alex held out his hands and tried to smile.

"I prefer to think that I went sane and disappeared."

"I have your poster on my wall at school."

All at once the penny dropped.

"Oh my God, earlier I said you just needed to apply yourself and you could achieve anything. You must have been laughing so hard inside. Jesus, I'm so embarrassed. How could you lie to everyone like that? How could you lie to me like that? And for months? Oh, Jesus, I offered to teach you how to play the guitar!"

Cassandra had started pacing, walking in small circles, her hands in front of her face and blushing various shades of crimson.

"I'm sorry, I did it because I didn't want anyone to know who I was … I—"

"So everything has just been a game to you?" Cassandra felt her world begin to crumble. "Rich and famous, playing at being a normal person for the fun of it! Can you even understand how devastating this is? I genuinely worried about you, and cared for you and wanted you to try harder because I thought you could really be somebody. Now I know you were just pretending. Was anything you ever told me true? You told me you couldn't sing!"

Furious tears streamed down her face. Alex just stood there, stricken and ashamed, confessing was worse than he thought it would be.

"All my feelings were real, all my interactions were real … but, no, my past is only very loosely based on the truth."

"Feelings? I don't even fucking know who you are, and I slept in your bed … Oh my God, I slept with a total stranger. You! Made me sleep with a total stranger!"

Her face flushed red, then turned grey.

"I think … I think I'm going to be sick … How dare you! How dare you have kissed me. I told you things about my life I've told no one else, and you … Oh my God!"

She turned around a few times and Alex saw the signs of a full-blown anxiety attack. He was scared, though, that if he stepped forward or touched her, that would make it worse. She spotted the door and stormed out – directly into Fredrik, who grabbed her, more out of reflex than anything else, and she crumpled into his arms, breathing too deeply and too fast as tears rolled down her face.

"Get me … away from him … Please."

In one quick movement Fredrik swept her up into his arms and back to her room. He held her as she cried, whispering calming words. It took about ten minutes before she managed to calm down, but she was also finished. So overwhelmed by emotion that she switched off and fell asleep. Fredrik had seen it before with people directly after a crisis and put her in the recovery position with a bucket in view and a glass of water; he then headed out to find Alex, who was squat on the floor outside her room.

"How is she?"

"Asleep, for now … What did you do, Alex?"

"It's kinda a long story. Maybe I should tell everyone at once."

"If they're all going to react like she did, you might want some protection."

Alex shrugged and tried to smile.

"I have a condom in my wallet."

Fredrik grinned.

"Okay then."

They made their way back to the bar, a hush immediately settling on the place as they entered, an awkward silence descending on them all. Alex wasted no time, and launched into as best an explanation as he could muster. Of the volunteers, Sagi was the least surprised and the most worried about Cassandra. Kristin, Aina, Ella and Fredrik had always known that he was running away from something but didn't know what, and felt it was not for them to ask. Naturally, there was still the sting that comes with being told someone you care for has been lying to you, but they all believed that just because he'd lied about who he was before didn't change who he was for them. That shocked and touched Alex so much that his lip trembled a little when, one by one they, they embraced him. Not surprisingly, it was Fredrik who lightened the mood.

"So, international rock star ... It's no wonder you have no idea how to pick up women. All this time you've been getting by on being famous. Makes so much sense now."

"You sound envious?" Alex grinned.

"Please, I don't need fame – I have charm."

Everyone laughed and for a few minutes everything seemed normal again, but in the back of their minds they all knew things had forever changed. The staff knew that Alex would be leaving and Alex was painfully aware of how much pain he had caused Cassandra, and that guilt wasn't going away.

"It feels good to finally tell you all the truth. I mean, you have any idea how much this beard itches?"

Their laughter sparked renewed conversation. It had already been late when all the excitement had started, so very quickly after it died down everyone drifted off, going their separate ways. Alex did his usual run down of closing the bar then headed to his sister's room. Annabel was sitting on her bed reading, patiently waiting for him.

"How did it go?"

"About as good as could be expected."

"And with the girl? Cassandra?"

Alex couldn't even force a grimace.

"Slightly worse than I had could have imagined."

"People just don't like being lied to, Alex – women with feelings especially so."

He sat down on the bed and stared at the wall.

"I know, but I wasn't ... I'm still not really sure who I am. So how could I tell them? I came here so that I could try to figure it all out. I'd like to be able to say I've found all my answers, that I'm ready to face the world again, but really I'm not. I'm sorry I didn't let you know where I was or what was going on but ... but I don't think I'm coming back with you."

Annabel moved closer and took his face in her hands.

"But we can help you, Alex. We love you and all we've ever wanted to do is help you."

"I know that, but ... you can't. No one ever really could. As much as the support has carried me – and it has, it really has, I don't know what I would have done or who I would have been without it, it's still always been me who has to actually go through it. And now it has to be me who needs to come to terms with being Alex Harris werewolf, not rock star, not uncle, brother or son ... As much as I love you, and I love you, werewolf is the most important part right now."

Annabel wrapped her arms around him and kissed his cheek.

"I know, I know. But I'm here for a few days; I haven't seen you in a looong time. So before you get back to wolf hunting, we're going to hang out."

He gave her a broad, honest smile.

"But before that, I'm going to bed. I promise to still be here in the morning."

He leaned over and kissed her forehead and headed back to his room.

Cassandra was standing at Alex's desk, flicking through his drawings. He could smell her through the door and stopped to compose himself for another onslaught before going in. She looked up at him, still tired and burnt out.

"Why do you only draw Muromtsevo?"

"What?"

"These drawings, why are they all of Muromtsevo Castle?"

"I, uhmmm … I didn't know that's what they were of. I've only ever seen it in my nightmares."

"You mean this is what you dream of? This place?"

"Yes. Where is it?"

"Russia. It's abandoned now, doesn't look like this anymore."

A rush of intrigue came over him but he held it at bay, telling himself that he would have time to deal with that new information in the morning.

"How are you?" He tried to change the subject, distract Cassandra from his drawings.

She sat down on the bed and looked at the floor.

"I'm hurt, and I'm confused, and I'm tired. You?"

"Ashamed and deeply sorry."

"Sorry that you lied, or sorry you got caught?"

"Sorry that you got hurt."

She turned to look at him; she appeared a little grey.

"What did you think would happen?"

He sat down on the floor and looked up at her.

"I think … I think I thought at some point I'd just announce I was leaving and go. Probably at the same time you left."

"Why?"

"Why would I leave, or why did I lie?"

Silence.

"I lied because I was running away, because there's something I need to do that is more important than being a rock star. Which is also why I have to leave here, because … I need to get back to it."

Cassandra rolled her eyes.

"Such cryptic bullshit," she scoffed. "It's fine – you don't have tell me. Just stop lying to me."

Alex's cheeks flushed red.

"All right, I'm not sure what to say, but I'll answer any questions you have. The whole truth."

She was clearly furious, and her anger quickly spilled over into tears.

"Was it all just a game to you? Just a stupid rock star playing with normal people for kicks?"

He moved with speed from the floor to wrap his arms around her and whisper in her ear: "No, no. God, no … I … You mean more to me than I know how to deal with, and I hated lying to you, and every day I hated myself more for it. I wanted to tell you, but I got lost."

She pulled back from him and they stared into each other's eyes, and for the briefest moment all seemed clear, that everything was okay. And then, like lightning, Cassandra pulled away and slapped him as hard as she could.

"No, no, no! No, too soon – I'm not ready. I'm not ready to forgive you."

She pulled away and stood up, grabbed her coat and dashed out.

Alex's shoulders slumped and he let a few moments pass, sitting in the shame of his mistakes. Then slowly he rose and headed to the bathroom, deciding it was time to own who he was.

Chapter 7

When Alex arrived for breakfast the next morning no one but Annabel recognised him. He had liked the beard but the time had come. Time to make some changes. He'd shaved the wild growth down to short trendy stubble, and neatened up his hair. To Annabel, he looked like her brother again. It took everyone else a few minutes to adjust but it wasn't a hard transition to digest.

As the shock faded, the volunteers recognised him – he was the world-famous rock star Alex Harris. Ken and Greg – and, to a lesser degree, Cassandra – were fans of Waterdogs, and now that he actually looked like the guy in the poster it was becoming more real. Fredrik and Ella were the last down for breakfast.

"That doesn't seem fair," Fredrik frowned.

"Why?" Ella laughed. "Because he's not only talented, rich and famous, he's also incredibly good looking?"

"Yes, it's overkill really. He doesn't even have to try."

Alex took a sip of his coffee, leaned back in his chair with a mischievous smile and admitted, "It's true. I really don't."

Annabel instantly rolled her eyes and without thinking agreed: "It's true. He really doesn't."

That, given the company and the situation, made Alex snort his coffee through his nose, choking a little, which made everyone laugh.

Greg then lost the run of himself and blurted out, "Oh God, it's so cool that we can just sit and laugh and joke with a real rock star! Oh man, wait until my friends find out I'm real-life friends with Alex Harris, they're not going to believe me. I mean, we are friends, right?"

Both Sagi and Fredrik patted him on the shoulder and shook their heads at the same time, but left Alex to speak.

"Yes, yes, we're friends. I'm still the same guy I was a week ago. But I'd rather you didn't start telling your friends about this just yet. Technically, I am still in hiding, after all. Remember, 'Rock Star Has Nervous Breakdown and Disappears'?"

Alex knew he'd been lucky to avoid any serious conversation the night before, but knew, too, that the sooner they got this it out of the way the better.

"Oh, oh, yeah. Right. Of course."

Kristin and Aina stole a glance at each other, then both turned to Cassandra and, finally, Alex.

"So … what are you going to do now?" Kristin kicked off. "Are we down one charming barman?"

Alex turned to Annabel, then back to them.

"Yes, I'm afraid so. I'm sorry it's all been so sudden, and I'm really truly sorry for having lied about who I was. The truth is I did have a breakdown and I did run away –from my life and my fame. And I found this place and you guys, and you've made me feel so accepted and welcome and let me make this place my home and I love you for it. But since the cat's out the bag, I need to move on."

It was at this moment Cassandra joined the conversation, a desperation in her voice that that she couldn't hide.

"You're just going to keep running?"

He managed a wan smile.

"No, I'm going to release a press statement saying that I took a sabbatical from fame to work here under an assumed name. That I'm well and happy, and not insane. That I'm going to continue my travels but not in hiding. I don't want to let my fears lead to anyone getting hurt again, my family obviously and, of course, all of you."

He had always been good at addressing crowds. Although he was, in a sense, performing to an audience, he was also being entirely frank, open and honest. He meant everything he said, and would miss them desperately.

Kristin nodded sadly. "So, when are you going to leave us?" she asked.

Alex looked at Fredrik and Ella, and raised his eyebrows. They looked at each other and said as one: "Next scheduled delivery is in four days and we can send you out on that, or you can wait a week and we can take you down."

"So, after the next party, I guess," Alex smiled. "If it's alright with you guys, I'll continue working, pay my dues."

"In that case," Annabel smiled mischievously, "when does the bar open because I'd like to place a few orders."

And so breakfast came to an end, the cue for Kristin to stand up to get everyone's attention.

"Right," she said, "as this marks our last week with the charming Mork ... sorry, Alex, I would just like everyone to know that we'll suspend morning activities on the day after he leaves, not only to get our heads around him not being here but also, of course, the inevitable hangover. Mork ... Damnit. Oh, to hell with it, I'm not going to call you Alex. Mork, if you and Fredrik could please make it happen, we'd like to honour you by hosting a special farewell dinner. And only then can Fredrik whisk you away."

Alex blushed and warmth filled him.

"Thank you, that's ... very touching."

"Oh, there's a condition," she raised her finger in warning. "You're not off that easily. You, naturally, will perform for us at the party."

Alex threw back his head and laughed: "You're the boss."

Excitement erupted on everyone's faces. Even Cassandra looked less conflicted and cracked a smile. She thought about offering him her guitar, but the idea reminded her of how embarrassed she was that she'd offered to teach him how to play and she blushed and kept quiet. She wanted to stay angry with him for lying to her, but she was admittedly sad that he was leaving and she had to admit that she was excited to hear him sing. All of which also irritated her because she felt like he was getting away with something terrible, she was just collateral damage.

Annabel could read the thoughts flickering across Cassandra's face and knew how she felt, having often found herself furious with Alex for charming his way out of trouble yet again. She waited until after breakfast to steal a quiet moment with her brother.

"You need to talk to Cassandra?"

"No, I don't."

"Yes. Yes, you do." Annabel eyed him in the way she always did, and sibling frustration flared. "Don't give me that look, she doesn't want to talk to me. She wants to be, and is perfectly justified being very angry with me."

"But you really like her I can see it in you."

"Yes, I do, and that's why I don't want to 'win her over'. Let her be angry with me. I'm leaving in a week so ... What difference does it make? If she hates me then maybe that'll be better for her, for both of us."

"Alex!"

"What?"

"That's really unfair."

"On who?"

"On her, dumbass. She wants to forgive you but doesn't know how, and if you don't give her the chance you'll just be that one regret she has to carry around."

He took a long breath to give himself a moment to consider Annabel's words.

"How could you possibly know that?"

"Because I'm a woman. And, more than that, I'm also your meddling sister." The room fell silent for a minute before she continued. "Alex, how has running away worked for you so far?"

His shoulders dropped; he really didn't want to have to accept that she was probably right.

"I have work to do."

"No, come on …"

He turned, his eyes flashing green.

"And what exactly do I say to her? Sorry, again? I won't ask her to just forgive me. I can't undo what I've done. I have to accept that. You … you weren't there when I told her, and even if you were, you can't see things the way I do, the total devastation. Jesus, Annie. She was … I don't know … disgusted. Disgusted with me, with herself."

They were standing at the bar, where Alex was supposed to start his morning checks and clean. She stared at him, and he let his gaze drop to the floor. She allowed a few moments to pass to clear the air.

"No, I wasn't there last night. You're right. But I was there today, and today she just kinda thinks you're a bit of a dick, which sounds to me like a step in the right direction."

"Again, how exactly do you know this?"

"We women have our ways."

"Yeah, I hear it's a lot like being a werewolf, except it's a myth that I'm a monster during full moon."

"See? You are a bit of a dick. Go talk to her."

"You've been here one day," Alex sighed, "and already you're telling me how to fix my broken relationships. I love you, but this is getting old." He looked her dead in the eyes and, in a direct and calm voice that made her think their father was speaking, said, "Annie, you need to let this one go."

All thoughts of trying to talk directly to Cassandra vanished from her mind; she realised that Alex had some genuine feelings for this woman, and that she was meddling in things she didn't fully understand.

"Okay, okay, I'm sorry, I'll drop it."

The room was silent when Fredrik walked in on them.

"Hey, rock star, just because your sister's here doesn't mean we don't have to do stocktake. Grab a clipboard."

Alex groaned, and pulled out the stocktake box from under the bar. Handing one of the sheets to Fredrik, he turned back to Annabel and smiled in way of apology.

"Wanna come watch me work?"

"It's all I've ever wanted. But I can't, I've got a temporary office set up in the main building and a pile of e-mails to reply to. Also, I need to report back to Dad that you're here. That you're safe. Happy. And I think you need to call him too."

"Actually, about that, can we do that together a little later? This and the orders shouldn't take more than a couple of hours."

The realisation that he could just pick up a phone and call his dad made Alex's heart jump a little and a broad smile spread across his face. He hadn't realised just how much he'd missed his family.

"I'll do this," Fredrik frowned. "Go. Go phone your father and tell him you're alive. It's okay. But when you're done, you come back and help me finish, you hear me?"

Annabel and Alex both turned and smiled at Fredrik, who could now clearly see the family resemblance.

"Man, thank you, that's really kind of you. And, as much as I'd like to leave you to get on with this alone, it's about three in the morning on the island. No one's going to be awake."

Fredrik thought about it for a moment and realised that he still thought of Alex as from Canada. How strange it was that he'd been lying for so long and for the first time Fredrik felt the sting of it all.

"Oh, well, in that case, get back to work."

So it was that Alex followed Fredrik into the back room to start counting stock.

Annabel was right though, he thought; he did need to talk to Cassandra, but he also didn't know how to go about it. In his many encounters with women, he'd never been in this sort of situation before, and wanted Fredrik's advice.

But Fredrik, who was there just a second ago, had gone. He could, however, hear voices in the bar.

"Oh, yes, of course we've taken great care of your brother." said Fredrik. "We knew he wasn't telling us everything, but this is a home for lost animals and he seemed very lost when he arrived."

"It's very comforting to know that he's been here the whole time and not somewhere destroying himself."

Alex moved quietly to the door and watched them, frowning.

"Could you not?" Fredrik poured coffee and, seeing the look on Alex's face, laughed.

"It's funny how quickly people adopt their old behaviour when their family is around."

For a brief moment Alex wanted to say something, witty and clever about Josh, but now was perhaps not the time for him to give in to his own insecurities. Fredrik was allowed to flirt with Annabel and Annabel was allowed to have fun and be flirted with.

After coffee she excused herself to head off to do some work and the moment the door closed Fredrik turned to Alex.

"So, what are you going to do about Cassandra?"

"What?"

"Oh, come on man, I can see it's eating at you. What do you want to do there? And how can I help?"

"You're an excellent friend," Alex put his hand on Fredrik's shoulder. "But I have no idea. I was actually going to ask for some advice. I want to talk to her, but I don't think she wants to hear from me."

"Of course she does."

"What makes you say that?"

"Look, no one gets that hurt unless they're that emotionally invested. That's been the problem with you two for weeks, no ... forever. Casual friends don't get that angry with each other. I mean, yesterday, what was the first thing she did when she woke up after yelling at you?"

"Uhmmm, came to my room?"

"Exactly. You are her go-to person. She wants you to be the one with whom to vent her anger, even when it's you she's angry with. It's a very confusing time for her."

"Yes, yes, it is ... How does everyone seem to know more about this stuff than me?"

"Don't take it too personally, man. It's a lot more to do with us watching you, than it is you being a lying shitbag. From the outside we can see both of you; from inside you can only see the other person. And, besides, you can't see the whole solutions because you're right in the middle of it. Problems are always easier when they aren't yours."

Alex sighed again.

"I take it that when you say 'we', you mean Cassandra and I are the topic of everyone's conversation?"

"Naturally. We live in the middle of nowhere; it's going to be super boring here without you creating drama. I swear, having you here is more interesting than any TV show."

Alex raised an eyebrow.

"Season three's big reveal ... What will happen when a person from Mork's past walks into the bar? Stay tuned for another exciting episode. That kinda thing?"

"Exactly. It's great, horrible, hurtful, and totally insane, but it is also what it is."

The room went quiet for a moment before Alex responded.

"But ... I think she kinda hates me."

Fredrik's turn to put a hand on Alex's shoulder.

"Well, it's good that you're not totally clueless. Man, you lied to her, to all of us, but mostly to her. She doesn't hate you; she's just hurt, bad. You need to go to her, talk to her, let her yell at you all over again, and you need to take it. Until she's got the noise out of her head and she can start thinking clearly again, this is important. If you just disappear without doing it, you risk leaving her with that voice in her head, and yours, and there will always be questions. And that's not fair."

Fredrik's words hit home. Alex really understood what he meant, because he could already hear the whispers in his mind.

"Thank you, my friend."

Fredrik shrugged.

"Also, she's the only person here with a guitar, so you're going to have to borrow that."

"Ah, shit."

"Yeah, good luck. I'll finish stocktake."

"What do I ever say?"

"Man, look at yourself. You're a writer and a poet; you don't need some special line or clever trick to solve this problem. Just be honest with her. It was lies that got you here. Think before you answer, say the true thing, not the right thing. Let the cards fall where they may. Her problem is that you lied, and you can only fix that with the truth." Fredrik looked him over and shook his head. " Shit, man … I didn't realise you had it this bad for this girl. You're kind of a wreck too."

"Yeah, me neither, not until she lost it with me so badly and I realised I'd lost something precious."

"You haven't lost her yet. And you have one saving grace: you didn't lie to her to get something from her. You were in hiding, and just happened to meet her. Now go, she's in her room studying, as usual … when she's not in your room studying."

Alex forced a smile and grabbed his coat to head out. As he made the slower-than-usual trudge to her door he found the sensible, rational side of his mind telling him he'd already lost her, so he had nothing left to lose. But his heart refused to believe that. He took a deep breath, gritted his teeth, and knocked.

On the other side of the door Cassandra jumped. She put her book face down on the desk and went to open the door.

"Hey." Alex managed a half-smile.

"Oh, it's you …"

Her words cut at him.

"Can we talk?" She moved aside to let him in.

"What do you want to talk about?"

Alex turned to face her and gently sniffed the air. She wasn't angry, which was good, but she wasn't happy either.

"I don't know really," he said as he flopped down in his usual spot on the floor. " But everyone keeps telling me that I need to come talk to you, and apologise until the words sound strange, and give you the opportunity to scream at me all over again, and I guess I get what they're talking about, but at the same time ... I don't know if that's actually what will help or work or what you want either. So I think I'm here so that you can talk. To your best friend at camp maybe? This whole thing has been really shit, and largely my fault. I know that, and I am unbelievably sorry. I also seem to just make it worse ..." He looked up at her, his face pained but open. "I don't know how to fix what I broke, or even if it can be fixed, but I do know I can't fix it without you. So here I am ... Everyone says we need to talk and that I need to be totally honest, so here I am. What do we do?"

Cassandra harrumphed down onto the bed.

"Yeah, that's great and all, except my 'best friend at camp' turned out to be a lie, and I don't know how to deal with that because I don't know which parts of you I know, and which parts you made up."

"Does it help at all if I say that I wasn't lying to you specifically or trying to trick you into anything? You just showed up while I was in the middle of a lie to myself and got swept up in it?"

"Actually ... no."

Alex nodded his head and thought for a moment.

"Okay, well, my book is open. I want to fix this, and I don't want to leave things this fucked up between us. So ask me anything, full access, no restrictions. Because I think you ... I mean, you haven't kicked me out. I know that look on your face – I think you want to fix this too. I've missed you the last few weeks and—" Alex felt like he was simply repeating himself. "I honestly can't think of any other solutions."

"It's a little unfair to dump it all on me like that."

"Again, open to suggestion."

Cassandra slid down onto the floor to be at the same level.

"No. But still ..."

For just a second he could pick up something in her voice that gave him hope, and he leapt on it.

"Oh, don't pout, you love being in charge."

Then, as if seeing sunshine after a month of rain, she smiled, but that quickly faded. What he read now was rejection.

"So, were you laughing at me the whole time I was trying to teach you to play guitar?"

"What? No, not at all, mostly I felt embarrassed and deeply ashamed. That's why I kept making excuses not to do it. You were being super sweet and patient and I just wanted to die, but felt that confessing that I actually knew how to play would be, in my mind, a really obvious clue to my real identity."

"You have any idea how many people learn how to play the guitar? It wouldn't have made everyone go, "Ah-haaa! Has to be Alex Harris, we knew it all along." It's not like we suspected anything was wrong or were looking for clues."

A blush crept up Alex's clean-shaven face.

"Yeah, well, that's the sane and rational approach, but I was very self-conscious about what I said and how to keep up the charade. Which I hated, for the record."

"If you hated it so much, why did you keep it up?"

He sighed again and gave himself a few moments to feel out his answer.

"When I left Syn Island, I was running away from a fairly serious breakdown. So much so that I thought people were out to get me, actually, actively chasing me."

"What happened? Did you get in trouble with the law? Were you running from a crime? Drugs?"

"It's … it's really hard to explain now. My nephew was kidnapped, and my dog – Mork – and I … I found the guys who'd taken him. And, uhmmm, Mork being a wolf, and being very protective of my nephew, savaged the men who'd taken him, and in the wake of the terrible stress that I was already under, and having witnessed it all, I thought that … well, that I was going to get the blame; he was my dog, after all. It was an insane and paranoid response, I know, but that's what happened. So … I … ran."

Another lie for the pile, but it was also as close to the truth as he could get without saying the word 'werewolf'. The notion that he was a werewolf seemed so unbelievable that she would probably write it off as some rock-star fantasy and that'd only make the situation worse. Or at least that's what he told himself. He also knew that his version vaguely matched the story the press put out about the incident.

"Anyway, so when I got here I tried to think of every practicality that would back up my story. Alex Harris was a rock star, so obviously his alter ego Mork couldn't sing or play an instrument."

Cassandra just stared at him, neither of them saying anything.

"Jesus," she offered finally.

"Yeah."

Her face softened. He'd clearly been through something traumatic and had witnessed something truly horrible. But she was scared that if she got close to him now she might kiss him, and she still had the voice in her head telling her, no.

"So … what happened to your dog? Where's he now?"

"Mork? I don't know."

Her hand flew up to her mouth, stifling a laugh.

"You named yourself after your dog?"

"I love that dog."

"No, wait, hold on, let's just back up here for a second … You lied about being able to play guitar because you thought it would be too obvious, but took on the name of your pet?"

He couldn't tell whether he was seeing mock or genuine anger in her voice.

"His name was never made public knowledge – hell, even that he existed was never public knowledge. He's half wolf half Great Dane. Guy was huge and I … I may have smuggled him onto the island from Canada."

She chuckled and shook her head in disbelief.

"As for what I'm going to do now. Well, I'm going to pack up and head off on a pilgrimage. I mean, I'm still a little lost, but feel closer to myself than I've felt in a really long time, so I'm going to announce to the world that I'm not dead or insane, then head off quietly and see more of the world."

He shifted his gaze to her and they locked eyes. For a moment she held fast but her guard slipped a little.

"But why can't you stay?"

A strong compulsion washed over him to just tell her the whole truth, that he was a werewolf on the hunt for others like him to try to get a better understanding of what had happened to him as a child. That her recognising the drawing from his nightmares as a real place was the true reason he was leaving, and that he desperately wanted her to come with him. Perhaps he should try? But just as he was about to open his mouth, there was a knock at the door and Sagi peeked his head in. They both looked up in alarm as if caught in an intimate moment.

"You're needed at The Sanctuary.

Chapter 8

Fredrik was waiting at the stairs leading into The Sanctuary.

"What's going on?" asked Alex, spotting a Land Rover that didn't belong to anyone there.

"Two guys just showed up out of the blue from the forest. Something isn't right about them. They're in there talking to Aina. I wanted you guys in there – I'm going to check their truck."

"You thinking poachers?"

Fredrik narrowed his eyes, and a faint and familiar smell tickled Alex's nose.

"See you inside."

Aina was standing with the two men at the far side of the room, all drinking coffee. She was explaining the work they did at The Sanctuary. The men didn't seem fazed when Alex and Cassandra walked in; they continued to smile, nod and ask questions.

"So we didn't think this area had that significant a wolf population. Has it recently increased? Have you been introducing new wolves into the area?"

Annabel had left her office to stand just inside Aina's vision so she would know she wasn't alone.

"Well, with the rehabilitation work we've been doing, along with the nature conservation, we're helping to protect the population and that's created an environment where it can now begin to grow. But part of the reason we chose this location was because it already had a good, established wolf population. We'd like to reach a point where we can send wolves to other parts of the world where the population has taken a significant hit, either through climate or poaching."

"Oh, right. That's very cool. And have you had issues with rogue wolves much?"

Alex tried to place their accents, but again got the faint smell of something familiar, something wrong.

"No," Aina smiled, "But tell me, what brings you two up here?"

"Oh, we're just on a camping trip. We didn't even know this place was here until we happened upon it."

"Oh! These woods are beautiful. And what brought you to Norway?"

The men glanced at each other.

"We were sent here for work."

The door burst open as Fredrik stormed in, a massive wolf bundled in his arms and fury blazing in his eyes.

"These two fuckers are sports hunters!" he spat as he lay the wolf on the table. "Bastards!"

A cold shiver ran down Alex's body as he realised what the smell had been. He ran over to the wolf. The Alpha female of his pack back at the cave. He'd known her well and they'd run together. She was his friend and now she lay dead on the table. He ran his hands through her fur, his fingers tracing the three bullet wounds on her flank. His jaw set rigid and tears rolled down his cheeks. His heart was beating fast in his chest when he turned to face the two men.

The room had gone quiet.

The strangers had drawn pistols and both were pointed at him.

"If you were poaching for fur, you'd have skinned her already."

His eyes were shining bright green and he knew what was coming, and he didn't care.

"Yes, well, we read online that there's a wolf in these woods the size of a bear and wanted to add it to our collection."

The two men laughed, and Alex laughed with them as he slowly moved forward, stepping out of his shoes.

"It's funny, when I was a child my cousin called me the G'Mork, because it was the scariest thing he could think of."

His voice was rough and deep and he smiled a wide, toothy grin. The men pulled the hammer back on their guns.

"You don't want to be doing that, demon."

Alex's breath was heavy and loud, his muscles tensing and rippling with every breath. The volunteers and staff instinctively knew that the firearms were no longer the most dangerous things in the room and even the air seemed to grow still with fear.

The man's final word struck Alex.

"And why's that?"

"Two reasons: one, we'll be able to shoot you and at least one of your friends before you cross the room; and two, these guys have silver bullets."

That stopped Alex in his advance.

"Now, why don't you step outside with us and we'll make this clean and simple for you?"

Alex shot a glance at Annabel who'd gone a ghostly pale at the mention of silver; he could see her muscles fighting against themselves – she wanted to intervene but was being held in check by fear. Everyone else looked on at the exchange with a mix of fear and confusion. Alex scowled, forced himself to breathe slowly, then slowly raised his hands.

"There's a good boy."

The men walked around him, never taking the guns off him, determined to get to the door first to make sure he didn't bolt. All the while, Alex was experiencing flashbacks to when the wolf had bit him and the state the creature was in when he'd found him. When the men reached the door one spotted Fredrik clenching his jaw and slowly flexing his fists.

"Don't try to be a hero," he warned, waving his firearm at Fredrik. "This isn't a movie."

The words snapped Alex back to focus and a deep terrible chuckle rose up out of the back of his throat.

"What are you laughing at, monster?"

"Do you know that when I was sixteen I tried to kill myself?"

"So?"

"You know what I learnt then?"

The two men shot nervous glances at each other and Alex's face elongated slightly, making his voice darker, more sinister.

"Silver just makes me itch."

Then, in what seemed like an explosion of thunder and violence, the wolf Mork burst forward as if leaping out of Alex and slammed into the two men, sending the three of them tumbling head first down the stairs. Mork moved like lightning, violent and powerful, lashing out, snapping and clawing in every direction. His ferocious anger was driving him wild so that by the time they hit the bottom of the stairs both men were little more than broken bags of dead meat. Mork stood up over them, fury burning through him as he threw his head back and howled.

Inside The Sanctuary the howl was the trigger that turned everyone's paralysing fear to panic. Sagi caught Cassandra as she crumpled to the ground, taking him with her. Fredrik stumbled backwards, lost his footing and hit the floor hard. He promptly gagged, rolled over and vomited into a plant pot. Only Annabel and Aina managed to keep themselves upright and sprinted over to the door – something they both instantly regretted. Aina froze as she watched the wolf take another deep breath as though to howl again. He checked himself mid-breath when the sound of Annabel's voice reached his ears.

"Mork! Mork!"

Slowly she began making her way down the steps towards him, her hands outstretched, speaking calmly.

"It's okay, it's okay ... It's over. Over. Just ... just calm down."

His eyes wide with both fury and adrenaline, Mork took hold of himself and turned to face his sister, then down at the bodies sprawled at his feet. Immediately his jaw began to snap, his teeth grinding against each other, breath fast and erratic. Slowly his deep breaths turned to soft whimpers.

"It's okay, Mork, they were going to kill you, you were just defending yourself, defending us."

Mork turned to her and then looked past her at the others. Aina, Fredrik, Sagi and Cassandra had gathered at the top of the stairs watching the drama unfold, and had at some point amid the flurry of limbs and blood been joined by others, their hands over their mouths, eyes wide, gasping at the horror that had just played out in front of them.

Annabel could tell that things were about to take a turn for the worst when the look in Mork's eyes began to change. She sensed that he felt caged, surrounded, vulnerable, and that was never a good thing. At this stage, he could pose a serious danger to everyone. Then she spotted the bleeding hole in his shoulder and realised that, during the chaos of the scuffle, he must have been struck by a bullet. She straightened up, retreated one step and yelled at the others.

"Everyone stay back! Go back to your rooms, go back inside, please … Please just go away!" She'd only just found her brother and was now terrified that he'd turn and run again. She took a slow, cautious step towards him, her hand still outstretched, heart pounding in her chest. "Look at me," she urged him. "Look at me! It's going to be all right. Please, just stay calm."

Mork could see the fear in her eyes, smell it wafting off everyone.

While everyone else had appeared to have been turned to stone, Ella immediately recognised the danger they were in and was taking Annabel's warning seriously. Hurriedly, she motioned to Kristin and the two guided a reluctant Ken and Greg into the bar. The others at the top of the stairs, though, remained fixed on the scene in front of them. They wanted to help, but felt powerless. There was nothing they could do to diffuse the situation, and they knew it. So, following Sagi's lead, they sat at the top of the stairs with their hands open and visible. During his stint in the military, he'd had learnt that if you're ever captured, make yourself look as little like a threat as possible; this was just a modification of that protocol.

Mork lay down and heaved a sigh, allowing his instinct to run, dissipate. As the urge lifted, the pain in his shoulder grew, and he let out a low groan as he tried to turn his head to lick at the hole. He looked back at his sister, then closed his eyes.

"No, don't, the facilities here are perfectly suited to wolves, not people. Let them get the bullet out first."

Annabel was still panicked but refused to let it get the better of her. Behind her she could hear the others start whispering, frantic at the realisation that Mork had been shot. Fredrik stood up and walked closer.

"He's sane? He can understand us?"

"Perfectly, and his memory basically carries over. It's only when his emotions are high that he can be a little dangerous, but even then, he's never hurt any of us."

"Can he talk?"

"No."

Fredrik cautiously stepped closer to Mork, who sat up slowly as he approached. Fredrik could now clearly see the bleeding wound in his shoulder and his mind started putting together what needed to be done for a wolf in that condition.

"Mork, my friend, can you walk or do you need to be carried?"

Slowly Mork stood up and tried putting pressure on his hurt leg. A bolt of pain shot through his body and he let out a yelp. Fredrik stopped in his tracks, watching him carefully to see what he would do next. Balancing precariously on three legs, Mork hopped and nodded.

"This is so fucked up, man! You're a werewolf? I mean, it explains a lot, but still ... And who are those guys? The way they acted, with silver bullets and guns and everything, I think they came here looking for you."

Mork frowned, then snorted and shrugged, which sent another wave of pain through him.

"Right, yes, okay ... We need to get you inside.'

Fredrik then turned to the others.

"We have a wolf with a bullet in him – let's go, people!"

Everyone sprang to life. Cassandra went to fetch the others and explain the situation as best she could, while Annabel, Aina and Fredrik followed Mork inside. Sagi calmly and gravely volunteered to cover the bodies and try to preserve the scene. In his mind, they had one dead wolf, and two dead poachers killed by a wolf – it balanced. He'd had to deal with this kind of violence before and knew exactly how horrible it was, and didn't want the others to deal with it if they didn't have to. Fredrik turned to Mork.

"You know the drill ... First we need to X-ray your shoulder to check the location of the bullet before we can decide how best to remove it. If ... I can't believe I'm saying this ... if we put you under, will you change back?"

Mork took a deep breath and moved his head in a 'so-so' fashion he really wasn't sure, then leapt up onto the X-ray table. Aina started to prepare for the scan but knew she needed to wait for Kristin, who was their lead surgeon. Meanwhile, Cassandra stood exasperated, trying to explain in a way that wouldn't make her seem completely insane that their friend Mork, Alex, wasn't just an international rock star but a werewolf, and that he'd been shot by two random guys who appeared to have been hunting him down and he now needed a bullet removed from his shoulder. It didn't take long before fear and frustration started getting the better of her.

"Look, Mork's been shot and now we have a wolf with a bullet in his shoulder ... It doesn't matter right now that they're the same person. Move!"

They all hurried to The Sanctuary to find Sagi pegging a large tarpaulin over the crime scene – in part to preserve it but also to hide it from everyone else. He stopped Ella as she passed; they needed to discuss how they were going to move forward with the bodies, but hung back until the others had made their way inside. Where they encountered the biggest wolf any of them had ever seen, lying calmly on the examination table. His X-rays were up on the light box.

"Right," said Aina as they came in, "now that you're all here we can begin. We're going to try to look past all the strange aspects of this for a moment and focus on dealing with the situation as we see it. This animal is injured and needs our help. As you can see, the bullet is lodged in the scapula, so ... What's the next step? Where do we take it from here?"

She was presenting the information as she would any other lecture she'd given on the subject, hoping that that would sterilise the situation and get people thinking clearly and logically, herself included. Kristin stepped forward to stand next to her and together they waited for someone to answer. Greg, who hadn't yet looked at the X-ray as he was mesmerised by the wolf itself, suddenly found his voice.

"Assess the condition of the animal, then sedate it in preparation for surgery."

Mork let out a groan, which Aina ignored.

"Well done, Greg. Now, looking at him, what can we say about his situation?"

"Uhmmm, he seems very calm and tame for a wolf. Makes me wonder if he's a pet."

There was a low growl in Mork's throat, which made Greg feel a little uncomfortable, embarrassed even.

"Again, very good. It's important to note these kinds of things, as we generally deal with wild animals that are frightened and in-jured; most are already tranquilised when they arrive, but if not, or if they've recovered from the tranquiliser, we'd need to see if we can administer the drugs safely. Out in the wild we'd obviously use a gun; once they're here though we'd either put something into their food to calm them or, if they become really hostile, we'd have to dart them once again. But in this situation we can simply inject the animal."

She quickly turned to Annabel: "Right?"

Annabel had been standing with Mork, gently stroking him the entire time and fighting off her impatience at the others going through the motions instead of just helping her brother, but she also knew that for them him being a werewolf was a little world shattering.

"Yes, he's fine as long as he's not surprised. Also, uhmmm, you can talk to him."

Kristin handed Greg the sedative and he nervously extracted it into a syringe. Mork looked at it, then up at his sister and let out a snort.

"Oh, right, that's probably not going to be enough."

Greg quickly looked back to Kristin, who frowned and turn to Annabel.

"We know what we're doing," Kristin assured her.

"Oh, I know, but he's really resistant to this kind of thing. Ever since he was bitten, whenever doctors had to put him out he'd wake up in half the expected time. If you give him the normal amount of an animal this size, he'll wake up sooner than you think."

Everyone started looking around uncomfortably, still struggling to come to terms with the idea that the animal on the table was in fact their friend. That was the final straw for Annabel.

"I don't care what you believe," she insisted through gritted teeth. "Could you all stop standing around staring and actually do something. My brother has been shot! If you want my family and my company to help fund this place you'll pull yourselves together and help him!"

Fredrik put his hand on Annabel's shoulders in an attempt to calm her. Mork leaned over and licked her hand to try to reassure her that he was all right, and then turned to Greg and snorted again. Greg in turn drew more sedative from the bottle and walked over to him.

"You're, uhmmm, you're going to feel a slight pinch, a stabbing sensation at the base of your neck. Please, uhmmm … please don't eat me."

For a split second Mork thought of bearing his teeth as a joke, but thought better of it considering that the pain in his shoulder had been growing steadily worse. He closed his eyes as Greg administered the injection and in less than a minute he could feel it starting to take effect. For a few moments everyone stood staring as he resisted, then quickly gave up and dropped his head slowly onto the table. At that point Fredrik and Aina led Annabel into the main lounge away from where the surgery would take place. She had managed to calm herself a little but remained anxious; she wished she could have had the rest of the family with her for support.

Waiting for news from the adjoining room, time seemed interminable. Her nerves were shot, helped in part by a few too many cups of coffee, and she struggled to maintain her composure. She knew, too, that it was time to call home, she couldn't put it off any longer, especially now that matters were out of her control. She needed to report back. When she turned her laptop on she found a message from Josh waiting for her, asking how it was going and if she'd found anything and then Josh must have seen her come online and the screen immediately flashed with an incoming call.

"Hey, honey, how's Norway treating you? Any news on Alex yet?"

Annabel's urge was to burst into tears when his image appeared on her screen, but managed to mostly hold herself back. She couldn't allow herself to crumble, not now; she knew there was no way of explaining the situation to him without also telling him that Alex was a werewolf. A stray tear ran down her cheeks and she forced a smile.

"I missed your face so much ... And, yes ... Yes, I found him. How are you? How's Bastian?"

"Awwww, honey, Bastian's just fine. I spoke to your Dad last night, says he's being a real champion about you being away. I miss you too – I should have come with you ... So, where's Alex? He all right?"

Logically, Annabel knew Alex was going to be fine. She'd seen him survive a devastating car accident, but between missing her son, her boyfriend, the relief of having found her brother after hunting for so long, coupled with watching him savage two men and then be shot, she was fighting hard to hold herself together. Josh narrowed his eyes at her.

"Annie, you okay? What's the matter?"

She blushed. Clearly, she wasn't as good at staying outwardly calm as she had thought.

"Oh, no, it's just … uhmmm … they found a wolf that had been caught by poachers this morning and it just got me, you know. Dead animal and everything. Also, you know finally finding Alex after all this time, the relief has taken the wind out of my sails a little."

"Ahh, that sounds horrible. I'm sorry you had to see that kind of thing. I hope those guys get the same treatment – that sort of thing is just fucking sick."

Annabel felt a little nauseous thinking about what had happened.

"Yeah, well … As for Alex, he's sleeping; he works at night here. He did want me to wait before contacting you and Dad, but you called me so that doesn't count, and I'm really glad you did."

"Oh right, yeah, I guess that makes sense. So has he said what he's been doing, what he's going to do?"

Annabel palmed off the question and steered the conversation back to Bastian before making an excuse to end the call, and continue to worry about her brother in peace. She missed Josh, but realised too that she had no answers to his questions and it wasn't helping her de-stress.

Chapter 9

Alex woke on a gurney in The Sanctuary, wondering at what point he had returned to his human form. He blinked a few times and turned his head to see Kristin sitting nearby, watching him.

"How do you feel?"

"Fine, all things considered."

"Physically, you're perfect, there isn't even a mark. I had to take the stiches out as soon as you changed back."

"Ah, yeah, I could have told you that was going to happen."

"Your body is ... well, it's amazing. I've seen it do things today I wouldn't have believed possible if I hadn't seen it with my own eyes. And I don't just mean the transformation, which was, I mean, I've seen some really abnormal things in my years as a veterinary surgeon but ... that ..."

"I know ... It's a different sort of thing. I'm told you get used to it." And then, worrying where this conversation would take them, Alex tried to move the conversation along, and added, "By the way, did everyone see me naked?"

"No," Kristin laughed a little, "not everyone. Your sister and Fredrik were out of the room at the time."

"Oh ... Oh good."

She laughed again.

"No, I'm just joking, you were covered. Annabel had warned us that you might change while asleep. But, uhmmm ... I want to ask you a few things."

Alex took a deep breath and waited, hoping this wasn't going to be the conversation he'd been dreading.

"We took some blood to check for infection, and then you just healed when you changed so I started a few little experiments to see how your blood responds to infected tissue samples we have ..."

Alex's muscles tensed. He swung his legs off the bed so that he was facing her, his eyes shining bright green, which stopped her in her tracks.

"I really, really, really need you to destroy those samples."

His words were as calm as he could muster, but there was no mistaking his seriousness.

"But, Mork, the potential for good here is extraordinary, for humans and—"

He cut her off again.

"No. No, it isn't, believe me... Me being a werewolf is not going to help anyone."

"But what if we can synthesise a 'cure-all' from your blood?"

"And what if you infect people with lycanthropy along the way?"

"Well, then, we have other sources ... where we can get more blood for testing."

A deep growl rumbled out of Alex's chest, filling the room.

"Do you hear yourself? You want to make other werewolves so that you can harvest their blood? And, in the process, brush aside the almost comical supervillain nature of that plan. Kristin, I lost my temper at the sight of a dead wolf and killed two people! Is that want you want to make more of? I was ten years old when I was bitten. I've spent my entire life learning how to try to stay calm.

Destroy those samples, and the experiments and forget about it … Please. This thing isn't a blessing, I promise, and it's not something to play around with. I'm begging you. The idea of spreading my infection terrifies me. Don't … don't try to claim it's for science and then make me responsible for this happening to other people. You can't just have my blood – and you can't take it by force."

They stared at each other for a long time, both thinking without speaking, trying to find a way to push their points further.

"But, Alex, think of the poss—"

"Kristin, just because there are monsters doesn't mean there also needs to be mad scientists."

The mental image got to her, but it was less the prospect of being the mad scientist than the realisation that the man she knew and loved believed himself to be a monster. She searched his face for a sign, a faint glimmer of hope that his stubbornness was just part of his argument, but couldn't find it.

"You're not a monster, Mork. I … I really want to use this information, but you're right of course, I'm not going to steal your blood. I'd never do that. I … I don't fully understand, but I'll respect your wish and I'll get rid of what I have."

Alex could finally breathe again.

"Thank you."

She had been waiting for him to wake up so that they could have this conversation but now, feeling somewhat defeated, she excused herself to inform the others that he'd woken up. Alex watched her walk off and wished the conversation had never happened; he wished even more that he didn't feel the need to get Fredrik to make sure that all traces of his blood were destroyed. It had been something Dr Cooper had thought of very early on when discussing the original bite all those years ago and how it had healed so quickly, the potential in him for medical research, and how dangerous it might be for Alex when confronted by someone who believed they'd found the key to cure all diseases. What they could justify doing to him with that as the end prize. Above all now, Alex really wanted to believe that Kristin wasn't really that type of person. The drugs were still toying with his mind so he closed his eyes and eased his way through to what had just happened, the prospect of maybe offering himself over to science for the greater good. Perhaps it would be better for everyone if he became a science experiment. Again, he remembered a conversation with Dr Cooper.

"What if there's a way to turn my blood into some kind of magical potion, Doc? What if I can cure cancer? Am I being selfish hiding that from the world?"

Dr Cooper had been turning this very point over endlessly in his mind since it had first been raised, and he had come to a clear personal decision on the topic.

"Alex, look at it from this point of view. So far everything that has happened with your lycanthropy has followed its natural course. As unnatural as it seems to us, it remained true to itself. You were bitten by another werewolf, so you became one. Your transformations are based on your emotions and on the stages of the moon. And, in keeping in tune with nature, you have found balance and control. Now if we take that out of nature, and turn towards science, distilling it, reducing it to its very essence, there's no way to know exactly what will happen. Not without a barrage of tests and years of thorough research anyway ... And could you face the consequences of the potential outcomes? Say they reach a point where all tests in labs come up safe and it is given to a patient with cancer, only to find that when actually in a living human body it doesn't attack the cancer it bonds to. We don't know what sort of creature could be born out of that, what the combination of your werewolf DNA, the chemicals added to suppress the wolf, and the patient's DNA will mean. Even if it works one million out of one million and one times, is that a risk you're willing to take? Also, there's always the possibility that after years of testing and experiments it turns out there isn't a way to synthesise a safe version of your blood into a magical cure."

Alex had never really liked the idea, but he had thought about it as a child. What pushed him over the edge was when Dr Cooper asked him one simple question.

"What does the wolf think of all of this?"

That was all he had needed, all anyone had ever needed to say. Mork knew it was wrong, knew it should never be done, and when Alex looked at that, so did he. He had played the conversation over in his mind a few times over the years, usually around the anniversary of his mother's death and ... The spell broke as soon as the scent of his sister reached him and he opened his eyes just as she peeked from behind the door. She rushed forward and wrapped her arms around him.

"Hey, hey, what's the matter?"

"You got shot, you arsehole."

He held her tight for a few seconds, comforting her.

"No, I mean it, what's going on? What's really going on?"

She sniffed back her tears.

"It's just ... just everything. I've missed and worried about you so much, and now you're going to have to run again, and I miss Bastian. I've never been away from him for so long and, well, seeing the animal inside come out like that is also ... well, it's scary and I think I'm just a bit overwhelmed. Besides, you did actually get shot, you know."

Alex paused for a moment and Fredrik, who was hovering at the door with Ella and Sagi, jumped at the opportunity.

"You can't run off just yet though."

Alex turned to look at them and raised an eyebrow.

"Well, we have rangers and police on their way to deal with the bodies. Obviously, our victims were poachers and were killed by a wolf. Karma. Makes sense to us ... But we can't actually let anyone leave until they've been through. It would look really suspicious."

Alex and Annabel both knew that Fredrik was telling them the official story and it warmed Alex's heart to know his friends weren't abandoning him.

"Also, man," Sagi stepped forward, "you're going to want to come look at some stuff with us before they get here."

"How long do we have?"

Fredrik looked at his watch and shrugged.

"Distance, weather, Sagi's military training making him an officially trained crime-scene person ... They should be here in about twelve hours."

"And how long is it going to take to see what you want to show me?"

"If we do it right, an hour."

"Great, then I'm going to sleep a little longer. Let the last of these chemicals work their way out so I can be clear headed. That cool?"

Fredrik looked back at the other two then back at them.

"Yeah, man, that's cool."

Annabel took that as her cue to leave and followed the others, but Alex reached out and caught her arm.

"Stay with me, please."

"Okay, okay, I'm right here."

She could see in his eyes that he was tired, but she wasn't sure whether it was the effects of the drugs, the stress or both. She sat down on the bed next to him and waited. Fredrik smiled to himself and closed the door behind him as he left.

"I've killed four people now."

Alex's eyes welled up with tears.

"No, sweetie, Mork—"

"I am Mork! We're the same, Annabel. I can't use that as an excuse anymore because it's exactly that. It's an excuse. Mork and I are one ... We ... I killed those people."

Annabel thought for a moment, trying to hold back her own tears for the sake of her little brother.

"The first two had taken my son and I would have done exactly the same; and the other two had shot you, had killed that wolf and come here for you. I think ... I think they were werewolf hunters. You're not a monster, Alex; you're not turning into a Hollywood werewolf, I promise."

Alex lay back down on the bed and stared at the ceiling. They sat in silence for a while.

"You know what I really, truly miss?"

Annabel smiled at him as he tilted his head to look at her again.

"The full moon."

"What? What do you mean? The full moon has been one of the key factors in your life since forever."

He smiled sadly and his eyes grew distant again.

"Yes, but I haven't seen a full moon in real life since I was ten years old."

The thought struck Annabel – she'd never really considered that before. But of course there was no way he would have been able to see it, or see it ever again. A flood of memories from their childhood rushed over her of Alex loudly proclaiming that he thought the full moon in a pale blue sky was more beautiful than anything. At the time, it had sent the family into fits of laughter. Now it sent a shiver through her and she finally lost her battle within herself as tears streamed down her face.

"I'd ... I'd never really thought about it like that."

He rubbed his face and tried to push out thoughts of miracle cures and dead bodies.

"Most of the time, I don't hate what I am, I actually love it. I don't admit it much but I really do – it's like having super powers. But every now and then it creeps up on me and hits me, out of no-where, and I just want it to be over, to be done. I don't want to be this thing anymore."

The drugs were allowing him to swim to a place of half-remembered dreams, and he knew that he wasn't making perfect sense. But talking helped. Annabel lay down next to him on the small bed and listened to his mindless ramblings until he finally drifted off to sleep. She considered staying for a while, but eventually slipped off, careful not to disturb his sleep.

The second Alex's eyes had closed, they opened again into his dream, and he was already running. Only, instead of sprinting to-wards something, as in most of his dreams, this time he was run-ning away, and panic gripped his heart. He was consumed by a desperate need to get away, to escape from whatever it was that was after him. But there it was, gaining on him, and as it drew clos-er he could tell that it wasn't just one thing but many, a crowd of people. As the thought hit him, he realised too that he was running through a city with cobbled streets and narrow alleyways. Sud-denly he took a wrong turn and hit the dead end he'd been dread-ing. He turned to face the mob that was now gathering around him. His heart raced and the sound of it filled his ears as he saw the face of all those people reeking of hatred. Only then did Alex become aware that he was still human; maybe, if he could change, that would scare them off and give him a chance to escape. The transformation began almost instantly. He ripped off his clothes, and fell onto all fours, letting out a deafening howl. Eyes wide, the mob stared on in horror and, to his own surprise, he began gnash-ing his teeth, fury gripping his racing heart. As he leapt forward at them, he also threw himself out of bed. For a moment all he saw was bright white light, the images from his nightmare flash-ing through his head. Then, when his eyes adjusted, he realised that he was standing naked in the middle of the room, Cassandra blushing crimson in the corner. Lowering his arms, he cleared his throat and said as confidently as he could.

"So ... this is my penis."

Chapter 10

"That somehow doesn't make this any less awkward."

Cassandra couldn't help but glance down.

"If you think it's bad now," Alex continued bravely, "just give it a second."

For a moment Cassandra felt a mild panic set in, but before she could get any words out, the door burst open and Fredrik, Ella and Annabel appeared.

Alex sighed again.

"See?"

"Christ, Alex, we can all see – cover yourself up!"

He reached for the sheet that had slipped to the floor and wrapped it around his waist, then turned back to Cassandra.

"Sorry," he shrugged.

Then he turned to his sister.

"How long was I out for?"

"About an hour."

He ran through things in his mind for a second.

"Groovy, now can we have a few minutes?"

The others looked at the situation, smiled and left without a word. Just as Annabel closed the door, Alex called out.

"And, for the record, it's cold in here!"

"Sure it is, rock star," Fredrik's voice came back from the other side of the door.

Cassandra giggled and Alex frowned in mock offence. The room fell quiet and they just looked at each other, until a single thought bubbled up out of Cassandra.

"So ... you're a werewolf."

It wasn't a question, and Alex nodded in affirmation.

"You're the massive black wolf we saw during the blizzard. You were coming home after realising a storm was on its way?"

"Yea, well, it was full moon. I ... aahhhh ... I have a cave I stay in. I went there after not being able to sleep here and when I woke up I realised what was going on and decided that being snowed in was a bad idea, so ran for it."

"This is, well, honestly, this is terrifying. How long have you been like this? I mean, is this the real reason you ran away from your normal life, because you became a werewolf?"

Alex clenched his jaw and thought back to that night, before his mind flashed forward to what he'd done to those men earlier that day. He realised, too, that this was the first time in his life he'd ever been able to talk about it with someone who hadn't always known.

"Six months ago some people kidnapped my nephew and I ... well, I lost control. It was the first time it had ever happened, but well... Okay that's not entirely true. It was the first time it had resulted in death. But I've been like this since I was ten years old."

Cassandra gasped and covered her mouth with her hands.

"Ten years old. What happened?"

"I was ... I was playing in the woods on my grandparents' farm when I found this massive wolf tied down. It looked dead, and being ten I decided that it couldn't stay tied down, that to do nothing would be wrong. So, I pulled out a little penknife I had and tried to cut the ropes, which ..." A thin smile spread across his face for a second then faded and his eyes glazed over with the memory. "I can still remember how hard I had to push to make any impact, the rope was so thick and the knife so blunt. But I was going to cut him free. Only, before I managed to get through the rope, the knife slipped and the wolf turned out to not be as dead as I thought. I didn't know then, but I'm sure thinking back on it now that the look it gave me was an apology. We locked eyes for a moment, while I begged it to let me go ... Even then I thought it looked sad, but, sad for itself not me. Ha, I haven't told anyone this story since it happened."

With his last sentence he brought himself back into the room and realised that Cassandra was quietly crying.

"How does a ten-year-old deal with something like this?"

"I remember feeling very isolated, both from my family and the rest of the world. And guilty that I had done something that so clearly distressed them. Ha, I even said to my grandfather that I should stay on the farm so my parents and Annabel could live normal lives. I don't know what kind of monster I'd be without my family; these last six months have been the longest I've ever been away from them, and the first time I've not spoken to them."

The room fell back into silence, reminding Alex of those first few days when his family, who were normally so loud, with hundreds of stories and anecdotes and jokes had fallen silent because of him. It reminded him of his mother and a cold shiver rippled through his body. Cassandra gasped, her eyes flickering at his face.

"Your eyes?"

"Green?"

She nodded, and he closed his eyes and rubbed them gently.

"Yeah, that happens. They were originally dark brown, like my dad's, back before all of this happened."

But then he also remembered that he was naked, so scanned the room for some clothes.

"So, those guys, the so-called poachers, they seemed to know what you were. You think there's a connection between these guys and your ... uhmmm, sire?"

Alex raised an eyebrow.

"Maybe. Sagi and Fredrik want to show me something – maybe they've found a connection? I honestly don't know more than that. The wolf that bit me disappeared, but the area where he had been was burnt up. I've just presumed it dead my whole life."

"And you never looked into him?"

"I thought about it, but we've been researching werewolves my whole life and never once found a thread to pull on. They all seemed to lead to either ancient untraceable legends, Hollywood movies or weird romance novels. There's so much pop culture around it that it's all but impossible to filter out what could be real or what's just myth."

They were silent again for a moment, both thinking, Alex about his past, Cassandra about what might happen next. She ran through a few things in her head then seemed to come to a conclusion.

"I'm still not one hundred per cent with the lies, but I guess ... I guess I understand. Can you just promise me you'll never do that again, and then can we dial us back about a month and I can just hug you and not miss you and then at least something can feel normal?" Her voice had started out confident but started to crack as she went on. "I have never, in my entire life, shared secrets with anyone like I have with you right now."

She leapt up from her chair and wrapped her arms around him, allowing herself to cry a little into his shoulder.

"Okay, good, because today has been really fucking scary and I need my friend back."

He put his arms around her and for a few seconds the rest of the world melted away and it was just them, together.

"Right," Cassandra took a deep breath and pulled herself together. "Pull on some clothes and let's go see what there is to see and work out what the next step is going to be."

Once ready, they headed out together to find Sagi, Fredrik and Annabel waiting for them. Sagi stepped forward and handed Alex a thick file.

"Take a look at this, my friend. I found it in their truck."

Alex opened the file and found detailed backgrounds on each and every person at The Sanctuary, photographs, family history, Sagi's military record. Each profile was pages long, starting with a red stamp that read 'Clear' and ending with a short paragraph explaining why they weren't a suspect.

"Jesus, what is this?"

"There's more."

Sagi handed Alex a second folder, which he opened to find pictures of himself at The Sanctuary, printouts of Ken's blog posts, and a short handwritten bio:

Subject known as Mork (alias) has no personal or import documents. Studies have shown that his movements can be erratic and he is prone to disappear for days on end, always around full moon. It is clear to us that he is our target. Unfortunately, we do not have enough signal here to run a photo analysis to determine true identity. Will have to make arrangements soon to entrap the beast and deal with him accordingly.

Addition: Suspect the sister has arrived. Now know him to be Alex Harris, the famous musician who disappeared from Syn Island seven-ish months previous. Possible connect to murders around the time of his disappearance. In fact, we're certain of it. Arrival of sister has pushed him to make plans to leave. So no time for procedure and planned trap – we're going to have to improvise. If we fail, may God forgive us for our failure and admit us to heaven knowing we do His work to rid the earth of Satan's demons. And if we succeed may God forgive us still.

On the next page Alex found a few diagrams detailing how they planned to trap and execute him, which involved having him tied down between trees and set on fire. He looked up at the others and passed the folder to Cassandra.

"Would it be too on the nose to say Jesus?"

Sagi and Fredrik smiled weakly. Annabel just frowned.

"So, what else did you find?"

"Illegal hunting traps, two dead cellphones and a laptop, some spare batteries that also appear to be dead. It looks like they've been following us following you for a long time now. Oh, and also what looked like a branding iron?"

"Any clue as to who they are? Where they were trying to report back to?"

Annabel lay her hand on his shoulder.

"We're charging up the phones and laptop now to try to see if we can find answers to those questions. We've decided …" Her eyes flickered to the others. "We've decided to keep a lot of this stuff from the police when they arrive."

Alex turned his gaze to Sagi.

"Oh, don't worry my friend," Sagi assured him. "The crime scene is secure and everything that should be there is there."

Alex took a deep breath in and tried to clear his mind, his heart turning to stone.

"You're all being very calm about the fact that I just murdered two people."

The thought had been bouncing quietly around his mind since the incident, but the guilt and the scent of fear meant that he needed to drag it out into the light of day. They all, Cassandra included, stared at him.

"I mean, I'm grateful, but still …"

Sagi, instantly recognising the look in Alex's eyes, stepped forward and placed a crushed silver bullet in his hands. Alex looked at it and winced.

"This is the bullet you pulled out of my shoulder?"

"No, this is one of four we pulled out of the wall around where Aina and your sister were standing … These men weren't just poachers they were here to kill you and they were willing to kill the rest of us to do it. I also don't think they were the type who left witnesses. You saved our lives."

Alex looked down at the bullet again, took a long breath in, trying to hold himself together.

"So, what's our official story then?"

Fredrik finally took his turn: "It's simple. We were in The Sanctuary when we heard a car pull up and suddenly there were men shouting. We ran to the window, only to see a wolf leaping from the truck onto the men and before we could do anything it was too late and the wolf ran off. We've compared it with images of other wolves we know of in the area and it doesn't match. We've concluded that the men were poachers, that they had captured two wolves, presuming that both were dead. One woke up and attacked them as they were driving through, and then it ran off."

"And that'll work, you think?"

Fredrik smiled: "Hey, we're the experts. Why wouldn't they believe us?"

"Can I see the branding iron please?"

They all walked out to the truck and Sagi carefully retrieved it for Alex. A dazed expression came over Alex's face.

"What is it, my friend? Something wrong?"

"I've seen that symbol before." He turned to Annabel. "You remember when I was bitten? The wolf that bit me, he was branded with this symbol when I found him."

Annabel frowned deeply.

"Alex, you were so young, how can you be sure?"

Alex's expression grew dark and serious.

"Trust me, I've thought about that day a lot. Plus, I wasn't bitten right away, remember? I sat there for a while before it happened. I know what I saw, and it was this. Whoever these guys are, they hunt and kill werewolves. They killed the wolf that bit me and now they're after me."

In his head, he finished that sentence with "And I've got to get out of here", but kept it to himself. He knew there were things that needed to be done first and announcing to all that he was about to bolt now struck him as a bad idea.

The next few hours passed slowly as the group waited for the authorities to arrive. Everyone was questioned separately and those who had witnessed the incident gave slightly personalised versions of the same story, the others explaining that they had been in another part of the facility and had seen nothing. Because they had been involved with the crime scene, Sagi and Fredrik were questioned more extensively. One by one, after questioning, everyone made their way to the bar to find coffee and tea waiting for them. Fredrik and Sagi were the last to arrive, both more interested in alcohol than hot drinks. With everyone in one place, Alex took the initiative. He poured himself a drink, turned on some music and smiled at the crowd.

"Welcome to my bar, everyone, what can I get you?"

Unsurprisingly, they all wanted to know more about werewolves. Having never openly discussed the topic with anyone outside of his family, Alex felt a strange mix of excitement and anxiety as he retold the story of when and how he had been bitten, what changing felt like and how much control he really has as a wolf. The line was drawn when Greg, after a few beers, started asking if he would change so they could see.

Cassandra realised before anyone else what was actually happening and disappeared to her room to grab her guitar, presenting it with a flourish to Alex with a smile, in part to actually hear him sing but also to change the topic, and because she had guessed that it might be their last opportunity. To everyone's surprise, Alex blushed when he took the guitar. The cheer that went up from everyone reminded him that performing was something he knew well. So he hopped up onto the bar and checked the tuning, then waited in silence to allow everyone to settle and build some anticipation.

Then, all at once, he erupted into song with a joyous howl – there was no mistaking that Alex Harris was a rock star. His voice filled the room with warmth and excitement. He worked his way through four Waterdog numbers he knew would have the whole bar dancing and laughing. As he hit the final chord, he stretched out his arms and took a bow, to cheers and applause. As he straightened up, he could immediately pick up the change in the way everyone was looking at him. They saw him now as Alex the rock star, and not as their friend Mork the barman. Better, he supposed, than them seeing him as a murderous monster, but it did put another brick in the wall between them. He'd liked being just another guy; it was nice to not be anyone specifically special or different. And although that persona had been slipping away over the last couple days, it was now finally gone. The only people who regarded him with any kind of normality were Fredrik, Cassandra and Sagi. Greg and Ken, on the other hand, were practically foaming at the mouth with excitement.

In that moment a thought occurred to Alex that now he really could just up and leave. Performing had cut the strings between him and his friends and now he could go. Then he did something he never thought he'd do in public. He plucked at the strings a couple of times to get everyone's attention then started to play "The Night They Drove Old Dixie Down", the song so closely linked to his memories of his mom that he'd learned how to play it just for himself. It had been a way to keep her memory alive within him, and he'd never performed it before. Annabel hadn't even known he knew how, and instantly started crying. Again, his voice rang through the room, but this time it was different; goosebumps erupted over everyone in earshot and it felt like a mist was drifting through the bar, blanketing them all in a soft, cold melancholy. As the last bars of the melody faded, everyone stood and clapped. No loud cheering, just a subdued clapping in admiration of a rendition that clearly emanated from the heart, from the very depths of his soul. This time everyone, including his sister, looked at him through wide shining eyes. He handed the guitar back to Cassandra and smiled a thin smile.

The room was quiet and he knew that it was time.

"I'd like to thank you all for everything you've done for me – not just today but over the last few months. Obviously, today you all learned something that only eight other people in the whole world know. My closely guarded secret. I know you're all good people and I know I can trust you, and I do. But, with that said, if you can I'd like you to forget all about it. I'm not asking you to forget about me, this evening or who I really am – just about what I am and what really happened here this morning. Tomorrow you can tell yourselves it was just a bad dream, and let it drift away with all the other nightmares. I also want to take this moment to tell you that when you wake up ... When you wake up, I won't be here."

A look of shock and sadness spread across their faces.

"Apparently, people have been keeping an eye on me and I don't want to put anyone else in danger. So at some point tonight I'm going to head off. I'm not going to tell you where I'm going, but I am going to make a statement to the press before I go, to let them know I'm alive, that I've been in touch with my family and I'm not insane but thanks for asking. Maybe in those exact words, actually. Anyway, the only thing I ask really is that when I resurface – and I will – please get in touch, stay in touch. We are still friends after all. Thank you again … I'll miss you all.'

He slipped back behind the bar and grabbed himself a beer, downing half of it straight away.

"Now, what can I get you?" He made a feeble, half-hearted attempt to lift the mood, but it didn't really work, so he walked around the bar to Aina and Kristin and wrapped his arms around them both, holding them until he could feel their sobs against his shoulders. Ella was the first to join in and it very quickly turned into a sombre group hug. They stayed like that for a minute or so before Alex flexed and straightened up. He looked around, taking it all in for a moment, the comfort, the kindness, the sadness of the goodbye. He could feel it coming off everyone in waves and it touched him, made him smile. Then he went back behind the bar, put on some cheerful music and started handing out drinks.

"Come on, folks, this is a celebration of the time we had together, let's party!"

Everyone else quickly fell in line and the mood lifted. Alex didn't stay behind the bar, though; once everyone had been served, he started making his way around the room, chatting to people. His first stop was back with Aina and Kristin, who were sitting away from everyone and thanked them personally, apologised for all the trouble he'd caused and promised to come back once everything had settled to some kind of normality. "That's if I'm actually wanted back after today," he added shyly.

Alex detected no fear, no resentment from them, the ones who had offered him a home.

"Today has been a very strange and stressful day," Aina said calmly, "but it's over now and we can start to put it behind us."

"And of course you're welcome here. Always," Kristin interrupted. "You will always be family."

Over their shoulders, Alex spotted Sagi sitting a little away from everyone and went to sit with him.

"Sagi, man, what you doing sitting here alone?"

Sagi smiled to himself.

"And all this time I thought you were trying to pick up Cassandra."

Alex let out a low laugh but waited for the real answer.

"I'm actually just taking some time to watch everyone," Sagi offered.

"Yeah, how are they?"

"I think they're fine. Sad about you leaving, but fine."

"And you? How are you?"

Sagi turned to Alex, deep in thought.

"I ... I'm glad that I was here to help with everything today, in part to help and in part so that no one else had to do it. I'm also glad that such things are not part of my normal life anymore. Today has brought back some things I was glad to have forgotten."

"I'm, I'm sorry—"

Sagi raised a hand to cut him off.

"No, please, my friend, you have no need to apologise. In truth I am more glad that I could help than I am sad."

Alex put his hand on Sagi's shoulder.

"Thank you, my friend, today would have been very different and much worse had you not been here."

They smiled at each other and Alex got the distinct impression that Sagi wanted to be alone. His next stop was the crowd of Ken, Greg, Ella and Annabel – mostly to save Annabel who was fielding all the usual fanboy questions.

"You know you can talk to me instead of about me, right?"

Fredrik and Cassandra, who were sitting away from them all, watched Alex play the crowd like a master and realised how much practise he must have had over the years, and how often he had used similar tactics as a barman. Alex fielded questions for a while until he was finally able to make the excuse that people needed more drinks and was happy to find Cassandra and Fredrik moving to join him at the bar – the two he really wanted to spend his last night with. Annabel too quickly excused herself from the group conversation and joined the group at the bar. Alex handed her a beer and they all raised their glasses.

"To you, my friend," Fredrik tipped his glass at Alex. "It won't be the same here without you."

"Thanks, man, gonna miss you guys too. But before we get back to having fun, I have a very serious favour to ask you."

Fredrik put his drink down and narrowed his eyes. Alex's face told him that he wasn't joking around.

"What's that?"

"While I was out, blood samples were taken. I asked Kristin to destroy them and I want to, with all my heart, believe that she did. But I also need to know that you'll double check. It doesn't matter what she says, or what's to believe, my blood is dangerous."

Fredrik's look grew deeply concerned and he looked across at Cassandra.

"Consider it done."

A weak smile spread across Alex's face.

"Thank you," he said with some relief. "I would hate for something stupid to happen, for someone to be infected by my blood."

"We're not talking about a normal infection here, are we?"

"Being what I am is not as much fun, or amazing as I make it look."

There was no humour in Alex's voice and it almost sucked the air out of the room. Quickly realising what he'd done, he tried to turn the conversation.

"So, as soon as I'm back on Syn Island you guys must come visit. All on me. We'll do some cheesy sightseeing then take the city by storm. Fredrik, you can finally prove to me how good you are at picking up the ladies."

"That wouldn't be fair," Fredrik scoffed.

"Why, because I'm a rock star?"

"Well, yeah, that – plus home-field advantage. But it still won't be fair on you. I'd feel bad for you sitting alone in the corner with only guys trying to talk to you."

Everyone laughed and the conversation slipped from the deep contemplation to the usual friendly banter.

One by one, everyone excused themselves, until it was just Ella, Fredrik, Cassandra and Alex remaining and Ella had to practically drag Fredrik off to bed. Fredrik finally got the hint and, with both hands on Alex's shoulders, said with great drunken seriousness: "What's the first thing you do when you meet a girl you really like?"

Alex smirked. "Delete your internet search history."

Everyone laughed and Fredrik was finally defeated; they hugged and he left. Cassandra, who had been strategically drinking water throughout the night, was still in a fairly reasonable state and for a long time the two just stared at each other.

"So, where are you going to go next?"

"Russia."

"Why?" Cassandra raised an eyebrow.

"Remember when you spotted that drawing in my room? Well, I've been dreaming about that place for months now, and I've always had some form of shared dreams with my werewolf heritage. And … I don't know, it just feels significant to me, and as you pointed out, it turns out to be a real place, so I figure that's the path to follow."

"Manor Muromtsevo. How do you plan to get there?"

"I was thinking I'd run."

"Run?" Cassandra stifled a laugh. "You can't run to Russia!"

"Why not? I basically ran here. Wolves can travel great distances and as long as I stay away from cities, I should be fine."

"Why can't you just fly there?"

"I'll probably fly to as close as I can get, but I imagine I'll need to leave Norway the same way I entered." Seeing the look on her face he smiled and said. "Illegally. Also, if I am bring tracked I don't want to leave a distinct flight path showing where I'm going."

For a moment she thought he was just being paranoid, then realised that maybe he was right and suddenly wasn't sure what to think. She looked up at him and found him staring at her … And then they were all over each other.

Alex scooped her up, pulled the bar door behind with one hand and carried her back to his room where they tore frantically at each other's clothes, mouths open pressed against each other, hands flailing and tugging and pulling. Finally, with his jeans crumpled around his ankles, Alex stumbled backwards and hit the edge of the bed. They both tumbled onto the mattress and erupted into fits of giggles. Half naked and laughing, Alex rolled onto his side and looked at her. He'd gotten as far as removing her shirt and bra and let his hands slip slowly over her thighs to pull her in close. He wanted to feel her skin against his and again they kissed, this time with less frantic energy and more care and passion. The rest of the clothes came off easily and the hours melted away.

Chapter 11

The next morning Annabel woke up to find a note pinned to the door of her room. Her brother was gone, along with his passport, his wallet and his phone.

***

Good morning, this is Barbara Barker and you're listening to K505, Syn Island's number-one hit radio station. Top story around the world today: Alex Harris has loaded a video on the internet, explaining that he's fine, not crazy and actually just taking a break from fame. In the clip, he apologises to his friends and family, promising to be less of a, well ... we can't say the word he used, but less of it. And also promises to keep communication open. He has gone as far as to say he might not always share where he is, because he doesn't want people trying to follow him, or the press pestering his family to know where in the world he is. But he's alive, well and not missing.

***

Alex knew that because of some of his previous tour destinations he would not be able to enter Russia legally, certainly not without serious visa applications, something he was determined to avoid. He was, however, fairly confident that he would be able to run across the border, as long as he packed enough provisions. The plan was that he would run into Sweden and from there fly to Krakow in Poland where he planned to set himself up in a small hotel and work out how he was going to get to where he wanted to go.

The Waterdogs were particularly famous in these parts of Europe and he had to smile when the hotel receptionist recognised him instantly and momentarily forgot how to speak.

"So … it would be great if no one found out I was here. Maybe we could even have the booking done under a fake name? How much would that sort of thing cost?"

She stared at him star struck, and Alex's smile turned a little more genuine as he realised that she possibly hadn't even heard a word of what he had said and was trying not to laugh about it.

"Had you not heard that I resurfaced?"

"What? No, no, of course I heard. I'm a huge fan. I love you. I mean … uhmmm … I love your music." Alex's smile broadened, and the girl blushed. Then she reached under the desk and slowly turned up the music. Gradually the sound of WaterDogs' first single filled the room. Alex winked and extended his hand.

"So, I'm Alex Harris, which I guess you already knew. What's your name?"

She was wearing a name tag, but he decided to ignore it.

"Oh, uhmmm … Paulina."

"Nice to meet you, Paulina. Now, is there a room available here for the week or so? And can we check me in under a false name?"

Paulina suddenly lost her smile and started tapping away at the computer, chewing frantically on her bottom lip.

"Yes! I mean, yes, we do and, yes, we can. Uhmmm … What name would you like to book in under?"

Alex thought for a moment.

"How about just Alex Smith – it's different, but simple and it means I won't do that thing where I forget what my fake name is."

"Certainly, Mr Smith," she smiled coyly. "I can put you in either a standard room or our premier suite, which is only 50 złoty more."

"Sold! Let's do that."

Paulina blushed again as she quickly ran through the description of the hotel and its services.

"Unfortunately," she said, "we don't have a phone in that room, so if you have any questions you'll need to come to reception. Sorry. But if you need a hand with your luggage, I'd be happy to help."

Alex lifted his only bag.

"No, I think I've got it, thanks. Two things though … Is there a bath in the room or just a shower? And can I have a couple of beers to take up with me?"

"Yes, and yes."

Alex grabbed his beers and the room key and for a moment thought about asking the girl to show him up to his room, just to keep the game going a little longer, but decided against it. This was not the time to be messing with someone's head – least of all his own. So he headed up to find his room alone.

To his utter joy, the bath was huge and hot water plentiful. He immediately stripped off and lay there soaking, allowing his muscles to relax for the first time in what felt like forever, finally drifting off to sleep, only about halfway through his beer.

Suddenly, he awoke. A knock at the door. He quickly clambered out of the now icy bath, wrapped a towel around his waist and headed for the door. Paulina turned crimson, her eyes so wide that Alex though they might actually pop out of her head. They stood in silence for a few seconds while he waited to see if she'd regain command of herself or just continue to stare.

"Hi, how can I help?"

She quickly stuttered back to life.

"Oh, oh, yes I … I just wanted to know if you wanted to order some food. It's getting a bit late and things will start to close soon."

Alex did a quick glance around for a clock.

"Sounds great. What are my options?"

She held out a stack of menus and he smiled, gesturing with his head down his own hands were holding the towel in place.

"Tell you what … Come inside quickly while I go put some clothes on and we'll continue this conversation in a second."

He stepped back and waved her in, then ducked back into the bathroom. Paulina stood for a moment, a little apprehensive about entering the hotel room of a rock star, and not fully sure she knew what she was getting herself into or what he was going to come out wearing. But he'd smiled nicely and was being polite and cool so she slowly stepped into the room and let the door close behind her. A couple of minutes later Alex reappeared wearing the clothes he'd had on while checking in, but with hair neatly brushed.

Together they flipped through the menus, which were mostly in Polish, and found him something to eat. Paulina hurried back downstairs to place his order and for the first time Alex really took in the room. It wasn't the largest hotel room he'd ever stayed in, that was for sure, but compared to where he'd been living it felt like a palace.

In the morning Alex was pleased to see Paulina at the reception desk again; it saved him from being recognised and having to explain again that he had checked in under a different name.

"Morning, Mr Smith."

"Morning, Paulina, and how are you today?"

"Good. A little tired, but … Oh, no, I mean fine. I'm fine."

She blushed again.

"It's all right," he reassured her. "You were here late last night so you're allowed to be tired."

"It's not so bad. My shift ends after breakfast, so that's good. Then I can go home and sleep."

A thought crept into Alex's mind and his smile broadened.

"Hey, you wanna hang out a bit after work? I could use a guide-slash-translator."

A look of pure excitement erupted in her face and she failed dismally in her attempt to look cool. She jumped at the idea.

"Oh my God, yes!"

"Groovy. So, I'm going to go back to my room – just come and knock when you're ready. Also, I don't know how far away things are, but I need to get a laptop and some more clothes, so if we need to get a taxi or something, can you organise that?"

"Yes, yes, of course, don't worry."

It didn't take him long to start questioning his decision. Not because Paulina was drawing attention to him, or being overly fangirlish, but because she shopped exactly the same way Annabel did. He wasn't allowed to buy anything that he just saw. Everything had to be checked against similar items in other stores that might be cheaper or a better deal. They had to be of reasonable quality so they would last, and no amount of reassurance from him that he was happy with what he had in his hand would placate her.

"But I can afford it it's fine."

Hours passed as they trudged from shop to shop, trying things on, asking places to hold onto things so they could check other places. On one level, he did rather like that he didn't really have to make any decisions. Paulina had ideas on what kind of clothes he should be wearing, which sunglasses suited his face, and what shoes fitted his style. She quizzed him on what he needed the computer for and worked out which laptop would best suit his needs and in what price range. She also seemed to know his size so perfectly that he started to believe that she could have done the whole trip without him and he would have ended up with exactly the same stuff. But eventually enough was enough and Alex sat down in the middle of the mall with far more bags than he was expecting, his head in his hands.

"Is ... Is everything all right?" A growing sense of anxiety filled Paulina.

"Yeah, sure, everything's fine … but if the next place we go to isn't a bar, I think I'm going to start to cry."

"Oh no, yes, I mean, we can grab a taxi and drop everything back at the hotel, then go to a bar. Please don't cry."

Alex smiled to himself at the thought of her worrying that he might actually be about to cry.

"Great," he sprang to his feet. "Let's go."

On the way back to the hotel he made a point to thank her.

"Don't get me wrong, I had a lot of fun, but now it's time for a beer."

Paulina felt her whole body go hot and found herself suddenly lacking in words. Waterdogs had been the first band she had been really obsessed with and still couldn't believe that she was spending the day with the Alex Harris. Her bedroom walls were covered with their posters; she'd seen them play twice and cried when she missed getting tickets for their third trip through Poland. The idea of going to a bar and having a drink with Alex was almost more than she could handle. But she did have to force herself not to think about the cover of the schoolbook that read 'Mrs Paulina Harris'.

What started as a quick beer break turned into a night-long bar hop through various districts in search of the city's emptiest bars. Paulina was a slender nineteen-year-old who desperately wanted to keep up with him, and even announced at their fifth bar stop:

"I'm Polish! We know how to drink!"

Unfortunately for her, her staying power just couldn't compare to his tolerance levels. He mercifully pulled her hood up to mask her face when he walked her giggling through the hotel lobby and up to his room.

A shrill alarm sounded, filling the air with a loud, long-winded screech. Alex leapt out of bed, his eyes darting around the room and found Paulina stabbing at the buttons on her phone, desperate to make the noise stop. The alarm clock on her phone.

"Oh my God," she stared at him through wide eyes. "Oh my God! We're in the hotel. What happened? What happened last night?"

"Well, you decided you needed to prove you could outdrink me."

She swallowed, her throat dry, her tongue clinging to her palate, as the hangover kicked into full gear.

"How did I do?"

"Really good, considering you weigh about as much as my arm."

Paulina paled slightly and her voice came out a little shaky.

"And then ... Then what happened?"

"Well, when you stopped being able to speak English and I couldn't figure out where you said you lived, I brought you back here. Don't worry, no one recognised you on the way in."

"And ... and then what?"

Alex disregarded the hidden meaning, the potential accusation. Hers was a fair question given the circumstances. She didn't know him and clearly had a few blank spots in her memory. On top of that, she had just woken up in his bed.

"Nothing. You passed out."

She stared at him, her built-in distrust starting to flare up; as much as she wanted to believe he was one of the good guys, just as she'd always thought and hoped, how could she be sure? Alex could see her mind ticking over, her eyes dart around the room looking for clues, so he waved his hands down over his body and she realised that, except for his shoes, he was fully clothed. She realised too that she was also fully clothed under the blanket, which she had slowly been pulling up over herself. Memories of the previous evening began to trickle back and her cheeks suddenly flushed.

"Oh my God, I need to call my mother! If I didn't tell her I was staying at work she might have called the police!"

Paulina leapt out of bed and started frantically tapping her phone; she started speaking almost instantly and although Alex didn't know the words, he perfectly understood the tone of someone giving a panicked apology while also trying to sound relaxed when they really weren't. As the conversation started to drift to why she hadn't come home or let anyone know where she was going and what she was doing, Alex decided to excuse himself for a quick shower.

By the time he was done Paulina was sitting nervously on the edge of the bed.

"You all right?"

"My head hurts, and I ... I don't feel too good."

Alex opened one of the bottles of water from the bar fridge and handed it to her.

"Here, small sips and go take a nice, long shower; it'll open up your pores and help relieve some of the tension. I'll order room service. What would you like for breakfast?"

She stared up at him and smiled, realising that she was possibly still a little drunk.

"I'll have whatever you are going to have, and ... thank you. You are even cooler than I imagined."

She took the bottle and made her way into the shower. The hot water did help and by the time she stepped out again she was feeling much more settled. She pulled on her clothes from the previous evening and stepped into the bedroom where Alex sat tapping away at his new laptop. He turned when she entered.

"Feeling better?"

"Yes."

"Food shouldn't be much longer. I hope you like eggs and coffee."

"I do, thank you."

She stared at him for a bit and he smiled back, waiting for the obvious questions to start.

"Why are you being so nice to me? I mean, there isn't anything special about me."

It wasn't the first time he'd been asked a question like that. Something about being famous made people think you were different to them, made them feel like they needed to deserve your kindness. Also, teenage girls come with their own set of internal issues and the combination of the two always seemed to come out eventually. He walked over to her and took her hands in his.

"You're my best friend in Poland. That's pretty special, right?"

She blushed from head to toe, hoping and fearing that he was about to kiss her. It was strange and made her excited but, at the same time, a little uncomfortable and even slightly sick. Alex laughed a little at the cocktail of emotions she was giving off, and she frowned at him, but didn't pull her hands free.

"It's true, we spent the whole day yesterday shopping together, then all of last night drinking together and then slept in the same room. That says friendship to me. You're also welcome to tell people, I'll happily back it up. We can take some selfies and you can send them to your friends. Just, if you could wait until after I leave, I'm still trying to avoid a crowd."

Her frown deepened, her voice a little sad.

"Oh, you are leaving soon?"

"I have to I'm afraid; I'm a man on a mission."

Alex's ear twitched and he let her go.

Knock-knock.

Paulina narrowed her eyes, wondering what he was up to, when there was a knock at the door to announce the arrival of room service.

"How did you?"

"Magic ... Would you like to hide in the bathroom?"

Her face took a devilish smile, the kind Alex had not seen on her before.

"And come out wrapped in a towel just in time to be seen here with you?"

Images of it flashed through his mind and instinctively he ran his hand down her side in a way that gave her goosebumps.

"Absolutely."

They both knew that his mind had stopped on her in a towel, but they were interrupted again by another knock. Alex jumped up.

"Just a second."

As he headed for the door, Paulina slipped into the bathroom. She realised that his comment had been more to do with her being seen by co-workers than him seeing her in a towel. Their minds did linger on the idea, though, and when the main door closed and the bathroom door opened to reveal her fully clothed Alex couldn't help saying,

"Damn."

Paulina bit her bottom lip. She was a pretty girl, if a little awkward at times. She was also a massive fan, and right there clearly there had been chemistry, a chemistry that he could detect from across the room. His heart rate shot up and he considered what would happen if he moved towards her. He took a long in breath through his nose and the wolf started to push against his mind. Quickly he closed his eyes and turn away. Either he would need to calm down or she would need to leave.

"Is … is everything all right?"

"My … uhmmm … my hangover has just kicked in with a vengeance."

She stepped closer and placed a hand on his back. He screwed his eyes shut and raised his hand to his mouth.

"The … smell! Food might have been a mistake. I'll … I'll be right back."

He quickly stepped into the bathroom and closed the door behind him – but he'd made a terrible mistake. The room was filled with her scent, from the long hot shower to the temptation to strip and appear in a towel, he could smell her desire and it pushed his heart rate up even higher. Hurriedly, he filled his hands with cold water and splashed it over his face, thinking, 'Get your shit together, man. There's no way you can transform here and get away with it. How do you explain walking into a bathroom and then suddenly … wolf.' A gentle knock at the door roused him from his thoughts.

"Alex, are you sure you're okay?"

He looked at the face in the mirror – glowing green eyes stared back at him. He swore and started to gulp down handfuls of water, then stepped over to the toilet and stuck his fingers as far down his throat as he could until the water and any remaining alcohol came rushing back up. For effect, he made a show of exaggerating the sounds. He then swore just loud enough that she could definitely hear, and called through the door in a much deeper, darker voice than expected.

"I … uhmmm … might be here awhile. Sorry, this is not as cool as I wanted to be right now."

"No, no, it's okay."

"Are you going to be all right to sneak out and stuff?"

"Yes, yes, I'll be fine. Just want to make sure you're all right."

"I'll be fine. I just need some time. Sorry … Oh God."

Alex's whole body tensed as he tried to hold the wolf at bay long enough to finish the conversation. Paulina waited behind the door, listening. Perhaps he needed some help?

"Don't worry about me," she responded a little nervously. "I'll be all right. I need to start work soon anyway, but call me if you need anything, okay?"

"Sure," he said, the anxiety rising in him now as he realised that he'd be unable to hold the wolf back any longer. "Will do."

Alex pulled frantically at his clothes, trying to rip them off in time and almost succeed in stepping out of his jeans before the full transformation hit and his claws ripped a few new holes in them. He huffed, sitting quietly listening, ears pricked up, hoping Paulina wasn't going to natter on or, thinking he'd passed out, come rushing into the bathroom to save him. A minute or so later he heard her back at the door.

"Okay, bye then! I hope you feel better and … thank you for a fun night. And for being such a gentleman."

Mork wracked his brain for some kind of sound that would indicate he was alive and eventually settled on a sneeze. At the sound of the door closing behind her, he dropped down onto the floor in relief. Slowly, his heart rate began to drop and he closed his eyes.

Chapter 12

It wasn't the first time Alex had woken up confused and naked on the floor of a hotel bathroom. He slowly got to his feet and stepped right into the shower. The hot water brought clarity and focus. What he needed to do was plan his route and then get moving. The near miss with Paulina had reminded him of Cassandra and a deep feeling of shame crept over him. He knew he might not see Cassandra for a long time, or maybe ever again, but it was too soon for that sort of game. Both she and Paulina deserved better than that.

Still dripping, he turned on his laptop and set about plotting his course: first of all, a bus to the Polish border. As Mork, he'd sneak into whichever country made sense, then back on a bus and get as close to Russia as he could, and then quite simply run the rest of the way. The route didn't take long to work out, but it did make him realise how long it was actually going to take. He booked his tickets, got dressed and picked up his phone.

"What?"

"Oh shit!" Alex laughed. "Sorry, I didn't think about time zones."

"Alex?"

Annabel's voice came both angry and surprised.

"Where are you?"

"Krakow, but I'll be leaving soon."

"Where to? Where are you going?"

"It's a long story, but I wanted to let you know that I'm still fine and that I'm not just disappearing again for months on end, and I'll be in touch when I can be."

She sat up and blinked away the sleep, taking mental notes of what he was saying.

"Well, that's good, but could you please consider time zones next time you check in."

"Sure. So, how are things?"

"Good. I'm back on the Island."

In the background Alex could hear the shifting of sheets and the murmur of another voice, which he instantly recognised.

"Josh is with you."

"No!"

"I can probably hear him better than you can."

Annabel blushed, grateful that neither Alex nor Josh, in the darkness of the room, could see.

"I know, I know … It just feels weird that you're so okay with all of this."

"Why? It's like I said, he's been in love with you since school."

"No, no, that hasn't been said yet so I'm rejecting that statement."

"That's cause you luuuuurve him, and know he luuuuurves you."

"I think I preferred it when you were missing."

Her voice had taken on the unmistakeable tone of the unimpressed older sister and the familiarity of it warmed Alex's heart.

"How's Dad?"

"He's all right, relieved to know that you're actually okay and not just presumed fine. You should call him. I mean, not right now obviously but, yes, you should call him."

"I know, and I will."

"So, where are you going anyway?"

Alex thought for a moment, trying to work out whether his phone may be tapped and whether people were actually hunting him.

"Russia. There's a castle there that keeps popping up in my dreams, and I want to investigate, see if I can find out anything useful."

"What exactly are you looking for, Alex? I mean, I know why you ran in the first place, but why are you still running?"

"I need to learn more about being a wolf; I need to know if there are others like me, and where they are. Aaaaand if I can find out anything about those guys from The Sanctuary, that wouldn't be such a bad thing either. Running is one thing, but learning that you're actually being chased is weird."

The conversation fell silent.

"Well, stay safe and stay in touch. And let me know if there's anything I can do to help."

There was a muffled sound on the phone and Josh's voice came through the line.

"Alex, man, that you?"

"Hey, man, how's it going?"

"Dude, it's good to hear your voice. How are you?"

"I'm good. It's ... it's good to hear you too and sorry I hadn't—"

"Don't sweat it, man, it's cool. When are you coming home?"

"I'm not sure, but I'll stay in touch. I promise."

"All right, all right. Cool. Damn, it's good to hear your voice. Anyway, man, I'll hand you back to Annie."

"Oh, that reminds me, if you hurt my sister, and it'll break my heart to do it, but if you do, I'll rip your throat out with my teeth."

"Please don't threaten my boyfriend like that Alex."

"Oh, goddamn speaker phone. Doesn't matter. I stand by what I said. But I'm also going to love and leave you. One, because I need to get moving and, two, because I'm not afraid to say, I love you. Bye!"

Alex hung up, happy to leave them in the most awkward situation he could manage from so far away. He knew he was being a bit of a dick, meddling in his sister and best friend's personal affairs, but he also knew that they were good for each other, had known each other for a long time and really did love one another.

The guilt over almost falling back into his usual ways and bedding Paulina still lingered like a bad taste. It was a new experience for him, pining after a single girl, that feeling that appeared to extend further than the time they were actually together. It was a slightly uncomfortable feeling but not a bad one, just strange, and he found himself hoping she was all right. Slowly, his mood began to spiral downwards and suddenly he felt the acute loneliness of not having family nearby. On a deep and instinctual level, their absence weighed heavily on him. A physical ache within himself that left him vulnerable.

He was relieved when there was a knock on his door, and smiled when he heard Paulina's voice on the other side.

"Hey, I'm about to go home I just wanted to check on you, make sure everything is okay?"

Alex swung the door open with a smile.

"That's sweet of you, thanks. I'm okay. I took a nap, drank litres of water and feel much better now. How about you? How you feeling?"

"Like I can't wait to get home and fall into bed. But it was really fun spending the day with you."

"For me too, and I think we both deserve a good night's rest. I'll still be here in the morning, don't worry."

The smile and lift in her voice warmed his heart.

"Good to know. Couple of things: if you get hungry, there are some menus at reception. You can just go down and the night receptionist will order for you; or there are some lovely restaurants in the city and we can make reservations for you."

"Awesome, thank you."

"Oh, and there were two guys asking for you a little earlier."

The blood in his veins turned to ice and his body stiffened.

"What?"

"I think they might have been reporters or something; they were asking if we'd seen you, that they'd heard rumours that the missing rock star had been spotted in the city and at this hotel. I told them we didn't have you here or anyone booked under your name. I ... I'm not sure whether they believed me but they seemed to give up and left."

Visions of the two men at The Sanctuary and what had happened to them surfaced again and his muscles tightened. Anxiety slipped a cold knife under his skin and his breaths grew long.

"Th-thank you, I appreciate that. And thanks for letting me know."

She shifted a little uncomfortably.

"My pleasure. You definitely seemed like you didn't want to be seen yesterday and I know that you've never really been the kind of star who relishes being in the spotlight or being hounded by the press. Are you sure you're okay, though?"

"Yes, yes, I'm just ... Thank you for not telling them about me. I appreciate it."

Alex's heart slumped at the idea of being hunted again. He felt like an animal being backed into a corner and the hair on his neck started to stand up. He faked a smile.

"I hope you have a lovely evening and sleep well. Get home safe, and thank you again."

He held out his arms for a hug and she wrapped herself around him. The physical contact made him feel a little better and for just an instant he thought about inviting her to stay the night again. But he immediately pushed the notion out of his mind.

Instead he said: "Oh, wait, get a picture then you can blame everything on me if your mom's still mad."

Pauline laughed, pulled out her phone and snapped a few selfies with him. Alex then quickly turned and tore a sheet from the notepad on the desk in the room and scribbled down his number, knowing exactly what he was doing. He handed it to her.

"Here, this is my private number. Send me the pictures."

Paulina looked down at the piece of paper, not fully able to process what was actually happening. Slowly she reached out a shaky hand to take it, and without realising it held it to her chest.

"Now I know you won't share that around, but it's still something I always say. That's my private number; I'm giving it to you because I trust you – you're my friend. Please don't give it to anyone else."

She threw herself at him again and hugged him with all her might. If she could have formed words, she was sure she would have confessed undying love. Instead she stuttered something in Polish, blushed, waved goodbye and hurried off.

Alex watched her go, feeling hope fade as she did. He closed his door and dropped onto the bed. For a moment he just lay there, not thinking, not feeling, not fearing. His body told him that if he just closed his eyes, he'd fall asleep, but his mind had sparked a cacophony of doubt and paranoia, and just before he transformed he remembered clearly tearing through the men at The Sanctuary.

As Mork, the fear and threat of imminent danger grew and the large black wolf paced impatiently around the room. He stared at the door, begging it, daring it to be opened. Hours passed, and his frustration grew, the sensation of being chased giving agency to his need to leave.

It took a few more hours before he was able to turn back into a human, and without wasting another moment he penned a quick goodbye note to Paulina and left it with a small pile of cash in an envelope at reception. He then returned to his room, packed the essentials and slipped out through the window. The night bus took him to the edge of the city, and from there he walked. It took a while, but at least he felt safe enough, and far enough away from others – to make the change. He double-checked his directions, suddenly overcome by a cold, desperate loneliness. He looked at the nothingness around him and realised he didn't have family, a pack. He was alone and running from a faceless nightmare. Just like he'd always dreamed. A shiver ran over his body for a moment as he fought against the transformation, determined to retain at least some control over when it happened, but the loneliness and anxiety got the better of him. He grabbed his pack and disappeared into the night.

Chapter 13

By the time he reached Russia, Alex's paranoia had all but taken over. Every strange scent was an attacker, every crackle a pursuer and no matter how much he tried to fight it, a deep terror gripped him. The trip itself had been uneventful, but that hadn't stopped him from running most of the way, taking as few breaks as possible. Exhaustion had, however, begun to play a part in his day-to-day life and when he finally stumbled into the city of Vladimir the idea of sleeping rough threatened a panic attack. He checked into the most nondescript hotel he could find, registered under a false name and locked the door to the room behind him. A part of him considered moving the bedding into the bathroom to set up a second door between the world and him, but sleep came so quickly that he barely made it under the covers.

***

Mork burst through the heavy doors of Muromtsevo Castle at full gallop, deep in the forest, close behind him the sound of horses. A familiar nightmare, but this time his grip on reality seemed undercut by fear. The sensation of being chased had already taken hold while he had been awake and had followed him into the nightmare. He had pushed himself to sprint as fast as he could through the forest, weaving between trees, employing every trick he could to lose his pursuers, but it never worked. He ran until he turned into a small clearing. As he reached the centre, men on horses appeared out of the forest all around him. His first instinct had been to attack, or find a weak point and escape, but lances had rained down fast.

Alex found himself awake, sweat pouring from his body and his breath coming in small, staggered gasps. As the nightmare faded, the paranoia returned and he checked the time, counting the hours he'd been asleep. Regret reared its ugly head as his aching muscles, pushed to the limit, began to protest. Throughout his life he had always been unnaturally capable physically, but over the weeks he'd learned that even he had limits and that he simply wasn't able to recover in a single day.

He'd gone to bed early and, despite feeling like he'd fallen directly into the nightmare, had slept for almost fourteen hours. The realisation filled him with a sick feeling of helplessness, of stupidity, and he ran over the potential unknowns that could have gotten to him in that time: those men hunting him down or whatever was waiting for him in the castle. Alex pulled off his clothes and stepped into the shower where the cold water hit him like a hammer blow and knocked him to the floor. Tears welled up. He knew he was being stupid, but also had nothing left to deal with it. He felt desperate, alone and vulnerable. He'd always treasured his private time, and had never connected that to the fact that he had had his pack – his people – when he needed them. The first thing he'd done when he reached Norway was to establish a new group, a new pack to live with and he had felt safe there. The water eventually warmed up but the tears continued and he had to fight back the urge to lash out, break things and scream. For an instant, his thoughts drifted to his mother and the laughter they had shared in her last moments alive, but still Mork lurked heavily in his mind. Alex pushed back and managed to hold him off. In the back of his mind he could feel the need to collect himself, to think rather than react. If there was someone or something chasing him, he needed to be far more in control than he was right now. Sitting around wallowing in self-pity and paranoia wasn't going to solve anything. That idea mixed with the hot water seemed to help clear his head and bring him back to some sanity.

It took a bit of research to discover that he could catch a bus to a town by the name of Sudogda and walk to the castle from there. He still wasn't sure what, if anything he was going to find there, but he knew he had to go. The many days of travel and fear couldn't be ignored though. The services in the hotel were sufficient to make sure that provisions could be delivered straight to his room in a relatively short amount of time, and he'd decided that he would be better off taking some time to rest and prepare himself, both physically and mentally – a far better idea than blacking out from exhaustion on the steps to the castle.

The food helped, water even more, and despite his best intentions, sleep came easily. Each time he woke up, his body ached slightly more and his muscles burned when he tried to move, and each time he realised how vulnerable he'd made himself. Two days passed as he ate and slept and recovered. On the morning of the third day Alex woke with the sunrise and could already feel that he was more himself. The nagging sense of loneliness still sat like a dark cloud in his mind, but with the recovery of his body he felt the fear and paranoia lifting – not entirely gone, but not as overwhelming as it had been. He felt in control again, able to handle anything that he might face. He could also feel that the end to this journey was near.

The bus ride dragged on and seemed to take forever. It was strange, but also a relief to be doing something so normal, so everyday. Even in his usual day-to-day life he didn't often get to just be a commuter on a bus.

He'd waited until the afternoon to start moving. The castle had been fenced off and he didn't think trying to break in at midday was a particularly good idea. Once the sun had set people started to hurry back to wherever they had come from, and Alex tried to tell himself that it was because of the cold, but couldn't help but think there were other reasons. For the first time in a very long time his sense of anxiety changed from fear to excitement. His child-like sense of adventure had started to creep in, and as he jumped the fence to start the walk to the castle, he felt a little like he had on the morning just before he had been bitten. A hero making his way through the woods in search of adventure.

Muromtsevo Castle was hauntingly beautiful. Built following a bet with an eccentric Frenchman after an argument about whose country was better, it now had nature knocking on its doors. Coming face to face with something he'd only ever seen in a dream sent a wave of cold down his spine. Part of him still believed it had always been no more than a dream, but still it renewed his fears. Which other parts would turn out to be true? Slowly he started exploring the ruins, working his way methodically around the perimeter and then carefully from room to room. As the hours slipped by, Alex found himself at odds with his adventure. Part of him was pleased that nothing had happened, but he was also growing frustrated. The urge to rush through each room and then leave angrily had started to intensify, but he managed to control himself. Even if there was nothing there, it was important to look. That way, no matter what happened, he would know, and not just wonder.

Finally, reward came in the form of a trapdoor and a smell. From the moment he crouched down he knew he wasn't alone. The scent shot through his body like a lightning bolt and he staggered backward, aware only of a desire to flee. But he fought it, pushed himself forward, dug in his heels and, with the courage of a child, called out to whatever was lurking in the shadows.

"Halt, who goes there?"

The castle fell back into still silence, and Alex felt like he could hear his bones creak against each other. Just as he opened his mouth to call out again, a low growl slipped through the darkness, as from all around him.

"Go ... away." The voice seemed to fill the void.

Alex's skin crawled, but he stood his ground.

"Who ... who are you?"

The darkness seemed to grow more intense and, despite a level-headedness that insisted otherwise, Alex hoped this was just in a nightmare. Despite his ability to see in the dark, he struggled to focus on specific shapes or figures around him. Then the voice came again, pressing on him as though it was physically pushing him backwards.

"Boy," it echoed through the ruins, "you don't belong here. You do not understand ... Go! Go back to where you came from."

Alex clenched his teeth and took a deep breath.

"Not without answers. Who are you? What are you? And why do I keep dreaming about this place?"

He continued to stand his ground, fighting the urge to run. For a moment the darkness softened and he heard the unmistakable sound of a man sighing. The pressure slackened and, despite himself, Alex relaxed a little. But it was for only a moment. Then came a long, sharp inhale and it felt as though a dark hand had reached out of the ground to pull him down into it. Alex collapsed onto his hands and knees. Wave after wave of emotion hit him, tears pouring from his eyes as his mind was dragged into a well of guilt and sorrow and regret. Footsteps came out of the darkness.

Suddenly, out of the murky shadows that hung heavily around him, a man emerged. The figure crouched over and leaned in to whisper into Alex's ear.

"Go home."

In the same instant Alex sat bolt upright in bed back in his hotel room and burst into tears. The intensity of the voice echoed in his head and it was a good few minutes before he was able to form clear thoughts. Drained, he swung his legs off the bed and put his head in his hands, going over everything in his mind again and again.

When the sun rose, Alex got reception to call him a taxi and headed for the airport.

Chapter 14

Although still anxious, paranoid even, this had become secondary to the idea of returning to the farm. Of course, that didn't stop Alex buying tickets from two different airlines to two different destinations. And all the while the voice lingered in his head, driving him, intensifying his need to be with his family. Even though he had slept well after getting back to the hotel, he knew it wasn't enough and drifted off almost immediately after boarding the plane. For the first time in what felt like a lifetime there were no nightmares. Instead he dreamed of Cassandra, first the memory of their time together, then the moment when she was standing right in front of him smiling.

"Excuse me, sir, we're about to start our descent," the stewardess was nudging him awake. "Please fasten your seatbelt."

It wasn't hard to get around in Canada. If anyone had followed him there, it would be pretty clear where he was going. So he hired a car and headed straight to the farm. As the landscape grew more familiar an excitement crept over him. The loneliness he'd felt before started to melt away and a sense of belonging took its place. He was returning to his pack, even if only a small part of it, and he was really looking forward to see his grandmother, with only a vague concern that she might have a heart attack when he suddenly arrived on her doorstep.

When she did see him, she burst into tears and threw herself at him, laughing and crying and occasionally pulling away to look into his face and make sure it was really him. Only to then hug him all over again. Alex couldn't help but laugh, touched by it all, and had to resist the urge to tear up himself.

"Oh my dear sweet boy, what are you doing here? Your father said you were off in Europe somewhere. I was so worried when I heard you'd disappeared."

"Sorry, Grandma, I didn't mean to do that to you. I just needed to get away."

"Yes, well, I also heard what had happened just before that and I understand. I understand completely." She sighed and looked at him thoughtfully, trying not to imagine what it must have been like for him. "But you should know you could have come here. You didn't need to run off to goodness-knows-where."

Tears again touched her eyes.

"I know, I know, and so here I am. I ... I needed to try to find out some things about myself, but now it's time to come home so, so here I am."

Marie smiled broadly.

"Also, I haven't been here since the funeral and ... and ... Well, it was long overdue. I'm sorry that ... I didn't come sooner."

"Nonsense, you're a famous musician. You're busy, I understand. I wouldn't have visited me in your situation either, don't worry. I might be old but I'm not stupid, you know."

She gave him a smile that made her look almost youthful and just a little mischievous.

"So, how've you been?"

"Oh, you know, a little older every day. Your uncle comes up every other weekend to make sure I haven't burned the place down or done myself an injury. It's like he forgets that I have help here."

Alex frowned and she laughed at him.

"Boy, I'm 82 years old; you honestly didn't think I was still doing this all on my own."

His face flushed a deep crimson, and he felt a little stupid.

"No, no, come, let me introduce you to my right hand. Her name's Nuria and she's a lovely woman – Spanish – too old for you and too valuable to me, so don't you go sleeping with her."

Alex's blush deepened and mischief spread from her smile to her laugh.

Taking his hand, she led him into the kitchen and there, turning towards them as they entered, was an olive-skinned woman. She was slender but well-toned – fit, in every sense of the word – and had a kind smile. For an instant their eyes locked, and he saw the briefest green flash appear and disappear. Goosebumps erupted over his body and tears began to well up in his eyes as his grip on his grandmother's hand tightened for support. They stared at each other for a long moment as the doubts slowly faded from Alex's mind, leaving him certain of who she was.

"I ... I never thought I'd see you again."

His voice trembled in a way that his grandmother hadn't heard since he was a child and she gasped when she turned to see his face. The sudden, nearly overwhelming rush of emotion that played across his face turned Nuria's smile a little sad, but her voice was gentle, the faintest accent no one could place on first guess.

"If I'm honest, at first I was too ashamed to let you see me. I ... I hated myself for what I'd done to you, and I crawled into a hole and stayed there. I owe you an apology, I know that, but I also need to thank you, and to tell you how unbelievably proud I am of you."

Alex took a moment to steel himself before croaking, "Thank me for what?"

"You saved my life. Which makes my actions even more unforgivable."

"I ... I don't understand."

"When you found me, you tried to cut the ropes that held me and then I did the unspeakable in return. At that moment, seeing the look on your face, knowing what I'd done ... I wanted to die. Then those men who had captured me returned and set me alight. The pain ..." She paused for a moment, fighting the painful memory. "The pain was incredible and, as I thrashed, the rope you had cut finally broke. Suddenly I knew I stood a chance and was able to free myself and ... and, well, survive. You saved my life and I ... I ruined yours. For that, and for everything, I'm so sorry."

Tears touched the corner of her eyes but she stood proud. As Nuria spoke, it dawned on Marie what was happening, and who Nuria was.

Alex stood, taking long, slow breaths. All this time he had been unable to shake the memory of that small child staring into the eyes of that monster. He wondered for a moment what his life would have been like without ever encountering her. Would he have ever been in the band? Would his mother still be alive? Would his nephew still be alive if he hadn't been able to help his sister in the way he had? What sort of man would he have become? And, curiously to him, as an echo of an afterthought, he wondered if he ever would have met Cassandra.

"My name is Alex Harris, and you didn't ruin my life. You changed it, in ways I don't even know how to form thoughts around, but you didn't ruin it."

He stepped forward letting his hand slip free from his grandmother's and threw his arms around Nuria.

"And I can't tell you how happy I am to see you."

The series of flights, the seemingly endless drive seemed to hit him all at once, sapping the strength from him, but he refused to let go. Dully, he heard his grandmother's voice.

"Why didn't you tell me?"

Alex let the world around him vanish in the comfort and safety of that embrace, and for the first time in many years, he allowed himself to remember the warmth of a mother's hug. It was something he'd run from for so long that he'd forgotten what it felt like to just let go. And finally, after years of trying to ignore it, his heart broke for the death of his mother.

Alex dragged his sleeve across his face, dabbing at his eyes.

"I'll make us some coffee, shall I?" He managed a wan smile.

Immediately, the mood lifted and they took their usual spots at the kitchen table. Naturally, questions hung heavily in the air but they knew too that there was no longer the sense of urgency that had threatened to overwhelm them all these years. They had time on their side and were going to use it wisely.

When Alex returned with the mugs of coffee, the three sat in silence, thoughts and memories churning about in their heads. The two women waited patiently for him to be ready. They both knew it was coming and were happy to wait it out rather than him stampede right into it. Alex took a sip of coffee as his thoughts found their places in his mind.

"I always knew there were others. I mean, I knew there was at least one more, and I also saw others in my dreams. In Norway I had an encounter with, I think, the same people who'd attacked you. You know much about them?"

Nuria's face grew sombre.

"Actually, no, I'm afraid not. I've only ever really had to deal with them that once and ... and I try to avoid people who so completely hate me. What I do know is that they like to appear as though they have right on their side, some ancient religious order set to save the world. But I've been around a long time and they have not."

Alex turned to his grandmother and then back to Nuria.

"How did you end up here?"

"I decided I needed to come out of hiding, and I knew that you would eventually find your way back here. Also, I wanted to help your family in some way and this seemed the most positive way I could do that, spending time with Marie, helping her out."

Nuria leaned across the table and took his hand thoughtfully. "Alex, we live a very long time. Much longer than other people, than normal people."

He looked up and into her eyes.

"But not forever."

She smiled softly and shook her head.

"No."

He nodded and breathed a sigh.

"When I was in Russia, I followed a dream and it led me to a castle which ... where I encountered a voice. It felt like a dream, but I know it wasn't. When he or it, I only ever saw a shadow, spoke I could feel the words like a pressure building in my mind. Like everything he said became my will."

Nuria shot a worried glace at Marie.

"Vincent, after all this time. How on earth did you find him?"

"I think ... I think it all started when I met a girl. I was in Norway and from the day she arrived I started having these dreams of this place in Russia and, if I think about it now, she was also the one who identified it for me."

His vision came back to focus on Nuria.

"Tell me more about this girl."

Before she could stop herself, Marie cut in: "If he can remember her name, that is ..."

"Grandma!"

"What? You seem to go through them so quickly."

"This one was different."

"So, you mean you didn't sleep with her?"

Alex opened his mouth to reply but saw the naughty glint of triumph in his grandmother's eye and decided against it.

"Her name's Cassandra."

"Cassandra who?"

Again, he opened his mouth to speak but as his eyes grew wide the two women both rolled theirs.

"Why don't you just tell us the whole story rather?"

Alex took a sip of coffee. For a moment he considered leaving out what happened moments before boarding the boat back on Syn Island, but Marie already knew and he had no urge to hide anything from Nuria. Occasionally, someone would get up to refill their mugs, but neither woman interrupted with questions. Once or twice, either Marie or Nuria would interrupt with a snide comment, but there were never any questions, at least until Alex reached the point when here arrived in Canada.

"And now I'm here," he concluded, waving his hand around the room.

The room fell silent for a moment until a thought occurred to Marie.

"Oh, I need to tell your father you're here. Or rather, you need to tell your father you're here."

"I also need to eat and I really, really need to sleep. I feel like I've been running nonstop for months and I can finally just let go and rest. It's ..." He let out a long sigh. "It's finally over."

A tired smile spread across his face.

Nuria rose first.

"I'll make us some dinner, and then put together a bed for you."

Marie smiled at her friend and then her grandson.

"And you, young man, will go call your father."

Alex smiled at the women; he could practically smell the affection from them. But that scent quickly changed to something all too familiar, something uncomfortable. He blinked a few times, trying to name that which has crept up on him, but it was only when his head hit the floor and his eyes closed that somewhere in the back of his mind he remembered what fear smelt like.

Chapter 15

When Alex opened his eyes he could just make out his grand-mother's face through the blur. He opened his mouth, but couldn't seem to find words. In the distance he could hear someone in-struct him to lie still, that everything was going to be all right, and to close his eyes again. An idea that sounded like the best thing he'd ever heard. As the darkness rushed in a sense of weightless-ness wrapped around him and he floated up out of his body, out of the room and into the night sky. He seemed to drift there for a life-time. Then suddenly he began to plummet back to earth and land-ed back in his body with what felt like a thud. He sat bolt upright and looked around, only vaguely remembering that he was at the farm, in the spare room. Slowly, he crept from the bed and made his way down the hall, feeling again like he had on the day he was bitten. Nuria and Marie sat in the kitchen, drinking wine and dis-cussing the chores that needed to be tended to in the morning.

"What day is it?"

They both sprang to their feet and Marie hurried over to him.

"You're awake. Oh, thank God."

"What happened?"

"You just collapsed. I wanted to rush you off to the doctor, but Nuria assured me that you were going to be fine."

"I ... I remember being super tired, but I guess it was worse than I thought."

Nuria stepped into the conversation with a smile.

"It's possible that with everything you've been through the last few weeks you just reached the end of your rope. You can push yourself until you have nothing left to give, you know ... It's not healthy."

Alex scratched his head and yawned.

"Funny that it doesn't feel healthy. Now I seem to remember someone saying something about food?"

The women looked at each other and laughed.

"That was yesterday. But, yes, don't worry, there's food."

The two women sat him down and started bringing plate after plate of leftovers, which he happily worked through. It didn't take long before he sat, still a little hungry, looking over a sea of empty dishes and two very shocked women.

"Oops."

"That ... that was three days' worth of food."

Alex looked down at the plates and grimaced.

"Double oops?'

Marie rolled her eyes and began clearing the dishes.

"You get hold of Dad, Grandma?"

"No, I decided that if I called him to tell him you were passed out he would only worry more. Which, all things considered, didn't seem very helpful. So you can call him yourself. Now. It's about 10 pm on the Island so it should still be fine."

Alex smiled nervously and excused himself. He dropped down into his usual spot and dialled the number he knew best in the world. A slight pang of guilt ran through him as he sat waiting for his father to pick up, realising that it had been around eight months since they had last spoken.

A tired slightly annoyed voice answered.

"Harris speaking."

"Hi ... Dad."

For a moment there was a stunned silence.

"Alex, my boy, how are you? Where are you?"

"I'm good … I'm on the farm with Grandma. I got here yesterday. At least, I think it was yesterday. I'm … I'm rejoining the world."

Over the new few minutes Alex gave his father a much-abbreviated version of the story he'd told Nuria and his grandmother, only his father asked a lot more questions, and probably ended up with less information.

"So, when are you coming back? To the Island, I mean. Or, here's an idea, why don't I grab Annie and Bastian and we all head down to the farm. Maybe Josh can come along as well if you're not ready for the city yet."

Alex smiled. He pictured an old-school family holiday on the farm and liked the idea, but he quickly pushed it out of his mind. Nuria was another werewolf, and he wasn't sure how that would play into keeping his secret from either Bastian or Josh. At the very least, he knew he needed to float the idea by her first, and learn a bit more about himself before bringing other people in.

"If it's okay with you, Dad, let me have a few days here and then I'll come to you. I … wanna ease myself into it. But I don't want to stay hidden either. I have a lead on my condition and I'm not sure it's a good idea to have others around while I investigate it, you know what I mean?"

"All right, my boy, just keep me informed. It's lovely to hear from you, so don't you go disappearing again."

"I won't, Dad. Don't worry. Otherwise, how are things? I take it Annie and Josh are still a thing?"

"You haven't been keeping up with rumours, have you?"

Alex frowned and it showed in his voice.

"No?"

"They were outed … We all think it was Stacy, but there's no proof. But it's been all over the tabloids lately. People are saying that it was the discovery of your best friend and your sister's affair that pushed you over the edge."

Alex clenched his jaw.

"Jesus, how angry is she?"

"Spinal tap."

Alex baulked at the idea of a furious Annabel.

"I can see why you'd want to come to the farm. Not sure why you'd want to bring her with, though."

"You think I'm dumb enough to do something that might make her angrier?"

"Fair, very fair. I'll give her a call now and pretend like I don't know and let her yell it all at me. That usually makes her feel better."

"There's a good boy."

They continued to chat for a while, relishing the opportunities they had missed in the previous months. And Alex, of course, was avoiding having to face up to Annabel. The truth was that they had gone without talking much longer before – when Alex was on tour it was virtually impossible to stay in touch – but this time had been different and Kyle had really missed his son. Eventually, though, they reached the end of the conversation and had to say their goodbyes.

As soon as Alex hung up, he took a deep breath and dialled his sister's number, then sat quietly waiting.

"Hello?"

The nuance in her voice was unmistakable and Alex almost flinched.

"Hey, Annie?"

"Alex?"

"Yeah, it's me, I'm on the farm and ... uhmmm ... just wanted to check in." He was preparing himself for what was coming. "Find out if anything interesting has happened since we last spoke."

What followed was a stream of consciousness: complaints about everything from the entertainment media, print media, the evils of the internet, the lack of privacy that she never wanted or asked for, why it was actually all his fault, why it was definitely 100 per cent that bitch Stacy and eventually about how professional photographers seemed incapable of taking a nice pictures of her.

"It's like they're going out of their way to get the worse possible angle, like they spent all the time learning when and how to take the worst picture. I am not fat, but you wouldn't think so looking at any of the pictures they've published."

As Alex sat there listening, he realised she was most hurt by an article comparing her to Josh's ex, which by the sounds of things was also the most unfair writer, the one with an axe to grind. More so, from Alex's point of view, knowing exactly how Josh felt about his ex, and how he'd always been a little in love with Annabel. Annabel presented it from the point of view of how uncomfortable it had made Josh, but Alex knew his sister well enough to hear her pain in every word.

"And I know it was that bitch Stacy, but there's no proof and she obviously denies all allegations because ... Oh, she would never do such a thing, how could we even think of it, all hurt and wounded by the accusations. Bitch, I fucking hate her. Alex, I! Hate! Her!"

Annabel let out a long frustrated sigh and the two sat in silence for a bit, she to catch her breath and he for her to calm down a little. Alex listened carefully to his sister's breathing, waiting for it to slow down before talking.

"Has she had the baby yet? Do we know whether it's Brandon's?"

"No, not yet. She's as big as a house, says it's just pregnancy and her body making sure their baby's safe and has everything it needs, but we all know that she's actually just fat … and ugly and a bitch."

"How's he holding up? Brandon, I mean."

"Yeah, he seems good. Same-same, but a bit more stressed that usual, apologising a lot more, but really excited to be a dad. God, on so many levels I hope we're wrong about her."

"Yeah, I feel you there. What about Danny?"

"He's around, everyone's around … Actually, everyone other than you."

"I know, I know, but I'm coming back. I just needed to hit the farm first, and I think I might hit up the USA for a bit as well."

"You going after Cassandra?"

"Yeah, I was certainly thinking about it."

"You so sure you're welcome?"

"Why? She say something after I left?"

"Well, no, not exactly. But a lot did happen in a very short space of time, and then you just left. I mean, I'm not saying don't go, but maybe call first?"

"Yeah, yeah, okay. I mean, I know that, on some level. Also, I'd have to anyway, I don't know where she is or how to get hold of her really."

"I've got her on social media. You can find her that way."

"What?"

"We had time to chat after you left. She's a very nice girl; we bonded."

"Oh dear God."

"What? It's not like I can reveal your deepest darkest secrets. You did that already, and she is nice and you left a mark on those people and then disappeared, like you do with everyone you meet."

"No, no, no … Please can we not have a relationship lecture right now. I had things I needed to do, I'm coming back to reality, I'm looking to contact a woman I've spent time with and I really like, I'm doing the things you've all been on at me about. You don't have tell me to do the very thing I am doing. You don't get credit – you just make me angry."

"Okay, jeez, calm down. So how are things on the farm? Have you met Grandma's helper? She's super cool."

"Nuria? Yeah, yeah, we've met."

"You didn't sleep with her, did you?"

Another spark of frustration flared up inside of him that he wasn't fully able to bite back.

"Am I really that bad? Grandma said the same. Or is it just that I've been away from this kind of thing for so long that I forgot that my sex life is the butt of every joke."

In the same moment, Nuria appeared in the doorway, shining green eyes looking through him. Alex held up a hand in apology. Seeing the things he's done mirrored in someone else like him gave him a strange sense of authenticity to the way he'd lived his life. Annabel's voice broke the moment.

"Is it full moon soon? Like, what's up? That's twice now. I thought you called so that I could be the angry one."

Alex looked back up at Nuria, who smiled; he knew she could probably hear every word of the conversation and he raised his eyebrows. She mouthed a word at him and he nodded and turned his attention back to the phone.

"Tomorrow, which is lucky, because I'd lost track and just spent two days on aeroplanes. That could've gotten really exciting."

Nuria smiled broadly to show off her sharp teeth before slipping back out of the room. Annabel rolled her eyes, wondering whether she was still the focus of Alex's attention.

"All right, well, it's late. I'm glad you're home-ish and safe. I'll speak to you later. But, hey, be sure to call The Sanctuary. I think they'd also like to know you're okay."

"I will, but it'll have to be later. Anyway, say hi to everyone for me and tell them I'll be home soon."

"I will. Love you."

"You too."

Alex put down the phone and went in search of Nuria, whom he found sitting alone in the kitchen.

"This is going to be fun," she smiled at him. "I take it this will be your first time transforming with another wolf?"

"I've spent time with actual wolves. But, yes. I've never met anyone like us before. How many are there?"

"I've met a few over the years. I believe you met one. And another who died. Well, I presume died."

"So we really can die? Like really-really? Because I've survived some things that I didn't think I would and ..."

He awkwardly gestured at himself as a way to show that he was fine.

"Yes, and yes. At one point we tried to live in a community, a small pack of three, but the urge to travel came to all of us. But that was a very long time ago."

"How ... how old are you?"

"I don't know exactly. Few hundred years."

A sombre look spread across Alex's face.

"Jesus, I am going to outlive them all."

It had been something he'd been over a few times in his head, but was happy to not know for sure. Seeing the look on his face, Nuria ushered him into a seat.

"There are a few other things you might not know."

"Okay?"

"We can't have children. You can't make a woman pregnant. I can fall pregnant but … it doesn't last."

"Even between two people like us?"

Her face grew tired and for a moment she looked her real age.

"Even then," she shrugged.

"I'm … I'm sorry."

"No, it's all right. Like you, I had siblings who had children. I was able to be with them as they grew older. But eventually I needed to move on and it was a different time back then. I could never stay in a single place and then not really age. They'd have burned me as a witch. Or as a monster."

"I guess I'll have to eventually disappear too. So how old were you when you were bitten?"

"How old do I look?"

"Not a couple of hundred and something."

"I was around my forties."

"So did you not have children before?"

"It was a different time, and not all children born grew up to be adults. It was not long after my last child died that I was bitten, wandering alone, searching for answers to my prayers, for some direction in my life."

Her voice trailed off and tears welled up as she thought back to the green eyes rushing towards her in the darkness, set to collide with her life and change it forever. Alex put an arm around her for comfort and took her hand.

"I'm sorry, again."

"It ... thank you, it was a long time ago."

Alex sighed and laughed a little.

"I went all the way to Norway, and chased a dream to Russia to learn more about being a werewolf, and in the end all I had to do was come home."

"Sometimes," Nuria smiled back at him, "the best way to learn about yourself is to come home. When you change alone it's about how you feel; when you are with another werewolf, emotions are shared. What you feel I feel, what I feel you'll feel. When one of us starts the transformation the other will not be able to hold back."

Alex's back stiffened.

"Well, that sounds ... intense."

"I imagine we'll also run a lot more than you're used to."

"I don't know, I've done a lot of running just recently. But, that being said, it's true that over the years I've gotten very good at just relaxing during full moon. I also really got into the swing of just being Mork for extended periods."

"Mork?" She dropped her head to one side.

"Oh right. For the purpose of hiding in plain sight, I would pretend to be the family pet Mork. So I would spend time in between full moons as a wolf so that people got used to seeing me. And I often found that if I was having trouble sleeping, it really helped if I transformed."

"That's incredible. I had none of that, never had that sort of experience. Even now, I very rarely transform outside of full moon. You can still expect to run a lot more than usual this time though."

Her eyes sparkled, sending a tingle of excitement through him. The prospect of transforming with someone else, running with an actual pack rather than just dreaming about it, or being the lone outsider among the pack at his cave in Norway, it felt strange. It was exciting, but also very intimate. He'd never had the opportunity to share that part of his life with anyone, until now.

It was early the next morning when Alex sensed the moon on his back and when he stepped outside, he found Nuria standing waiting for him. She was naked but, in that moment, he was too fixated on the new smells, the new feelings, the connection that was forming to notice. The experience seemed to come over them at the same moment, and for the next few days they ran.

When they finally changed back, the moon's influence waning, Alex found it much harder not to notice Nuria and his own nakedness, the way the rising sun accentuated her body. She didn't look a day over twenty. She too noticed him noticing her and he blushed crimson then quickly turned away.

"You know," she laughed, "we've been naked together for a few days now."

"I mean ... yes, but still, this is ... it's different?"

"We come from very different times, I guess," she smiled.

"Yeah, also, people keep telling me not to sleep with you and, I mean, I'm not trying to presume but, you are also ... I mean, well ..." He waved his hand up and down her body but was careful to maintain eye contact. "You're an incredibly attractive woman." He blushed and quickly added. "Also, when you're not naked, just ... uhmmm ... I mean, for the record."

Nuria's smile broadened and her cheeks coloured a little.

"Okay, so ... are you trying to protect my honour, or just hide your embarrassment?"

Alex stammered.

"Both, I guess."

"Alex," she laughed, but held a tone of earnestness in her voice, "just because we're naked together doesn't mean anything's going to happen. I'm a lot older than you."

He shrugged.

"That's not been the case in my experience."

"Oh, to be young and famous."

She stepped to stand in front on him and gestured at herself, inviting him to see her in all her glory.

"Alex, I don't actually want to sleep with you."

He feigned astonishment.

"But, but do you know who I am? You know I'm famous, right?"

Nuria laughed and rolled her eyes.

"Honestly? When you reach my age you can take it or leave it. I don't think I've had an orgasm in three years. Also, I am best friends with your grandmother. Besides, aren't you a little in love with that Cassandra girl you told us about?"

He thought it over a little before answering.

"I mean, I guess, but I've also never really let that stop me before."

Despite knowing that he didn't actually want to sleep with Nuria, the idea that she wasn't interested made him curious.

Nuria stopped and turned to him.

"Maybe it's time. Maybe that's exactly what should stop you. You know that I can basically smell what you're thinking right now, right?"

Alex could no more hide what was going though him than he could fly and although part of him liked to believe that he was simply accepting a situation that he couldn't change, a part of him was excited.

"I'm young, handsome and horny. That's currently not something I can do anything about. Besides, you're the one who said we've basically been naked together for three days. Thoughts like that have an effect."

She laughed at him again, then stopped and smiled wickedly.

"You're right, let's do it then. Right here, right now."

She ran her hands over her body to highlight her curves. Alex turned away, stuttering: "I ... I mean ... It's not that I don't w—"

She cut him off laughing.

"You see, just a boy whose toy has been taken away. You don't want to have sex with me; you just don't like the idea that I'm not interested."

She stifled a giggle and continued walking. It took a moment but Alex followed, now slightly ashamed.

"Have you always looked like this? Since you were bitten, I mean."

"Basically, yes. Why?"

"Well, because I've obviously changed a lot since then."

"Some things firmed up, I lost some weight and gained some muscle. I already had the grey hairs, so those stayed. I don't think all of this 'de-aged' me, if that's even a word, it just put me in much better shape than I was."

"So at some point I'm going to stop ageing."

She rolled her eyes.

"Yes, sadly, you are going to look that good forever."

Alex chuckled.

"You are taking far too much pleasure in all this."

"I know, but you make it so easy."

When they arrived at the door to the kitchen Marie frowned at Alex. His face immediately dropped in defeat.

"What? I didn't do anything! It was full moon."

"Well, I know nothing happened because I know Nuria. I trust her."

"Alex was the perfect gentleman."

"I'm sure he was, but doesn't mean I don't enjoy making fun of him."

"And you people wonder why I disappear for months on end. I'm going to go shower."

He could hear the women laughing at him as he stomped through the house, pretending to be offended. He was, however, unable to shake the image of a naked Nuria from his head. After a long shower, some coffee and a lot of food, he finally hauled out his laptop and started his search for Cassandra. It wasn't difficult to track her down; she was, after all, on Annabel's friends list. According to her public profile, she had left The Sanctuary and had made her way home. He sent her a quick and slightly awkward hello, and then sent messages to Brandon, Josh and Danny, telling them he'd be back on the Island in a couple weeks and wanted to see them; naturally, he apologised for having done a runner and for a moment even considered telling them about his condition, but the moment was only fleeting. Now is not the time, he reassured himself. Cassandra replied to his message almost instantly.

Hey, how are you? Where are you?

Just up in Canada. You think it would be all right if I came to visit? I'd really like to see you.

The reply didn't come as quickly this time, which made him a little anxious, but soon enough an answer landed in his inbox.

I think I'd really like that. I'm not saying anything is going to happen but it would be nice to show you off to my friends.

He immediately typed back.

I can be there in about three days?

Oh, wow. Okay, that's soon. Technically, I'd need to ask my parents, but yes ... Sure. Let's do it.

Alex quickly opened a new window and by the time the conversation was over he had booked tickets and was smiling like an idiot. He beamed his smile at his grandmother who had popped her head around the door.

"You're leaving, aren't you?" She shook her head.

"Yeah, in the morning. But I'm not disappearing this time and I won't be gone for as long, I promise."

Marie wrapped her arms around him and held on for a while.

"I know you're still going to be around for a long time, but I am not, so you better keep that promise."

A wave of emotion swept over him and it took a moment before he could speak.

"When I get back to the Island, I'll make a plan to get the whole family here. A nice proper family holiday on the farm, like we used to do."

"I'd really like that."

She hung on a little longer.

"Is everything all right?"

"Yes, of course. It's a grandmother's right to hang onto someone she loves for as long as she likes."

Chapter 16

The news that rock star Alex Harris had been spotted at an airport in Canada spread quickly, and by the time he landed in Colorado he was famous again. Cassandra found him standing in a small crowd signing autographs and fielding questions without actually giving any information. She stopped when she saw it, giving him the opportunity to excuse himself without having to ignore questions about her or fear that pictures of her would appear online. He'd learned that if he was cool to the fans, chatting, signing things and allowing them to take selfies with him, it was more likely that no malicious gossip would surface unexpectedly. Cassandra was driving her parents' nondescript minivan, which helped them to make a clean getaway. It did, however, rob them of an opportunity to simply throw their arms around each other; secretly that's all they both wanted to do, all they wanted from each other.

"That seemed pretty nuts. I keep forgetting that you're actually this world-famous rock-star person."

Alex laughed and shook his head.

"Yeah, me too. Hasn't happened in a while and I think I prefer it the other way. But this was actually pretty tame in comparison."

She gave him a sideways glance, somewhere between pity, envy and sarcasm.

"So how was Russia? You find what you were looking for?"

"Sort of, yes ... But not in Russia, not where I was expecting to find it."

"Okaaay?" Cassandra frowned.

"Sorry, I guess I'm still not used to being open about things like this ... Uhmmm, I managed to find the wolf, the one that bit me."

"Jesus. That's got to be kind of intense. What was he like?"

"She. And really kind of sweet, if a little odd. It was good. Feels a bit like I've dropped a weight I didn't know I was carrying. I don't know, it's all been such a crazy week I don't think I've had time to really process it all. But ... hey, it's really great to see you."

He reached a hand out and placed it on hers. She looked down at his hand, then shot a glance at him.

"Okay, fuck it."

She quickly checked the mirrors, hit the brakes and pulled the car to the side of the road; then she threw her arms around him as she'd been wanting to do since the moment she saw him.

"I ..." Alex said, finally finding his voice. "I didn't realise just how much I missed you until I saw you. I'm ... I'm so—"

Cassandra leaned back to look at him.

"Oh, shut up, smooth talker."

Then she kissed him. After a few seconds a smirk spread across her face and she pulled back and away, slipped back into the driver's seat and they set off in a calm, comfortable silence. They were almost at the turnoff to her place when she turned red and said through an embarrassed giggle, "Oh, oh ... I've been meaning to tell you. Also, sorry in advance."

"You have a bunch of your friends and family waiting to meet me?"

"I mean, they all swore they wouldn't tell anyone, and then everyone told everyone."

"So, basically, I'm about to meet you parents and all of your friends all at once? At a party so that they can all meet your ... friend? Boyfriend? Some guy you met while travelling?"

He could see even her ears turn red.

"Well, let's be clear on one thing, you're not my boyfriend!"

Her words filled the air around them, and Alex's eyebrows shot up. He wasn't sure whether he should laugh or be disappointed, but before he could work it out, more words started spilling out of her.

"I mean, we don't really know each other that well, and we live in very different parts of the world with very different lives. You're, I mean, a rock star who's also a secret werewolf and I'm still studying and that's really important to me."

"I know, I know, I was just joking. Mostly."

Cassandra let out a long sigh.

"I know, but there's also ... You did just jump on a plane to come visit me and, don't get me wrong, I'm really happy to see you, and excited and confused, mostly I'm really confused. And when you ask questions like that it just makes it worse. And, if I'm honest, it's not really fair."

What had started as a light-hearted idea had turned into a serious conversation neither had expected to be having.

"I'm sorry. For a lot of things actually. I know that I owe you an explanation or at least something like it. I'm not here to make your life more complicated or to try to stop you from being you. That's the last thing I want to do, but I did want to see you, and hang out with you."

"But what if just hanging out isn't enough? Or what if it's, maybe ... too much."

A new silence descended on the car.

"Before you say that perhaps I shouldn't have come, let me first say that you're wrong. Clearly, we have stuff we need to deal with and I think, I hope, we'd both rather get through that then let it loom bigger in the space between and end up never being resolved."

A genuine smile spread across her face.

"Oh no, you definitely should've come. How else am I going to prove to my friends that Alex Harris is my stalker?"

Her face told him that she was trying to steer the conversation back on track by making the same kind of joke that had derailed it. He didn't mind. She was giving him a pass and he wanted to take it.

"Okay, so that's my status. Got it."

"That doesn't mean you're allowed to flirt with any of my friends though, mister. I know your type."

"Don't believe everything Fredrik tells you. Just because he thinks it's real doesn't mean it is."

"When it comes to you it does."

They both laughed and realised how nice it was to be able to talk about The Sanctuary. Cassandra especially had felt a little like the door on that part of her life had closed the moment she had arrived home and no one really understood how important it really was to her. Alex reached across and squeezed her hand again and the comfortable silence returned, right up until she pulled into the driveway and he realised they'd driven past the house three times before she parked.

"That nervous, huh?"

"Oh shut up. And behave."

"Which one is it? I don't think I can do both."

"That doesn't make any sense."

"Yeah, well, you're not the only one who's nervous."

He stuck out his tongue and she made a disgusted face but still neither of them got out of the car. He sighed again and said.

"Count of three?"

"Count of five?"

"Too weird. It's just your friends and family, and I actually have training in this sort of thing."

"Really?"

"Yeah, legit … We became famous as teenagers, so the record company sent us to a week-long seminar on how to handle fame and fans and being accosted by strangers who thought they knew us personally because they related to something in our music. Its fine now, but if I think back to it, the things people said to me as a teenager, telling me about their hectic life issues, about death and suicide attempts and how my music saved their lives, it's strange what people will say to you when you're famous. I get that my music had a significant impact on them, but most of them don't realise that their lives have had no impact on mine."

Alex's eyes grew distant as if looking at something far off in the distance. A memory put in the very back of his mind. "And then there was Charlie."

"Who?"

"Fairly early on, a guy named Charlie committed suicide and when they found him, one of our songs was playing on a loop in his room. The media decided to create a link between the events and some social groups wanted us banned, claiming we had 'no empathy towards the destruction of human lives in the wake of our hostile music'. And asked, 'Is the band Waterdogs trying to make your children commit suicide? Some experts say yes.'"

"Jesus, that sounds ... How did that end?"

"In our infinite teenage wisdom, we decided to attend the funeral, showed that we did care, that we did pay attention."

"And?"

"And ... his mother met us outside the church, slapped me, called me a murderer and told me that because I had written the lyrics I was the one responsible and the one she was laying charges against. I was seventeen. It was at that point people stepped in, and we got sent away to learn how to better handle that sort of thing. The charges were ultimately dropped but I did have to make an official statement to the courts, stating that I in no way intended my music to cause harm. It was also brought up that his family had basically kicked him out when he was fifteen after discovering that he smoked pot, and the whole media thing was them trying to use his death to get money from us. It was just really, really bad, in a whole bunch of ways."

Alex blushed, realising he'd just opened up about something he'd not meant to. Outside of the band and his family, no one really knew the details about Charlie. He forced a smile and decided that they had been too heavy for too long.

"So, I'm fairly certain I can handle your family. I'll let you know if there are any problem people to watch out for though."

It wasn't as funny or laidback as he'd hoped it would be, but it was enough for them to undo their seat belts and head for the door.

The party was exactly how he expected it to be. He was introduced to fifteen grinning faces and pretty much forgot every name as soon as he heard them. He did try to hang onto what their connection to Cassandra was though. Mother, father, siblings, best friend, siblings' best friends, siblings' best friends' hangers-on. And then came the questions.

"Do you know Mick Jagger?"

"What's Hollywood like, you know, on the inside? The real Hollywood?"

"I thought you'd be taller."

"Can you introduce me to Stephen Spielberg?"

"So, what's the real reason the band broke up?"

"You look younger in the videos."

"Do you want to read my book?"

"... Listen to my album?"

"... Read my script?"

"I can't believe you drink coffee just like a normal person."

"Can you pass this on to someone important?"

Luckily, the barrage didn't last very long before Cassandra's mother took control of the situation and started giving people tasks to make sure the food came out faster. Teams were formed to chop things, toss salads and start a fire for a barbecue. The general chatter was still about him, and how awesome it was that they were friends with a famous person, but it was no longer directed at him. He turned to Cassandra's mother.

"Thank you," he mouthed

"That's all right, hon. I could see them getting a little overwhelmed and the best way to fix that is to get to work."

"I can see where Cassandra gets her level head."

"That little monkey? No, she's a mess like her father, always trying to do a hundred things at the same time, pretending like she's got it all under control. But she's a good girl."

Alex could pick up the subtle undertones of what she was saying and he raised his hands in surrender.

"I come in peace. I promise."

"I'll hold you to that, young man ... Now, you're a big strong boy; there are a few cases of beer and ice in the garage. Go fill the bathtub with water and get it all out to the back garden. Just because you're famous doesn't mean you don't get a job."

He turned his raised hands into a salute and smiled.

"Yes, ma'am."

Over his shoulder he could hear some of the other guests laugh at how he was being put to work like an 'ordinary person'. After that things pretty much slipped into a groove and the other guests seemed to forget that there was a celebrity in their midst. By the time food was ready and eaten most had either gone home or retired to bed, safe in the knowledge that Alex would be there in the morning, or at least satisfied that they'd met him. At some point in the evening, the barbecue fire had been moved into a fire pit and turned into a bonfire, where the remaining guests sat with the last few drinks. Alex looked across at Cassandra's best friend and smiled charmingly.

"It's Katie, right?"

His voice was a little tired and very apologetic.

"Right."

"Oh, thank god, I think yours is the first I've gotten right all day. So many names, so ... so many names."

He feigned exhaustion and put his head down for a moment before letting out a tired laugh and raising his beer.

"Very nice to meet you. Katie."

She smiled and they clinked bottles.

"Nice to meet you too. Surprising, still a little unbelievable, but very nice."

She downed the last of her beer and rose.

"Well, I'm gonna be getting home, but I'll see you guys in the morning."

Cassandra and Alex both rose to give out hugs and say goodbye, then settled back down for a final quiet drink together.

"So, how'd your training fare against my friends and family?"

"Fine. I've been asked most of those things before. For some reason, people think that all famous people know each other. Or know the secret to getting famous, like anyone can do it; they just have to be allowed in. I don't know. It was nice to meet them all, they're all pretty harmless."

They stared at each other for a while in silence until she smiled.

"Sleep with me? Like we used to?"

"I thought you'd never ask."

"I wasn't going to, but I'm drunk and you're warm."

She stuck her tongue out at him and for a long moment he thought about kissing her again, but didn't. He did, however, get up and scoop her into his arms to carry her inside, but had to put her down when they realised that they had to close and lock some doors.

As they crawled into bed and snuggled up together Cassandra whispered, "I'm still not having sex with you."

"I know, I know ..." He lay back on the pillow, thinking. "Sorry about bringing up some of that stuff in the car earlier. About Charlie, I mean ..."

"It's fine. I understand. That's a seriously screwed-up situation to be in, but it was also good to hear you open up like that. I ... If I think about it, I still think of you as Mork and kind of forget that you're Alex Harris. The Alex Harris, I mean. And if I think too hard about it, I still get a little freaked out."

He reached forward and kissed her forehead.

"You know more about me than anyone outside of my family. In some cases, even more than my band."

A tired smile spread across her face and she settled into her old sleeping position.

"I know, sort of ... Now, good night and sweet dreams."

"You too."

Chapter 17

A loud buzzing jolted Alex and Cassandra rudely out of sleep and back into the real world. A low growl rumbled out of him as he reached for his phone.

"What?" he spat.

"Shit. Time difference."

The voice was the slightly distressed voice of his sister, and a faint memory crept into Alex's mind.

"What's wrong?"

"You need to come home. Like ... now."

"Why? What's going?"

"Brandon's baby has been born, well ... no, Stacy's baby has been born."

"Okay?"

"Ah, it's a boy, and it's ... black."

For just a second Alex thought about laughing, then the reality of his friend's situation hit him and the humour abruptly dissipated.

"I'm on the next flight. I'll charter a plane if I have to. I'll call you once I have the details."

He said a quick goodbye and turned to look at the now confused Cassandra.

"Next flight?"

"I need to go back to the Island ... There's trouble at home."

Her shoulders dropped and her eyebrows rose.

"What kind of trouble?"

"My friend's wife just gave birth to a black baby."

Cassandra's eyebrows somehow managed to shoot up even higher.

"And that's a problem because?"

"Well, nothing really – except she's a bleached blonde white girl and he's equally skinny and pale. She is also a total bitch who we all presume has been having affairs every step of the way. And now it's confirmed."

Cassandra's face dropped, defeated. Alex rubbed his face and sighed.

"I mean, this isn't just a friend, he's a band mate, basically family. I've got to be there. He's just the nicest, sweetest guy and this has got to be destroying him."

She took in a long breath and nodded.

"No, no, I get it. I was just hoping we'd be able to have a bit more time together. Hang out and get to know each other again, properly."

A thought flashed through his head as he tried to work out how he was going to get there.

"Come with me."

"What?"

"Come with me. If you're not busy just come with me."

"There's no way I can afford—"

"I can."

A look of annoyed defiance came over her face.

"Call it arsehole tax for lying to you for so long, or just accept that you're really good friends with a very rich guy, who can and wants to fly you halfway around the world to continue to spend time with you. I mean, is it honestly all that different from me spontaneously flying myself here?"

"But I can't just up and leave again for ages."

"So, don't come for a week. I'll fly you home whenever you want. But I have to go, and I have to go today. Like, when we're done talking, it's coffee and go. But I do want you to come with me, so pack up quick and let's do this? Haven't you ever wanted to live the adventure of the rock-and-roll lifestyle?"

A faint glint appeared in her eyes and he knew he'd hit on the right chord. That and he could smell the excitement and slight arousal.

"Okay, okay, I'm in."

"Great. I'll go see if I can figure out coffee and you start packing."

Cassandra stretched, yawned and looked at the clock.

"Don't worry about that. My mom is probably already awake and that means you get to tell her."

Alex raised one hand and pulled a concerned face, but before he could say a word, Cassandra interjected: "Hey, consider it arsehole tax for lying to me for so long."

She stuck out her tongue then sprang from the bed.

Alex slowly pulled on clothes and cautiously made his way to the kitchen where Cassandra's mom was indeed drinking coffee and reading a newspaper.

"Morning, hun, fresh coffee in the pot. I wasn't expecting you to be up this early."

"Yeah, there's been a slight change of plan."

"Oh?"

Alex stuttered and stumbled his way through explaining that he was not only going to leave but was taking Cassandra with him, and to his surprise he was met with a smile and a hug.

"I'm glad you recognised the need to be nervous about telling me, and that she's going with you. I think it's a good thing she gets out of her shell a little. Norway was a big step for her, and I think meeting you was a good thing. But if you break her heart, young man, you'll have me to deal with."

She smiled sweetly but Alex knew better than to look cheerful; instead he nodded gravely.

"And if anyone else does they'll have us to deal with."

She smiled and he poured himself some coffee set to wait for Cassandra to finish packing. He pulled out his phone. A tired slightly defeated voice answered and Alex responded with a low, rumbling growl.

"Alex? Alex, man, is that you?"

"Of course it's me! Just heard the news, man, and I wanted to find out how you were and to tell you I'm coming home, like, today."

Alex could tell Brandon was a little choked up and had lost some of his resolve.

"Come to protect me again, huh? Just like always." Brandon's voice caught a little, somewhere between a laugh and a cry. "Thank you, man. I just … I just don't know what I'm going to do, or what I'm supposed to do. I mean, I can't ignore it, not anymore."

"Where you staying?"

"Josh's place. Danny's here too, and Annabel."

"Look at you, getting the band back together."

Just then Cassandra gently touched his shoulder and lifted a packed suitcase.

"Okay, Brandon, buddy, I'm going to get myself to an airport and find a flight. I'll keep Annabel updated and she can inform everyone else. But you can text me whenever. If I don't reply I'm on a plane."

"Okay, okay. Thanks, man. Appreciate it, honestly. I'll see you soon ... which ... which is fucking great actually. Can't wait."

Cassandra's mom drove them to the airport; she seemed far more excited about the whole idea than her daughter. They hugged goodbye and Cassandra decided it would be better if she went and found something to do while Alex went ahead and bought the tickets. She didn't have to know exactly how much international flights at zero notice cost. It also meant that Alex didn't have to justify First Class until after he'd already gotten them tickets. As he handed over his credit card, however, there was a sudden panic and the familiar sense of being chased slipped back into his mind. It wasn't overpowering, but it was there, that paranoid voice whispering that someone was watching him, hunting him. It sent a shiver over his body but he knew he was at an airport, with all the appropriate security, so he took a deep breath and told himself that they were fine.

When he rejoined Cassandra, she knew immediately that something was wrong but was distracted by the First-Class lounge and what that meant. In her mind, air travel meant wandering aimlessly around airport shops looking at things you had no intention of buying. Like being stuck in a shopping mall for hours on end then sitting in a slightly too-small chair for forever to get to somewhere amazing. When they boarded, she was somewhat dumbstruck by the free food and booze, the table servers and the most comfortable seats she'd ever sat in.

"Show off."

"It also means that I don't get mobbed by fans. The lady at the ticket counter said my photo is on the scrolling newsfeed all around the airport, so even if people don't know my music they're going to know my face."

"Oh, is that why you look so stressed all of a sudden?"

Alex turned to look at her and did his best to appear cool and confident, but was met with raised eyebrows. That clearly hadn't worked.

"How often do you think about what happened up at The Sanctuary?"

"All the time. Which bit?"

"The bit when I turned into a giant wolf and killed two people."

His tone was so flat and matter of fact that it sent ice through her veins. That particular thought was one she had put some time and effort into, trying to distance herself from. Once he wasn't there the idea had started to feel so unbelievable that she had almost forgotten that it was real – her and everyone else.

"Oh ... Yeah, that ...'

Her eyes grew distant and, smelling the fear rising from her, Alex wished he hadn't said anything.

"I don't know, after you left we all sort of decided to not let it become the focus of our time there and move on. I ... I dreamt about it a couple times though."

"You mean nightmares."

When he looked into her eyes he was surprised to realise she wasn't scared but sad.

"No, no, not at all. It just comes back to me in dreams.'

She studied his face for a moment, thinking about what she wanted to say, what she wanted him to understand.

'You're ... You're not a monster, Alex."

A smile spread across his face but it somehow made him look sadder, more thoughtful.

"I know, I just feel that way sometimes. It was worse as a kid. I'm actually really fine with it these days. I was mostly thinking about those guys and who they were and how they found me. Having my face everywhere again – that just makes me a little nervous."

"You have any run-ins with them while you were in Russia?"

"Not really, no. There were some people asking about me in Poland, but I never saw them. Thinking back, they could just as easily have been fans or journalists. I've not actually seen or heard anything from them since The Sanctuary. I think … I know I'm being paranoid but I also can't really help it."

She moved to sit down next to him and rested her head on his shoulder.

"You know, a wise man once said, everything is going to be just fine."

The flight was long but comfortable, and with some help from the free champagne they both managed to sleep. Alex spent the last half-hour giving Cassandra a crash course on what to do if a press and or fan swarm appeared. He was known on Syn Island and had often been spotted there before his disappearance, and this was his first trip home after reappearing in public. So the chances were high that if anyone noticed him, there would be a lot of excitement. And there was always the risk that one of the other passengers had messaged a friend that Alex Harris was on the same plane, and that friend would then have told a friend and that friend of a friend may have sent the news on to the press.

Cassandra listened intently, feeling as though she were peeking behind the curtain into a world she'd never imagined before.

"Once we grab our stuff, I'll head off first. That way, if there are people waiting, I'll be able to draw them off to one side. Just look for Annie when you walk out. If it's really crazy, though, security will meet us at passport control and escort us out another way, which would be ideal. Unlikely, but ideal."

"This all sounds a little insane."

"Yip, it's kinda fun for about a second or two, but then it just feels like work."

"I can't imagine it being fun or anything remotely normal actually. But, hey, have you ever considered the possibility that no one will be there waiting for you?"

Alex opened his mouth to make a quick reply but closed it again. Then, after an instant of hesitation: "Genuinely? No, not since I was a child. Wow, that would be … well, really interesting actually."

"Surely, with all the travelling you do now, you've perfected the art? Managing to get from place to place without being recognised."

"Yeah, but that still felt like hiding. Now that I'm back out in public and in the news, I just presume there is going to be some kind of reception waiting for me."

A curious look spread across his face and Cassandra wasn't sure if she should try to comfort him, but his face quickly turned to a smile when he saw the airhostess approaching.

"Mr Harris?"

"Yes."

"Sorry to bother you, sir, but since we're about to start our descent the captain would like to ask if you'd sign an autograph for his wife. She's apparently a huge fan." Alex's smile turned from a friendly smile into a victorious grin, which he pointed at Cassandra, who promptly rolled her eyes.

"I'd be delighted."

She handed him a small black book and pen.

"Her name is Lara."

Alex signed the book with one of his standard fan messages and handed it back to the hostess who smiled and winked.

"Thank you. And welcome home. It's good to see you again."

A flash memory of a flight to Canada popped into his mind but he managed not to blush.

"You too … Jenny?"

The hostess smiled in reply and quickly made her way back to the cockpit.

"What was that?"

Alex quickly turned his attention back to Cassandra with an undignified, "Huh?"

"Did she say that because you're out of hiding or because you two know each other?"

"No, I knew her once … She's worked for this airline a while, and we've spent time together. A long time ago."

"Dear God, what have I gotten myself into here with you?"

"Uhmmm?"

"I mean, I know intellectually that you're this big famous rock star – I know that because you've told me. But I guess I still think of you as Mork, the guy from The Sanctuary. And when that line gets broken by reality, I have to ask myself what I'm doing here. Do I really know you? What have I let myself in for? Maybe I shouldn't have come?"

"Cassandra …"

She put her hands up in protest.

"No, it's fine. It's just that sometimes I remember that for most of the time we've known each other you lied about who you really were and it makes me question my sanity for still allowing you in my life."

"I'm … I'm sorry about all that, still." The conversation had lost all sense of humour and Alex had to bite back the shame he felt as the smell of fear hit him full in the face. He tried to steady himself.

"But, like I said, you can go home whenever you want. If you want to get right back onto a plane when we land, that's okay, I'd understand. It sucks a bit for me because I'm excited to spend time with you, to share my real life with you. But I'm in the easier position, I know that. But I want to right what I did wrong and the only way I think I can do that right now is by showing you the real me and hopefully you'll see that the guy you got to know and I are very much the same person. Just with ... you know, slightly different back stories."

She knew he wasn't trying to make a joke out of it, but she had to laugh.

"Just ever so slightly, huh?"

Her smile filled him with hope and he took her hand.

"I regret every day that I had to lie to you. But the one thing that was absolutely true was how much I ... love having you in my life, and thank you for letting me try to make it up to you."

"Okay, okay, no need to get all teen drama on me. I get it, I'm sorry as well, it was just a moment. I think I know you are who I think you are ... which might not make sense to anyone but me, but that's okay."

Passport control was quick and easy and for the first time in her life Cassandra's bag was the first out the gate. Alex walked out first and, as expected, was met by a gang of reporters and fans all yelling questions. With the help of Josh and a few irritated airport security guards, Alex was led off to the side to hold a short impromptu press conference. Cassandra followed a couple minutes later and stopped, stunned, watching perfect strangers fight just to get closer to Alex.

Through the chaos she spotted Annabel and the two hurried to a car and Annabel drove off.

"Wait," said Cassandra as she caught her breath, "where are we going?"

"My place, so you can settle in. Josh will take Alex straight to Brandon. The boys need to have their time together. We'd only get in the way, and if it's just them they don't have to pretend to be anything other than themselves."

Cassandra understood that having strangers around forces people into a role, and from what she knew about the situation that wouldn't help anyone.

"So, is it always like that? When he gets off a plane somewhere?"

"No, people around here are usually pretty cool about it, but since his disappearance he's been in the news a lot more and it's caused some problems. It'll hopefully die down after this."

Meanwhile Alex was smiling for the cameras, patiently answering the same questions he had at Cassandra's family get-together, until Josh stepped in to questions relating to Brandon and the more obscure rumours that had sprung up around Alex's disappearance.

"I just want to thank you all for being here, but as lovely as it is to see you all, it's been a long flight, and all I really want to do is see my family. So I just want to ask that you allow me the space to do that in peace. I promise I'm not going anywhere soon, and if there is any Waterdog news, we'll let you know."

The two posed for a few more pictures, then Josh led Alex out to the parking lot.

"You've been driving my car?"

"Only today," Josh laughed, tossing him the keys. "I figured you've probably missed it."

Alex smiled as he ran his hand over the hood.

"You weren't wrong. So, where are we going?"

"Brandon's over at my place. Danny is there too."

"Getting the band back together ... nice."

Alex hadn't driven in a while so took a moment to check and re-acquaint himself with the car before speeding off, pulling a few choice words from Josh.

"Jesus, when last did you drive?"

"How long have I been away?"

"Oh dear lord."

Alex grinned wider than he meant to, showing his teeth, and let out a short laugh. An illegally short amount of time later they pulled into Josh's driveway and Alex stopped the car with a satisfied sigh.

"I missed driving."

Josh stared at him for a moment and raised his eyebrows.

"Yeah, yeah ... I thought I missed you, but I'm starting to have second thoughts."

Alex froze.

"I'm sorry, man. I know it wasn't the coolest thing I've ever done. Just disappearing like that."

"Your timing was ... well, particularly shit."

Alex thought back to the night on the docks, and the men in the warehouse.

"I know, man, I'm sorry. I ... I just needed to get away."

"And be a barman in the middle of nowhere?"

"That wasn't exactly the plan but, yeah, that's how it played out."

"How?"

"I bribed my way onto a ship, wasn't even sure what country I was in when I landed. Then just hid in plain sight behind a beard and a lie until Annabel found me. Well, until Danny found me."

"You could have told us, you know. We wouldn't have stopped you."

Josh's voice was matter of fact and it stung. He wasn't angry and it occurred to Alex that he was being told this in case it happened again.

"Thank you, man. I should've known but in that moment I didn't, I didn't know anything, and by the time I realised what I was doing I was already doing it and then just kept on doing it. There wasn't really a plan."

Josh's eyes grew distant for a moment.

"You know, I get it, man, that … does sound really nice."

"It is basically why we stopped the band after all. I mean, I wasn't planning to disappear, but it was nice to not be famous, to just be a barman. People judged me on who I was right in front of them, rather than who I was in their minds. I get why Danny goes on retreats and why Brandon wanted to live the lie. I mean, I love the band, I love you guys so much, but fuck, man. Out there in the snow, in the wilds of Norway, people liked me for me and not because I was Alex Harris."

Josh took a moment to think about what that must have been like.

"I get it," he sighed. "I really do."

A sly smile spread across Josh's face.

"But next time tell us, or take us along. Sounds awesome. Now, try to remember what you just said and come repeat it to Brandon. He's … yeah, well."

Alex nodded and they got out of the car. Danny and Brandon were sitting inside a massive pillow-and-mattress fort in the middle of Josh's living room. Beer cans and bottles littered the floor, sad music pumped from every speaker. Except for the alcohol, the scene reminded them both of a time when they were still teenagers and Brandon had fallen for a girl who was being really nice to him because she had a crush on Josh, and was hoping to step off Brandon to him. Josh, along with almost everyone else, quickly realised this and did his best to stay away from her. When Brandon eventually caught on, and had his heart broken, he hid in a pillow fort with his friends until he felt better.

"Request permission to enter!" announced Josh in a proud voice.

"What have you brought as tribute?" came Danny's reply.

"I present His Royal Douchebag, Alex Harris."

Alex played along.

"M'lords, I have travelled from far to visit this splendid fort and hope to beg the forgiveness of my band for disappearing. I pledge to never do so again and hope to find forgiveness in this most spectacular and sacred place. Also, I have brought vodka as tribute and penance."

Josh shot him a sceptical glace.

"You have?"

"Yeah, man, duty free. Also, come on ..." He pointed at the fort. "Did you think I wasn't expecting something like this? I've only been gone for a few months; I didn't die."

Brandon and Danny quickly crawled out the entrance, and threw their arms around Alex. Almost instantly, Brandon started to cry again and Danny, despite himself, joined in. Words spilled out of Brandon at almost the same rate as his tears.

"Oh my god, dude, it's so good to see you. It's so great that you're home."

Alex reached his arms as far around the two of them as he could manage.

"Hey, man, like I said, I wouldn't be anywhere else. Regardless of everything else, we've always got each other. Always be there for each other."

Josh quickly joined in the group hug and the four stood like that, hugging it out and feeling the gentle shaking of Brandon's sobs into Alex's shoulder. Between his own nearly overwhelming emotions at seeing his friends, and the scent of all the pain and fear emanating from Brandon, it took every ounce of his concentration to hold himself together. But he did it because he loved them, and was more interested in holding onto the hug than hiding himself. And that, in turn, gave him strength.

"All right, all right. I missed you guys too. But this Vodka isn't going to drink itself."

Danny immediately fetched beers and handed them around before they clambered into the fort. It took a couple of hours of catching up and a case and a half of beers before Brandon finally breathed a long deep sigh and looked up at his friends.

"So ... what do I do now? What am I supposed to do? I've spent forever standing up for her, believing her, but I can't ignore this. I just can't. She's ... I'm broken. And everyone saw it coming but me, and ... I don't know what to do now."

Josh put his hand on Brandon's shoulder and squeezed it. Brandon took another moment to breathe before turning to Alex.

"What did you do when your mom died? I mean, how did you handle it?"

A shiver ran down Alex's spine as he thought back to that time, and realised he'd never admitted it, never actually told them what happened.

"I, uhmm ... I tried to kill myself." The air seemed to get sucked from the fort and they all stared at him. "Well, obviously, I didn't try very hard. My doctor helped me through it, and then I wrote 'Scars in the sky.'"

Josh's eyes sparkled with realisation. "That's an idea, let's write a song? It's what we've always done before, it's how we've all worked through our shit."

Brandon looked around at his friends.

"I thought we were taking a break? And, I mean, I've never written lyrics before, not for any of our songs."

Josh looked at Alex who shrugged.

"Is that a no?"

Brandon smiled for the first time in what felt like a lifetime.

"Hell, no! Let's write a mother-fucking song! But not about me, and definitely not about Stacy, she doesn't deserve her own fuck-ing song. Let's do it properly, the way we always did it. Alex does the words, we write the music, we bring it together and, then rock the house down!"

The smile spread, and Josh put on his leader voice.

"Groovy, so we're not going home until it's done. Alex, you got any ideas?"

Cassandra immediately sprang to mind and his smile broadened.

"Maybe."

Chapter 18

Cassandra looked at Annabel.

"What do you think they're doing?"

"Drinking, probably."

The two women looked at each other and their smiles broadened.

"Red or white?"

"Beer?"

"I can see why he likes you."

Cassandra blushed and Annabel got up and grabbed two beers from the fridge.

"How are you, though, since everything in Norway? Going home after such a long time travelling is always weird."

They clinked bottles and Cassandra mulled the question over for a bit.

"Norway was amazing. Everything that happened, including ... It was just amazing. Really. But, yeah, getting home was strange. I felt like I'd changed so much and you get home and everyone just treats you the same and, you almost forget that you've been away and learned new things. Honestly, it was super frustrating. It's actually part of the reason I agreed to come here. I love my family and adore my friends but I feel like they don't know me anymore. Or at least not as well. You know what I mean?"

"Yes, well, mostly ... I never really travelled without family for a long period of time, because, well, Alex and then Bastian. But I did feel like that when I got back to work after Bastian was born."

As if he'd been waiting for a reason to introduce himself to the pretty girl sitting in the kitchen, Bastian walked in and straight to his mom to hide his smile while he looked up at Cassandra.

"Well, hey there, cutie. What's your name?"

Bastian rocked from side to side for a moment, summoning up the courage to speak, then gave up and hid himself in his mom's lap again.

"He likes pretty girls."

Bastian pulled his face in tighter to her legs, and Cassandra smiled down at him.

"So, you think I'm pretty? That's very nice of you. I think you're super cute."

Bastian blushed even deeper. Both women stifled their giggles and Annabel changed the subject.

"So, have you ever been to Syn before?"

"No. I've thought about it. I think everyone who isn't from here does. Just to see it, at least."

"Yeah, here and Japan. But in that case let's start with the best pizza place in the world, and they deliver. Also, it's my ritual when I get home after a trip to just have a chill day from travel and order pizza."

"That sounds amazing. Let's do it."

Annabel turned to look down at Bastian curled into her lap: "What do you say, little man, pizza for lunch?"

Bastian's smile turned from bashful to excited and then his face become very serious.

"Okay, but not the one with the chillies on it."

"No, not that one. We won't get you one with chillies again, promise. Do you want to call your grandpa and see if he wants to come over?"

"Yeah, grandpa!"

Annabel waited until he'd left the room before she sighed and looked back to Cassandra.

"You know, that boy used to love dogs, Alex as a wolf particularly, but since his kidnapping and Alex's daring rescue there have been nightmares, and … and I'm genuinely worried about how he'll react when he sees Mork again. And how a negative reaction like that could affect Alex. I'm grateful to have my brother back, but I can't help but worry."

Cassandra sighed thoughtfully and said. "I know how he feels, I've had a few of those dreams myself."

"How is my brother?"

"I don't know, or … I'm not sure. I know he wants to be fine, but there's something bugging him, weighing him down. I want to ask about it, but … I'm also not sure if I want to be the one he opens up to. I … I don't know if I want to be that person for him quite yet."

Annabel put a hand on her shoulder and smiled.

"I cannot tell you how relieved I am to hear that. So many people are just so desperate for his attention that they never stop to think about whether or not they actually want it. That, plus all the attention that comes with just being around him."

"I don't think the fame stuff bothers me, but he does shroud himself in mystery, and the lying is a big deal. And he's done a lot of that. I mean, I kind of understand where he's coming from. I don't know ... I want to trust him again, but I'm not sure if I do ... yet."

Annabel smiled again.

"I think you might just be the sanest girl he's ever brought home."

"How many has he brought home?"

"That's not a number anyone wants to know."

Cassandra made a part disgusted, part worried face but before she could say anything Bastian exploding back into the room.

"GRANDPA IS ON HIS WAAAAAAY!"

Then, spotting Cassandra, suddenly remembered that he was shy and almost spear tackled his mom as he dived into her lap to hide his face.

A few hours, a few beers and a few pizzas later the three adults sat quietly while Bastian, who'd gotten over his self-esteem issues, was explaining the plot of The Lion King to Cassandra in scene-by-scene detail. Annabel's phone buzzed.

"It's Alex," she smiled. "Hey, love, what's up?"

What came through from the other line was a loud, really bad, slurred chorus of something Annabel had never heard before, interwoven with laughter, followed by a few shouts, some cheers and the occasional expletive.

"Shut up, man, I'll tell her. Don't be gross."

"Alex? Everything okay?"

Annabel tried, albeit not very hard, to hide her laughter so as to not distract the obviously incredibly drunk men on the line.

"First, Josh says he loves you, cherishes you, and that you're ... Jesus, man, do I really have to say this?"

"Yes!" came a slurred voice in the background.

"And that you're the best thing that ever happened to him, ever."

Annabel smiled and felt her cheeks go a little pink.

"That's sweet. Tell him I feel the same way."

On the other side of the phone Alex shrugged and turned to look at his friend who had curled up into a ball on a table cuddling an empty bottle of something.

"She says she feels the same way."

Josh smiled, threw his arms out, hurled the empty bottle across the room and yelled.

"Hurray! Now ask her if she wants to marry me."

Fortunately, Alex, who was equally drunk, had sobered up just enough to take a second to think that comment over before speaking, giving Annabel enough time to process it.

"What did he just say?" She gasped with enough shock and alarm in her voice to turn the heads of the others in the room.

"He said ..." Alex felt another wave of drunkenness wash over him. "He wants to know if you'll marry him. But, personally, I question his timing slightly."

Annabel sat for a moment with no thoughts in her head, quietly hoping something would happen so that she wouldn't have to answer the question.

"How drunk are they?" she finally managed.

"On a scale of one to ten, I'd say about an eleven."

"And how drunk are you?"

"I'd say about a nine, but it's touch and go."

"How serious would you say he is?"

Alex turned around a couple times, trying to catch up with himself, then settled his gaze on Josh, who had gotten off the table and was now kneeling in front of Alex holding a small box holding a sparkling ring.

"I'd say he's fairly serious."

"I'm completely serious!" Announced Josh loudly and then he sprang forward and tried to grab the phone out of Alex's hand. "Give. That. To. Me!"

Alex did what he could to keep hold of the phone for just long enough to realise he had no good reason to try to put a stop to this, and handed it over. Josh smiled triumphantly, put it to his ear and in a suddenly soft, loving and drunk tone said: "I love you, Annie. I really, really do." His voice caught and tears welled up in his eyes. "I know this isn't the perfect way to do it, but I want to spend the rest of my life with you. Also, we ran out of alcohol ... Can you bring more?"

The sudden switch made everyone in the room with Josh groan loudly.

Alex playfully punched him in the shoulder and Brandon burst into loud tears.

"Oh my god, I just miss her so much!"

At which point Josh said quickly into the phone, "Oh-shit-gotta-go-love-you-please-bring-booze-thanks-bye."

And then he hung up, leaving Annabel to stare at her phone while her father and Cassandra stared at her. Kyle broke the silence first.

"Everything all right, honey?"

"I think ... No? ... No, so... Josh just asked me to marry him and bring them more alcohol in the same breath."

"What? Seriously?"

"I ... I'm not sure. They're all really, really drunk. But I think so. But then it sounded like Brandon started to cry again and Josh hung up. Well, not before repeating that they need more booze."

"Is that a good idea?" Cassandra asked from the sidelines.

"Probably not, but I'd like to know what's going on. Plus, I'd kind of like to see what carnage they've wrought."

217

A mischievous smile spread across Annabel's face, matched by an equally naughty glint in Cassandra's eyes. Kyle, on the other hand, rolled his eyes and said flatly, "Bastian, looks like it's just going to be me and you for a bit."

"What? But, I want to go with Mommy and—" He stopped himself before admitting to wanting to stay with Cassandra and, instead, blushed again. Kyle looked at the boy and shook his head.

"It's funny what's genetic. No, I'm afraid you've got to keep your dear grandpa company, otherwise I'll just be alone and sad, eating ice cream all by myself and with no one to share it with."

Bastian's expression changed, suddenly torn and confused, but before he could come to any kind of a conclusion about his sudden complex feelings, Cassandra knelt down in front of him.

"Don't worry, I'll be back later. I'm going to be staying for a while so you'll see me again at the absolute latest tomorrow."

She'd emphasised the words for dramatic effect, and it had worked. Bastian smiled broadly and nodded.

***

Josh, Danny, Brandon and Alex returned to their pillow fort, arm in arm and gently swaying to bad singing and the occasional mournful sniff from Brandon. Although getting rip-roaring drunk had made them all feel a little more cheerful, finishing their song and running out of alcohol had put something of a downward spin on the day and they all got quite emotional as they descended into the realm of 'I-love-you-drunk'. So, by the time Cassandra and Annabel pulled up, Brandon had passed out, curled up fast asleep, Danny was bravely attempting to clear up, and Josh and Alex set about hunting through the house for a second time for one last drink. A sheepish Danny met them at the door, with bloodshot eyes and an unusually cheerful smile.

"Careful," he whispered, "here be dragons."

Then he turned tail and went back to his chores, picking up furniture that had been knocked over, clearing empty bottles and dragging couches back into position. The two women looked at each other thoughtfully; had them rushing over been such a good idea, after all? Their line of thinking was interrupted by Alex and Josh, both roaring joyously at seeing them. Josh rushed forward, wrapped his arms around Annabel, lay his head on her shoulder and started crooning:

"I looove you, baby, and if it's quite or' right I need you, baaaaby ..."

Alex, ever the charmer, staggered up behind him.

"Hey, you come here often?"

Annabel tried to look serious, but couldn't hide her smile and pink cheeks; Josh's drunken attempts at romance were clearly working.

"How drunk are you?" There was a smile playing on her lips.

"Probably around seven, seven and a half."

His serenade interrupted, Josh cut his song short.

"Seven? How d'you figure that, man?"

"That ..." Alex smiled, "is because I'm secretly a magical mythical monster who burns through alcohol faster than a normal man."

Josh's face turned placid.

"Oh, right," he groaned and rested his head back on Annabel's shoulder.

"You bring up more booze? ... us. Bring us. More booze."

Cassandra raised a hand, holding aloft a shopping bag. The unmistakable clink of bottles.

"Beer?" Josh looked at her and grinned broadly. "I don't think we've met, but I feel like we're going to get along."

Annabel shoved him playfully with her shoulder.

"Bastard, one minute you want to marry me, next you're making bedroom eyes at anyone with a beer in their hand. Is this what I have to look forward to?"

Josh was stunned for a moment and then, prompted by the alcohol, scooped Annabel up in his arms, staggering slightly until Alex steadied him with a hand on his back.

"No, you have this to look forward to!" laughed Alex.

Josh immediately broke into song again and Danny, seemingly out of nowhere, launched himself into a remarkable dance on equally unsteady legs. Alex, not to be out done, offered his hands to Cassandra.

"May I have this dance?"

Laughing in a way that could just as easily been at them rather than with them, Cassandra took his hands and they began an exaggerated slow dance to fit the insanity of the moment.

"How?" she asked. "How are you guys still on your feet?"

"We're professional musicians, we can dance and drink and sing for hours."

"Hear, hear!" Danny and Josh called out behind them.

Feeling only marginally clearer than the other two, Alex herded the dancers out of the entrance and into the lounge where Josh carefully placed Annabel on the couch, and slumped down next to her. His intentions were a drunken kiss but she left him hanging and turned to Alex.

"Where's Brandon?"

"Asleep," Alex nodded at the fort in the corner of the room. "Throwing up can take it out of you."

"Always the lightweight of the group," announced Josh.

Cassandra looked around at the many empty bottles Danny had missed and wondered how a lightweight rock star measured up against a normal person.

"And how is he?"

Alex looked at Josh, who blinked himself back to sanity for a moment and pulled a face.

"Devastated. It's bad enough that we all saw it coming, but I think he did too but managed to convince himself he was wrong."

Danny plonked himself down on the coffee table.

"There was a personal trainer about a year ago, fucking clichéd bitch. Some ex-athlete or something. Hot and ripped."

Annabel nodded knowingly, remembering the stories. "Keith or something like that, I remember. They seemed to be together all the time and Brandon kept saying, 'Nah, they're just friends." Even though no one asked."

Danny nodded.

"Well, he was out of the picture again a few months after and, in my opinion, I think what happened was that Stacy discovered she was pregnant and then told him to fuck off because Brandon has more money, and we all know that that's her true love anyway. Not him, not the sportsman, her precious fucking lifestyle. Goddammit, I could kill her."

"Don't worry about that," Annabel reassured him, "I've got you all covered. All the money you guys have made is locked away. She isn't entitled to a penny of it. As soon as Brandon decides she's out, she's out."

All three men smiled.

"We love you," they chorused.

"So has anyone told the actual father?" Cassandra frowned, all too aware of Alex's arm over her shoulder.

Danny shrugged and looked at Josh.

"No idea … The way it played out was that when the kid was born, Danny, Brandon and I were at the hospital waiting. The doctor came out of the room and asked to speak to Brandon alone; he refused, said he wanted to meet the child. The doctor looked at us, and we explained that we were a band, together forever, and then ... then he said something like, 'In the interest of not causing a scene, I feel it my duty to inform you that the child appears to be of African heritage.' We asked him what he meant; that was when he came straight out and said it: the child is black. Brandon barged past him into the room and a few seconds later burst out of there, yelling that he was done and that we were leaving and fuck the fucking fucker. I called Annabel on our way here, and she called Alex, and you know the rest."

Alex, who'd heard the story a few times over the course of the day, shook his head, his rising anger making him a little more sober.

"How could she do that to him?" Tears welled up in Annabel's eyes. "I mean, we all knew she was a selfish cow but how could she do that to him? He's so sweet, so kind, and put up with so much shit from her."

She bit her lip and shook her head quietly, furious. Josh, recognising the look, put his arm around her, kissing her gently as he did. As if on cue, Brandon, a little bedraggled with his hair everywhere and a slight green tint to his face stuck his head out of the fort and slurred.

"Would it be all right if we spoke about something else?"

He staggered to his feet and dropped down again next to Danny.

"I'm ... not sure we've met?" He extended his hand to Cassandra. "I'm Brandon."

She reached out her hand and shook his.

"Cassandra. Pleasure to meet you. All of you, actually. It's been such a weird few days I've only just realised that I'm actually having a beer with one of the most famous bands in the world."

Josh and Alex smiled smugly while Danny took a long sip of beer and grunted, "Fourteenth globally, according to last year's stats, but number one in record sales in Norway, Sweden, Poland, here and Zimbabwe ... among a few other places. He then stood up slowly and in an official-sounding voice that, in his opinion, was an imitation of his father continued, "Now, if you'll excuse me, I'm going to go throw up."

Slowly, Danny staggered out, in one hand a beer, the other steadying himself against the wall as he made his way down the passage. Cassandra watched him go then turned to the others.

"Should someone not go with him?"

Alex shook his head.

"No, if he needs help there will be a crash of some kind and the sound of something expensive smashing. You wouldn't say so now, but he's actually very responsible about these things; probably just thinks he could be sick so is going to be by himself for a bit. He'll either come back in a few minutes or go off to bed."

Cassandra looked back towards the doorway, not entirely convinced.

Silence descended on the room as everyone considered the conversation Brandon didn't want to have. It had been a long, weird day for all of them. Alex yawned and stretched, fast reaching the point of a serious hangover; it was time to leave. Josh had already started to nod off. And Brandon didn't seem to be far off either. Recognising the signs, Annabel put her half-finished beer down and stood up.

"All right, I think it's time to call it a day—" She then walked over and gently kissed Brandon's cheek. "We love you honey," she reassured him. "And we're here for you always. But right now, I think it's best for all of you to get some sleep."

Brandon nodded, gave her a hug and waved goodnight before staggering down the passage. As he reached the bathroom door, he turned and called to Alex.

"You'll be here tomorrow, won't you? I mean, on the Island."

"Wouldn't be anywhere else," Alex smiled up at his friend.

Brandon smiled in reply and took himself to bed.

Annabel turned to the rest of them.

"Come on, let's get outta here while I can still drive."

Alex thought for a moment.

"There are rooms here, you know."

"Yes, but Bastian is with dad and I don't want to just disappear without warning him I won't be home. He still gets really anxious at night when people don't come home."

Alex's face flushed, feeling the sting of her words.

"What should I do then?"

Annabel looked at him slightly confused.

"What do you mean?"

"Well, I haven't been around and the last time I saw him was … well, you know, and I don't want to make things worse. I don't know what he's seen, what he remembers."

Annabel knelt down in front of her brother, took his hands and looked into the eyes.

"Alex, it's time to come home."

They sat like that for a few seconds while Cassandra stared at a moment so intimate, she felt privileged to witness it.

"Right," Alex let out a deep breath and smiled. "And I guess I'm carrying Sleeping Beauty over there?"

He squeezed his sister's hands for a second and winked at her before standing up and reaching down to scoop up Josh.

"Whose place is this anyway?" Cassandra asked as she helped Alex wrangle Josh into the back seat of the car. Alex gestured at the body on the back seat.

"His."

"Uhmmm, isn't it a bit odd then that we're carrying him out of his own house and leaving the others here?"

"Probably. In any normal situation, sure," said Alex as the rest all climbed in. "With that said though it's always been a sort of open-door policy with us. Well, until Brandon got married. Danny likes his privacy, but we all have keys to his place and occasionally get messages asking one of us to go around and eat his food because he's decided to take a sudden trip, or water his plants or whatever. But Josh and I have a very chilled my-house-your-house thing."

Cassandra wanted to ask more questions, to broach the subject of Josh one day busting Alex as a werewolf, but now was perhaps not the time.

When they got to the house Kyle was already tucking Bastian in, so Alex carried Josh into the house and to Annabel's bed. As the two met in the hallway they stared at each other for a moment before Alex broke the silence.

"Hi, Dad."

The words seemed to ring like a bell between them and tears welled up in their eyes. Alex opened his mouth as he tried to find words. He wanted to apologise, but struggled when he saw Kyle's jaw tighten.

"Long time. You've … you've been gone for a long time, son. And I know you've been gone for longer before, but never without so much as a word, a sign that you were all right." He swallowed and cleared his throat. "I've always known that at some point you might go off searching for answers, but I never imagined you'd leave us out of it."

Alex broke eye contact and hung his head, swiping at the tears that had started to roll down his cheeks.

"But even with that, I'm glad that you know you can always come home." Alex looked up as his dad wrapped his arms around him. "It's good to have you home. Good to see you again."

"You too, Dad," Alex choked. "You too."

Kyle stood with Alex at arm's length, and cracked a familiar smile.

"So how drunk are you?"

"About a seven."

"Oh good, not gone then ... Let's have a drink."

Chapter 19

Bastian's excitement at finding his uncle sitting slightly hungover at the kitchen table when he woke up was enough to wake everyone else in the house.

"UNCLE ALEX!"

"BASTIAN!"

The volume of both his and Bastian's voices booming through the kitchen and the rest of the house made Alex wince and remember his hangover in more detail. Before he had time to recover, Bastian had thrown himself at his uncle and wrapped his arms around him so tightly, Alex thought his heart might burst. Somehow in the boy's arms he finally felt safe, finally felt forgiven and that he could discard a weight he hadn't realised he was carrying. The idea that he might have destroyed his nephew's innocence faded and, despite his best efforts, he welled up. When Bastian saw he pulled a face.

"Are those the same tears Mom has when something good happens? Happy tears?"

"Yes, they're the same tears."

"Okay, that's good then."

Alex smiled and gave Bastian another quick squeeze, then turned back to his coffee while Bastian busied himself in the kitchen, going through his normal morning routine as if nothing had happened, as if Alex had never left.

Alex smiled. He could hear the movements of the others in the house, slowly getting up, and he knew that would change things. But for that moment he was enjoying a normal morning in the kitchen with his nephew.

Kyle was the first to make it downstairs, followed shortly by Annabel, both staring daggers at Alex as they walked in. Not only was he, in their opinion, not nearly as hungover as he should be and would get over it quicker, but he hadn't made enough coffee.

"What? I didn't expect anyone else to be up for hours. It's not my fault you didn't just roll over and go back to sleep."

Annabel searched her mind for a snide reply but was interrupted by Bastian.

"Is Uncle Alex staying for a long time, Mom?"

His words cleared the air and everyone smiled.

"Why not ask him instead, sweetie."

Bastian turned grinning towards Alex.

"I have no other plans, kiddo, no trips coming up so, yeah, I should be here for a while."

The boy's little face lit up and he turned back to his mom.

"Does that mean Mork is coming home too?"

For a moment Alex wanted to ask where Mork was coming home from, but stopped himself. He knew better than to participate in the stories parents tell their children. It did, however, start him thinking about Josh, and what Annabel might have told him about Mork, now that they were so close. Helped along by the hangover, Alex started to feel his pulse quicken and he had to close his eyes and start taking long slow breaths. Bastian noticed the look on his uncle's face and instantly burst into tears, convinced that something had happened to Mork and that the boys at school who'd told him that a dog 'going to go live on a farm' meant that it had died was in fact true. The scent of his fear reached Alex and it pushed him towards the edge. He drew in a long breath and he quickly got up to leave.

"I'm going to go be sick, but I'll send Mork down to say hello."

Alex burst into the room just as Cassandra was getting dressed. Startled, she yelped and stumbled backwards.

"Hey."

But as soon as the door closed Alex began his transformation. He clenched his muscles and closed his eyes, managing to hold onto himself just long enough to say.

"Don't … don't scream."

Within a matter of moments, he had transformed into a large, slightly frustrated, wolf.

"That, that's really strange to watch. What happened?"

Mork tilted his head to one side and raised his eyebrows. Cassandra nodded, more to herself than him.

"Right, of course … I'm talking to a wolf. What did I expect?"

Mork was staring at her, and she shifted uneasily.

"What?"

He thought for a bit, trying to think of a way he could remind her that Josh knew nothing about Mork. Then, realising that he simply had to rely on her being smart and capable, he shook his head and trotted up to the door to wait. When they stepped into the kitchen, Bastian's eyes lit up.

"Mommy, mommy, mommy, look!"

Despite himself, Mork's tail started to wag, and Bastian's face grew brighter.

"He remembers me!" he crowed as he wrapped his arms around the wolf's neck.

A wave of complex emotions washed over Mork. There was no hesitation in Bastian's eyes, no holding back, no scent of fear from him. There was a moment of introspection as he realised that Bastian was more excited to see Mork than Alex.

But Bastian broke the spell and yelled, "Come on, boy!" and took off down the corridor with Mork trotting merrily behind.

Cassandra looked up at the others: "How could he possibly have that much energy this early in the morning?"

Kyle handed her a cup of coffee.

"Something about the transformation, it's like he just resets. At this point his hangover and any potential liver damage is gone." He took another sip of coffee and sighed. "It really is quite unfair."

Mork came tearing back through the kitchen with Bastian in hot pursuit. Annabel yelled after them to slow down, be careful and not to break anything. Josh was the last to arrive into the chaos of a Harris family hangover and was almost as excited as Bastian to see Mork.

"Hey, big guy, when did you get here? Shit, it's good to see you." He grinned up at Annabel. "I'll be honest, a part of me really believed that 'gone to live on the farm' was just the line you feed kids and you were trying to spare my feelings. When did he get here?"

Without missing a beat and with zero indication of anything other than honesty, Annabel said, "Alex fetched him this morning."

Josh snorted.

"That man's ability to shrug off a hangover never ceases to amaze me. Where's he at?"

"I believe he's asleep at the toilet. The hangover hit with a vengeance. I expect he'll be gone for quite some time."

Josh let out a dry and tired chuckle, and a cold shiver ran down Cassandra's back. The family could lie, without blinking, without stopping to even think about it. It just came so easily to them and it made her question why she'd agreed to come on the trip in the first place. Josh downed his coffee, along with some painkillers, and stretched his neck.

"Well, when he resurfaces can you tell him I'm with Brandon? I'm gonna go take a look at the carnage and see if I can talk Danny into making breakfast."

Annabel smiled and kissed him and said wryly, "Try not get too drunk today."

Once he'd gone Cassandra said, "He seems awfully spry for someone that drunk last night. What's the secret?"

"Multivitamins and activated charcoal before bed," Annabel yawned. "Isn't a perfect cure and not great long term but does the trick in an emergency."

They moved from the kitchen to the lounge and Annabel caught Bastian, effectively ending the whirlwind of boy and dog and calming the whole house down instantly. Mork then breathed a sigh, and felt confident enough to go back to his room and re-emerge after a few minutes as Alex.

"Cassandra, I'm going to head over to Brandon ... Wanna come?"

He'd noticed something had changed in her, an uneasiness that wasn't there before. He could see it in the way she sat and smelled and he wondered if it had been watching him change or whether there was something else that he'd missed. It wasn't until they were in the car that he got the full force of it. He didn't know exactly what was wrong but she was afraid. It seemed to be coming off her in waves, as if she was calming herself down and then working herself back up and it wasn't very long before he was forced to pull over. She looked at him puzzled.

"What's wrong?"

"Funny, that's exactly what I was going to ask you. I can smell fear and anxiety ... and right now I'm practically drowning in it."

She shivered and he could immediately see her retreating into herself and wondered whether he'd done the right thing by bringing her to the island.

"Cassandra?"

Her jaw tightened and her lip trembled.

"Alex … you, you come from a family of liars."

The words seemed to shock her as much as him, but she believed in them and pressed on.

"I spent the morning watching your sister lie to her boyfriend without a moment's hesitation. I … I know it's to protect your secret and everything, but it's really …" She stopped for a second to order her thoughts. She desperately didn't want to say the 'correct' thing. Or accidentally say what she didn't mean. It was important and it meant as much to her that she was telling her truth, as much as the truth. "Alex I like you, and your family. I know it's been like … Jesus, only a day, but I feel so at home here and my guard is super down around you. And that scares the shit out of me, and the more I see how easily you and your family can lie like that, I just … I just don't know what to feel. Knowing the justification behind the lies." Again she stopped and he wondered if she was about to scream or cry. "I don't like liars, and knowing the truth makes me feel like I'm one too. When I see it happening and do nothing, I'm just as guilty. I know it's a big secret and a serious thing but, I'm not that person. I don't want to be that person and I don't know what to do about it." She put her head in her hands and groaned in frustration. "I don't know, I just … I don't know and that scares me."

Alex stared at her, taking long slow breaths to reassure himself that she would never tell anyone his secret and that that was not what she was saying. Then in a momentary bid to be charming, and hopefully ease the tension, he said, "I like you too."

She looked up at him and mirrored his sad smile. He had hoped more words would come to mind but none did and he again thought that maybe she should go. That maybe following a rock star to the other side of the world just for fun had been a little too wild for her, and too soon for them. Her shoulders dropped when she realised what he was thinking; then her focus turned from him to the driver's side window, at what looked like a black dot on the glass. Just as she realised that it was something coming at them, it smashed through glass and the car filled with smoke and darkness.

Chapter 20

The first thing Alex became aware of was how dry his mouth was and, still half in the dark of sleep, started plotting the shortest distance to a glass of water. Then, slowly, he began to realise he wasn't in his own bed. His memory of sitting in the car, of shattering glass and of smoke came rushing back and he bolted upright. A sharp panic pierced his heart as he realised he was on a single bed in the middle of what appeared to be a small cell, complete with bars. Pushing against the panic, trying to not lose control, he cleared his throat and tried to call out, but failed. Feeling the panic start to push against his vision and the fear of what might happen next, he closed his eyes and forced himself to take long, slow breaths. Transforming now would not help, and he needed to know where Cassandra was.

When he opened his eyes again, he found a well-dressed man sitting patiently just beyond the bars of the cell.

"That's an impressive amount of control for someone so young. I couldn't do that at your age."

Alex sniffed the air and growled, which seemed to make the man smile.

"Allow me to introduce myself," said the man with a bow. "My name is Edward."

Alex took another long slow breath and tried to measure him up.

"Boy, there is no need for that. I promise, you can't take me in a fight."

"What do you want?"

Edward's smile faltered as he thought.

"That is a complicated question. But, for now, all I want is to talk to you."

"And what? My agent wouldn't forward your calls? Or did you go straight to kidnapping?"

"Cute, but I want to know how you found Vincent."

"Who?"

Edward rolled his eyes and let out an exasperated breath.

"It's been a long time since I've had the pleasure of meeting one of us. I'd almost forgotten what we smelt like."

Alex could feel a prickle run down his back and although he actually knew what Edward meant, he wasn't in the mood to be friendly.

"That's just suuuuuuper creepy."

Edward shook his head and relaxed into his chair.

"I clocked onto you the first time I heard you sing. I don't know if you know this, but there is power in our voices. When we howl it's like a beacon, a flare to let others know who we are. For everything you'd done to hide your secret from humans, you literally stood on a stage in front of the whole world and announced who you were, told everyone you were a werewolf."

Alex's jaw tightened when he failed to find a reply.

"The one thing I couldn't figure is when you were bitten. You were, what, sixteen? Seventeen? At that first concert?"

Alex stared at Edward and considered his situation, considered the fact that he was in a cage facing the third werewolf he'd ever met face to face and whether or not it was true that he couldn't take him in a fight. Edward could tell that he was thinking and held his arms out to his side, palms up, suggesting openness and inviting him to look at his surroundings.

"I was seventeen at our first big concert, and ten years old when I was bitten."

Edward swore and shook his head in surprise.

"I am impressed, boy ... Couldn't have been easy in this day and age to keep it a secret like you have." He thought for a moment then nodded his head as if agreeing with an internal conversation he was having with himself. "You have earned my respect. I'll have some food sent and we'll continue this conversation later."

Alex's calm slipped and he rushed the cage door, rattling the bars.

"Hey! The fuck do you want from me? Let me outta here!"

Edward's calm smile sent a bolt of fear through Alex's body.

"I told you, for now, I want to talk. But we've got time. So relax, get a hold of yourself and eat something. I'll be back."

Unsure of what else to do, Alex staggered back and sat back down on the bed. He watched Edward slowly rise and leave, and a few minutes later return with a plate of food, which he slid through a gap under the door.

"Eat up, I'll come back later."

Edward had turned to leave when a sudden panic struck Alex and again he rushed the door yelling, "Hey! Hey, you! Where's Cassandra? What have you done with her?"

Edward stopped and for just an instant his back seemed to stiffen.

"That girl we found you with? We left her where she was ..." Edwards's eyes glazed over and he said in a near whisper, "I have no use for humans anymore."

He left Alex alone with the food. Alex sniffed at the plate a few times, trying to pick up whether there was anything wrong with it, but sensed nothing. Even so, he couldn't bring himself to try it. So he left it where it stood and went back to the bed. His mind started out blank, staring at the ceiling, desperate to avoid thinking about his situation. Then slowly it drifted to the voice he'd heard in Russia: Vincent, apparently. How he'd found him, the path he'd taken, the mental and physical exertion it had taken to get to him and to that voice. As his mind started to circle around, it occurred to him that it had been Cassandra. Cassandra had been the catalyst. From the moment she had arrived at The Sanctuary he'd started having dreams about the castle, and it was she who pointed out that it was a real place. She had been the turning point, but there was no way he was going to admit that to Edward. She had freed something in his mind, opened him up to something he didn't even know was closed; he still wasn't even sure what it was, but Cassandra had changed something in him.

It took waking up for him to realise that he'd fallen asleep and as he sat up, he felt his muscles tighten. Edward sat at the door of the cage, waiting for him. Alex blinked hard.

"That's also kind of creepy, you know that, right?"

"You didn't eat. Why?"

Alex swung his feet off the bed, face turned away, ignoring him.

"You ever hear the story of Hades and Persephone?"

Edward smirked and shook his head.

"Suit yourself. It doesn't matter. Tell me, though, do you know who bit you?"

Alex took a deep breath and channelled his 'rock star at a press conference' persona, then turned to look at Edward in a way that clearly said fuck off.

"Enlighten me."

Edward shook his head again and laughed, "I can't tell whether you know you're being a ridiculous child, or if you actually take yourself seriously. Either way, my patience isn't infinite and so far I've only been kind."

It occurred to Alex suddenly that he was still a famous rock star, and he'd been kidnapped, that witnesses had been left behind, so people would obviously be looking for him … All he had to do was wait it out.

"Are you asking me if I know who it was, or if I want to know who it was?

Edward seemed to relax and sat back in his chair.

"If you know who it was. But, then again, how could you? So, instead, why not tell me how you were bitten."

Alex thought about it for a second, somewhat relieved that Edward appeared to know nothing about him and Nuria.

"While I was playing in the woods, I found a wolf that had been tied down and hurt and I thought it was dead. I wanted to set it free and it bit me. Full moon happened about a week later and …" Alex mimicked Edward's gesture to the room from the day before. "Here we are."

Edward leaned forward and Alex could see his mind working, his eyes making quick jerking motions.

Then, almost to himself, Edward said, "Nuria, now that's interesting." He returned his gaze to Alex. "We're related," he smiled.

"What?"

"Well, you see, Vincent bit me, I bit Nuria and she bit you."

The room fell into a strange silence as Alex stared at Edward, unsure of whether he was being serious or if he was making some kind sick of joke.

"That reminds me," Edward continued, "how many people know your little secret? Actually, that doesn't matter. Have you ever been in a situation where someone asks you to share it with them?"

Alex's mind shot back to Kristin and The Sanctuary, and it showed clearly on his face.

"Ah, yes, see? There! You know that that feeling – the revulsion at the thought of it – is part of the curse. That need to protect it, to keep it to yourself. I bet you left wherever you were soon after that. The moment people start to want it, it drives you away from them."

A chill descended on Alex as he played the various conversations over in his mind; Edward was making sense and he didn't like that idea at all.

"Didn't stop you, apparently."

Edward's eyes suddenly flashed green and, without realising it, Alex's eyes did the same. Edward stared for a moment and Alex recognised the long slow breaths and the scent emanating from him, forcing his own heart rate up. Edward shot to his feet and stormed out of the room without another word. As soon as the door closed, Alex let out a long breath; it felt as though a weight had been lifted off his shoulders and he could breathe again.

It was a few more hours before Edward returned.

"You all right there, grandpa?"

"Don't call me that."

"You're the one who said we were related."

Edward sighed.

"There is so much you don't know, it's practically criminal."

"Speaking of which, you kidnapping motherfucker ..." For an instant Alex almost asked, "How did you know Nuria bit me?" but stopped himself. "What makes you think it was this ... Nuria? Who bit me?"

"That's easy – The Order of St Hubertus."

"Which means what to me?"

"Those men who attacked you in Norway, and the men who almost captured Nuria in Canada, they all worked for me."

Alex's blood seemed to flash boil and he could feel the glow building in his eyes.

"What?" he roared.

Edward was on his feet and snarling before either of them had time to register.

"I've been searching for Vincent since before your grandparents were born, boy! Don't presume to judge me! You have no idea what I've been through!"

Edward's words seemed to ripple through the room, sending Alex staggering back. He then let out a bloodcurdling scream that tipped them both over the edge. Alex had never actually seen someone else transform and he understood why others always looked so horrified. The crack of bones, the stretched skin, the spontaneous spouting of hair. It was haunting. The transformation was, however, over quickly and before either could do anything about it, Mork stood squaring up to a very large jet-black wolf, who let out a furious snort and quickly turned to leave. But even as he left, Mork could feel his words pushing down on his mind. Mork paced the cage as his temper rose until it boiled over and he threw his head back and howled with all his might, howling and howling until he was left breathless. Exhausted, he staggered a few steps to the bed and collapsed.

When Alex awoke a few hours later more food had been set out to him. This time he ate, the echoes of his howls still ringing in his ears. As he ate, he thought about how Edward said their voices had power and about Vincent, that voice in Russia, how Edward's words pushed on him. He wondered whether the reason his music had become so popular was because he'd subconsciously used it on the world and it made him feel sick. Later, when Edward returned to take up position in his chair, Alex, who had started to lose any sense of heroic bravado simply lay on the bed staring at the ceiling.

"Why did you bring me here? What do you want from me?"

"I want, as I repeatedly said, to talk to you and to know how you found Vincent. That is all."

"What good will that do? We both know he's probably moved on from where he was; we both know that I have nothing to say to you because I'm a fucking prisoner. What do you get out of this, Edward?"

Alex tilted his head to gauge the man's reaction, to see if anything was getting through. He found Edward staring off into the distance and when he started speaking, Alex again felt the physical pressure of his words.

"You have no idea what I've been through. What it's like to bite someone, to infect them, curse them to be like us."

His eyes came into sharp focus again and he turned to look at Alex, into him.

"You know that feeling of rejection that comes when someone wants to take the curse for whatever reason, that fear, that revulsion? Well, when you bite someone, it grows like a cancer in your mind and it takes over ... And it never goes away. As a human, I had, or I'd thought I had, saved Vincent's life. He was being hunted and I threw myself in the way of an attack, giving him the chance to counter and take down the hunters, but I was dying. I think the reason he did it was because I didn't ask for it. I didn't even know what I had got myself involved in. It all just seemed wrong to me, four men against one wolf. I liked wolves, you see, they were my favourite animal, powerful and scary but at the same time brave and noble, devoted to their families. I admired their spirit and, and then a living wolf spirit gave me his gift for saving his life. I was honoured to run with him, learn from him. But he never stopped trying to protect me from the dark secrets, the pain and the guilt that came from the bite. But I worked it out, I could see it and I confronted him to tell me the truth, and so he did. He said he could barely stand the sight of me knowing that it was he who had cursed me, and that he was infinitely sorry always. I was crushed ... And dedicated myself to finding a way to break that cycle, the horror of it, and came up with the idea that if I in turn bit someone perhaps that guilt would pass from him to me, and I would carry it for him ... And that's when I found Nuria." For a second Edward's eye shone, not green, but with the unmistakable glint of tears. "I ... was wrong. I was so wrong ... All I had done was infect someone else and Vincent now felt the guilt for my actions on top of everything else and it quickly became too much, the tension too great. I now carried the guilt of having bitten her and he for having bitten me, so he cast me out. It was then that I learned the next dark secret of our curse." He looked almost sorrowful. "We will always end up alone. Wolves who are desperate to be with others, with the pack, but cursed to be alone ... forever."

Alex had sat up to get a better look at Edward as he spoke. Everything he was saying was true, he could feel it, it rang familiar bells in his own heart, but there was one cold fear that lingered, one word that caught Alex's breath.

"Not forever. I ... I was ... we're not... no, not forever."

Edward cracked a sad smile, his gaze drifting away. "If there is a way for us to die, I would've found it. And believe me, boy, I've looked. I even threw myself into an active volcano once. It was the most spectacular pain I have ever experienced, bones and flesh melting as your lungs burst and your brain boils. And, like waking up having forgotten you were asleep, come full moon I was whole again, but still on fire. It took me ... It took me years to crawl out. It was—" A visible shiver ran over Edward's entire body and Alex could see dark rings form under his eyes. "It was mind shattering. I couldn't face people for a long time after that. Wandering as a stranger in a world I couldn't understand. Eventually I was able to form full thoughts again, and I came up with the idea of The Order of St Hubertus, patron saint of hunters. I knew I would never find Vincent on my own, so I amassed wealth, easy when you're a few hundred years old, and I founded the Order. I needed them to find him for me, or at least find others like us. They were remarkably unsuccessful – at least until they found Nuria in Canada. But, as you know, she got away and then a few years later you popped up out of nowhere."

Alex felt his temper flare, but managed to maintain control.

"If you were looking for ones like us, why did they try to kill Nuria and me? Actually, wait, you said you knew about me from my singing, and ... if you know we can't die, why are they hunters anyway?"

Edward shrugged.

"I needed to attract a certain kind of person, make it a crusade and let the fanatics work themselves to death for a higher power. I knew they couldn't actually kill anyone, that they didn't really stand a chance in a fight. I believe you proved that in Norway. But they could hopefully subdue you and bring back the bodies. You murdered my agents and Nuria somehow broke free, although now I imagine that might have been your doing as well."

Alex stared at Edward in disbelief.

"You haven't bitten anyone," Edward stared back in silence, his eyes flashing green. "You have no idea what true desperation feels like ... I need to find Vincent."

"Why? What are you hoping is going to happen? You think he's going to approve of everything, or tell you it's okay, that everything you've done is justified? Are you really just a scared little boy looking for Daddy's fucking approval?"

Edward shot to his feet, knocking the chair back as he did.

"You have no idea what you're talking about!"

"What are you hoping for, Edward? I'm not, not telling you how I found him, I can't! I don't know! I just found him. There isn't a big secret that's being kept from you. You're just a fucking crazy kid looking for his Daddy and I can't! Help! You! Not won't, not don't want to ... I can't."

"I have to find him!"

"Why?"

"So he can tell me how to die!"

The words echoed around the room like a gunshot, and Alex staggered back, his anger dissipating.

"What?"

Edward's eyes shone green and his jaw hung open, his breath rasping in a way that no human throat could. Alex held back his words and found himself having to start controlling his own breathing. Edward was apparently quicker at this than he was. Then after a few tense seconds Edward turned to pick up his chair and sat back down.

"Vincent isn't just the oldest werewolf I know. He's the oldest werewolf I've ever heard of. But someone bit him, someone who is gone. That wolf went somewhere and I want to, I need to know what happened, how it happened."

Alex threw his arms up in frustration.

"You want to learn how to kill werewolves? Why? So your dumb Order can start doing it right?"

"No!"

"Why do you want to learn how to kill us then, Edward?"

"Not you! Me! I want to learn how to kill me."

Again the words echoed around the room, sucking the air out of the conversation, and all they could do was just sit there, desperately trying to catch and control their breath. Trying to stay human. It took some time, but eventually Edward spoke, his voice now a sad, distant whisper.

"I can't live with this anymore. You ... you have to tell me how you found him, please ... I'm begging you."

Tears well up in Alex's eyes and ran down his face.

"I don't know. I can't help you, man ... That's the truth. Please just let me go."

Edward closed his eyes for a second and then took a long deep breath.

"It's around midnight ... You have until the morning to change your mind. I'm done talking – now I just want answers."

With that he got up and left, leaving Alex alone to think over his words. He knew he was never going to mention Cassandra, he knew it before he had even realised just how insane Edward was, and he knew it even more now.

The flood of ideas and fears that spilled through Alex's mind took him by surprise and it was a long time before he was calm enough to start trying to think of a plan. He looked around at the cage, trying to find any weak spot, or a gap large enough to fit through, any obvious way out, anything at all that he could use. But it was clear the only way in or out was the door, and just by looking at the lock and hinges he found himself feeling even more hopeless. Even if he did think he could break the lock, the effort and noise it would take would raise the alarm.

A few more hours passed as he sat trying to find a solution, an idea, an answer Edward might believe. He could, after all, just tell him he had been led by a dream. That was true enough, and he didn't have to admit the rest. The idea started his mind back down the path of why, what good would it do? If he told Edward it had been a dream, would he then be forced into some kind of dream slavery? With Edward trying to force another vision out of him? Every idea Alex had always led back to the thought of how Edward might respond and use that information against him. Edward terrified him, not because of his strength, or the way he could feel his influence push against him, Edward was genuinely insane. Alex had met some crazed people in his time, but nothing like this, and it frightened him. So much so that when he thought too much about it, a soft panic set in. He knew that for every rational, 'insane' conclusion he could think of, there would always be a chance that something entirely unexpected would happen instead, something he couldn't begin to imagine, because Alex was sane.

In the morning Edward arrived with another plate of food and waited while Alex ate, a scenario that became no less creepy the more often it happened.

"So, Alex, how did you find him?"

Alex swallowed the last mouthful and thought over his options one more time, took a deep breath and stood ready.

"I don't know what you want me to tell you. I don't know what good me giving you an answer would do anyway, even if I had one to give. I ... I apparently don't know a lot of things."

Edward sighed and stood.

"It doesn't matter, I have other ways of getting what I want. Are you sure this is the route you want it to take? I have no desire to hurt you – it doesn't need to be this way."

Alex's eyes flashed green with frustration and the thought of what might be coming.

"Motherfucker, you're not listening to me. I don't have an answer for you. I just found him, I wasn't looking for him. It was luck."

Edward clenched his jaw and pulled a key out of his pocket.

"So be it."

He slipped the key into the lock, turned it and swung the door open. For a moment, the two both just stared at each other. Then Alex rushed forward and, turning his shoulder forward, threw the full weight of his body at Edward. But in the last possible instant Edward pivoted, grabbed Alex by the belt and slammed him head first into the wall at bone-breaking speed. He then hooked Alex's arm back and pulled until there was an audible pop as the bone wrenched from the socket. Finally, Edward put his foot on Alex's knee and pushed until it broke. In the distance Alex heard the wail of his own voice as his vision faded to white. Effortlessly, Edward bent down and hoisted Alex onto his shoulder, stepped out of the cage and headed straight for the door.

"It didn't have to be this way, you know. Or maybe it did and you don't know how you found him, that you did just stumble upon him by luck." Edward stopped for a moment and sighed. "It doesn't matter. With news going around about your kidnapping and the way your voice carries, it won't be long. Or at least I hope it won't, for both our sakes."

Alex was only vaguely aware of what was being said. Through the thick fog of pain, he noticed a mountain of wood in the centre of a room he didn't recognise. He tried to open his mouth to protest, to struggle, to get away, but it was no use. With ease, Edward tossed him into the middle of the pile, took a deep breath and fished a flare from his pocket.

"Good news, and the bad news ... You're going to survive this."

Edward lit the flare and tossed it onto the pile. Within a second the entire thing, and Alex, erupted into flame. Despite the air having been sucked from his lungs, his head swung back and his mouth dropped open into a silent scream and he transformed. The flames tore into the wolf, but the intensity of the moment gave an instant of hope, of relief before the fire overwhelmed him and everything turned red and then black.

Chapter 21

Alex woke up violently, erupting into a scream. Wave after wave of memory and pain slammed into him. For an instant, he was still in the fire, still wrapped in flame, but as his screams grew louder and he found the transformation kick in again, he became aware that he was no longer on the pyre, but back in the cage. As Mork, he stumbled his way to the corner of the room and vomited, then blacked out.

Days passed in darkness and the next time he woke up he was once again on the giant pile of wood and tinder. Before he could utter a word, Edward, who looked like he had been waiting for him, lit the flare and it was all Alex could do to start screaming before the heat slammed into him. Through the pain and the blur and the growing sense of distance between his body and his mind, he was able to hang on to enough sanity to know that it happened at least eight times again after that.

It felt like a long time had passed before he opened his eyes. The world felt small and he struggled to remember how to be alive. When he searched his mind, he hit against walls of fire that actively pushed all consciousness away, and instinct began taking over. When he smelt food, he ate, when he needed the bathroom he crawled to the makeshift toilet in the corner; his body hurt, his mind ached from exhaustion, so he slept.

The next day the same, and the day after that.

On the fourth day when his eyes opened and he found himself still in the cage, he found that a degree of consciousness had returned, that a small corner of his mind had found some relief, some escape. He rubbed his face and gingerly pulled himself up into a sitting position.

Glancing at the empty chair, he wanted to hate Edward, and in many ways did, but he also felt a swell of pity for him. He understood that sense of loneliness. The notion of immortality was like a weight pushing him down, and he had to wonder what he'd be like after a few hundred years, after watching the people he loved die. How would he be if the only people like him had cast him out? Had he always been a monster or did he become one? As Alex, he contemplated what he might do to find a familiar face after being alone for a few hundred years, even if that face hated him. The desperation of the idea threatened to overwhelm him but he was determined not to transform; instead he put his head in his hands and cried.

Then footsteps and the clanging of the door being opened.

Without looking up, Alex whispered, "I found him in a dream, a recurring dream about werewolves and a castle. It came to me so often that I started to draw the castle and a friend at The Sanctuary in Norway recognised it as an actual place. I wanted to know more about that side of myself and I followed my dream ... and that's how I found him."

He turned to look at Edward who stood dead still, just staring at him. In his mind, Alex formed the words, 'I also know where Nuria is,' but just couldn't bring himself to say them. So, the two men just stared at each other. Edward looked away first and said: "For what it's worth, I am sorry," And turned to leave.

A thought rose to the top of Alex's mind.

"How long have I been here?"

Without stopping, Edward said quietly: "Three months yesterday."

Alex's heart sank, his shoulders dropped; he thought he heard, or felt words spill out of himself, but he wasn't sure. Then his body crumpled under the pressure of his mind. His eyes only half closed, he found the thought: "So much for the search party."

What little colour there was left in the world seemed to fade, taking all hope with it, and Alex slipped back into unconsciousness.

When he awoke it occurred to him that no matter where he blacked out, he always woke up in bed. He realised too that, on the very morning he had disappeared, he had promised his nephew that he would never leave again. As he sat up and spotted Edward waiting in his chair, a sharp pang of hatred flared in his mind, making his eyes glow and a low growl slip from his throat. All of which Edward ignored.

"How are you feeling?"

Alex ran his hands over his face and through his hair, realising for the first time that it had grown.

"You know we're not friends, right? You kidnapped me, tortured me, held me here for months, apparently just to get useless information, which I've now given you. And, I mean, I guess on some level I get it, and I can't help but feel sorry for you. Really, genuinely, but at the same time given half a chance I'd kick you back into that volcano. How are you feeling?"

Alex gave Edward the finger and lay back down, childishly turning his back on him.

"I think if I were in your shoes I'd probably feel the same way. But it's nice to see you're feeling better. I thought you might like to know ... I've disbanded the Order. After spending time with you, I realised I didn't need them anymore. So in the future you won't have to worry about them."

Alex rolled back and turned to Edward.

"You mean if you were ever planning to let me out."

"Evidently, and understandably, you don't like your role in all of this," Edward laughed. "But we're on a path together, one that has an end. An end that obviously isn't death. You won't be in this cage forever."

Alex sat up quickly.

"Then let me go now. What more could you possibly get from me?"

Edward stood up.

"Not yet, but soon ... Hopefully. Anyway, I'm glad you're feeling better."

Fury erupted in Alex and he rushed the cage door, throwing himself at it, screaming to be let out. He pulled and punched at the bars, kicked at the lock, while Edward stood silently staring at him. Alex felt his sanity fray, and his rage quickly got the better of him. Even after the transformation, he continued to howl with all his might until Edward was compelled to leave the room. And still he continued to howl, until he couldn't anymore and once again collapsed under the pressure of his situation.

When he opened his eyes again, he had been carefully dressed and, as usual, food had been prepared and was waiting on the floor at the door of the cage. Day by day, he felt as though the room he was in had become smaller and smaller. Thoughts made way for instinct and every memory he tried to hang onto only worked to drag him further down. He'd been told once that hope died last, and now that it seemed to be truly dead, he wondered what would happen next. He missed his family, his friends; he missed Cassandra, blue skies and freedom. A desperate need to get out of the cage hit him like a wave, but at the same time filled him with despair, a sense of hopelessness that he couldn't escape. The confines of his cage sucked the energy out of him and left him feeling hollow. Almost defensively, he pulled the blanket over his head and sobbed like a child trying to hide from his nightmare under his blanket. He didn't know or care if Edward was there; he just didn't know what else to do. Eventually his tears dried up and he pulled himself together, at least enough to eat. He sat on the edge of the bed, staring at nothing, thinking of nothing. Which is where he was when a new sound reached his ears, a different smell in his nose. For the first time since he arrived, he thought he could hear voices. There were footsteps, and he could smell other people, actual people, humans. It took him a moment to realise the difference, that there was one in particular – one he hadn't smelt for a very long time.

The door clicked and swung open, and in walked Frank Oslo, gun in hand, a serious look on his face. He shot Alex a look that clearly told him to wait while he and two other officers scanned the room. Feeling relatively secure, Frank slipped his gun into his holster and walked up to the cage door.

"You're a difficult man to find, Mr Harris." Alex's smile threatened to take over his face, but it didn't stop the tears. "Now just sit tight. We'll have this open in a second. You know what was going on here?"

Alex took a few long breaths in an attempt to steady himself and not lose control.

"No, I ... I don't even know where here is. I've pretty much just been in the cage, and ... when I wasn't ..."

His mind flashed with the memory of fire and pain and he winced. Frank recognised the look; he'd seen it on a lot of trauma survivors and his voice grew gentler.

"It's all right, son, we're here now and we're getting you out of here."

He waved a hand and a younger office started working on the lock. Once it clicked Alex was on his feet, but Frank put up a hand to stop him.

"Easy there ... We need a medical officer to check you out first. We also need to talk to you about a few things."

Alex closed his eyes, clicked his neck and let out a low growl.

"I've been locked in this cage for God knows how long. Can we at least do it in a different room?"

Frank looked nervously at the younger officer then back at Alex.

"What?" asked Alex.

"You really have no idea what's gone on in the other rooms?"

Alex felt his heart rate start to rise and tried to slow his breathing.

"No?"

Frank, who prided himself on being a no-nonsense man, cleared his throat and weighed up his words for a second.

"There are roughly thirty bodies littered across the other rooms. All of them looking as though they've been subject to some kind of animal attack … And not recently. You didn't see or hear anything?"

Alex staggered a few steps back, then fell back to sit on the ground, the words, 'I've disbanded the Order' ringing through his mind. Now feeling slightly nauseated, he looked up at Frank.

"How did you find me?"

Frank clenched his jaw and pursed his lips.

"Anonymous phone call."

Alex closed his eyes and took another long, deep breath, the smell of death tickling the back of his nose. He clamped his hands over his face to fight off the urge to scream.

"Please just get me out of here."

Two more police officers and a medic appeared at the door and with Frank's help they wrapped a blanket around Alex to shield him from the horror and lead him out of the building. Alex was then loaded into an ambulance and rushed to Syn General. Where his family waited anxiously. It took a few seconds for him to realise that Cassandra obviously wouldn't be there. He'd been gone for months. Why would she have stayed?

As he climbed into the ambulance, grimacing at how bright the outside world was, Annabel threw herself at him and wept into his shoulder. Once inside the hospital, he was placed into a wheelchair and whisked off to an examination room.

"Hello, young man. It's good to see you," said Dr Rajan Cooper.

Alex all but jumped out of the chair to hug him.

"Doc, oh my God, I can't tell you how good it is to see you."

Dr Cooper gestured for Alex to sit back.

"How are you, son?"

Alex closed his eyes.

"Confused, tired, scared. Tired."

"What actually happened? How did you end up like … this?"

Alex looked up at the man who'd stood by every mistake he'd ever made and never once walked away, and told him everything. From Russia to Canada to Edward and exactly how he had learned that he couldn't die. All he left out was that he was almost certain that Edward let him out in the hope that he would lead him to Vincent, or at least to his own way of finding him. He had left out those details not because he wanted to try protect Dr Cooper, but because he hadn't yet decided if he was actually going to do it or not. He knew where Nuria was; he could just go there. But first he wanted to at least speak to Cassandra, make sure she was all right. Despite proclaiming that he was probably immortal, Dr Cooper still did a quick once-over to make sure he was without any physical injuries.

"I've never seen you like this before," he warned Alex. "I really want you to just be at home for a bit, to be surrounded by those who love you and care for you. Like you originally planned to when the band decided to take a break, remember?"

Alex thought back and struggled to find a latching-on point for how long ago that had been, that they'd all sat down and decided to pump the breaks on making music. He thought about the magazine article about him dating Marina and how important that seemed at the time and how little he cared about it now. He ran his hands over his face and breathed in, trying to think of something wise and witty as a reply but even that seemed too much effort, so he pointed a finger at the doctor, smiled and said.

"Yes."

Then he covered his face again and groaned.

"Can someone please just take me home now, or to a home with a bed that has a door I can open and close at will?"

He found the dark behind his hands comforting and for just a moment thought about letting himself slip away into sleep, but at the last second remembered his situation and quickly tried to pull himself together. Dr Cooper stood looking at him.

"You all right?"

"Not really, no."

The doctor placed a reassuring hand on his shoulder.

"Sit tight," he said, "I'm going to grab your father."

Alex nodded but was only vaguely aware of what was happening when Dr Cooper stepped out to find Kyle. The family was sitting nervously in a waiting room when he appeared.

"How's he doing?" Kyle stood up.

Dr Cooper raised his eyebrows thoughtfully.

"Physically? Fine, exhausted, but no actual harm there, but you know him. Emotionally? Mentally? That's a very different matter. From what he's told me he's been through a lot, and it's been bad." He cleared his throat, but couldn't hide the catch in his voice. "Really bad."

He stepped closer and took Kyle's elbow, lowered his voice and steered him to a corner, Annabel following anxiously behind. "This is not the place to talk about it. But I think you need to take him home. Keep an eye on him, maybe even put him in a room with someone else so that when he wakes up he isn't alone. He's so out of it at this point that I think a lot of the last few hours is going to be a blur to him, and he'll need a reminder that he's not where he was."

Kyle's jaw tightened and tears welled up in Annabel's eyes.

"There's a spare bed we sometimes pull out for Bastian in my room," Annabel volunteered. "We'll put him there."

Together they walked back to the ward to find Alex asleep in the chair, and decided that it was probably safer to wake him gently than shock him by trying to move him while asleep. It took a little coaxing, but he eventually opened his eyes. Dr Cooper made sure the paperwork was in order as they wheeled Alex out the back of the hospital to the car and took him home.

Annabel brought in the spare bed for herself and Dr Cooper called his wife and told her he'd be staying with them for the night.

"I know," Mrs Cooper replied. "I expected as much."

There was a lightness to her voice that reminded him why he loved her so much. The great family-wide sigh of relief at finding Alex seemed to pull the wind out of all of them, and before long they were all asleep.

Chapter 22

Alex lay in the dark, telling himself over and over again that he was home and safe. Reassuring himself. He couldn't help fearing that he'd wake up in the cage in the morning. He fell asleep to those thoughts, and teetering on the edge of a dream he was too afraid to peer into in case it swept him back to the cage, or the field or into the twisted mind of Edward. But as the darkness spread around his words and thoughts, he found himself falling into the dream anyway. He landed on all four paws, racing through something to somewhere, neither of which mattered, as long as he could keep running. The feeling of freedom, of movement, of his muscles singing with the effort of propelling his body forward at ever-increasing speed. Eventually the darkness morphed into a desert, which in turned melded into forest and soon Mork found himself on a far too familiar path towards Manor Muromtsevo. As he approached the clearing he slowed to a trot and stepped out into the gardens approaching the front door, and there waiting for him was the same large black wolf as always, but now Mork spotted a second wolf with human eyes standing over the larger one's shoulder. It tilted its head to the side and in Edward's voice said.

"Hello, boy."

The words rang in Mork's mind like a bell and in a flash of light and chaos the manor began to crumble, a cacophony of splintering wood, smashing glass and fear. The forest behind him burst into flame, and as he spun around, Mork could make out other wolves amid the flames, circling and gnashing their teeth. In an instant, they rushed at him and pounced.

Alex leaped out of bed screaming, his heart racing as, wide-eyed, he searched the room, desperately trying to find something familiar, to catch his breath, and to not transform.

"It's okay, it's okay Alex, you're home."

Annabel's words washed over him and for an instant he thought they were a dream. Then he turned to look at her standing at a safe distance on the other side of the room. With a few gasping breaths, he managed to regain control of himself and slumped back down, deflated and defeated. Seeing him shrink, she chanced a few steps closer.

"It's all right, it's all right ..." she said, taking the last few steps until she could wrap herself around him. "We found you – you're home." Alex leaned into his sister's embrace, taking in the warmth of her body, the first kind touch he could clearly feel or remember in what felt like a lifetime, and the memory of their mother holding him tight to calm him as a child came rushing back.

"When Mom died and you guys had to go to Canada, after I transformed back after full moon I had healed, whole, no marks, no scars, nothing to show for what happened. Just the memory of pain, the shadow of what happened, of our last moments together, and it tore me up inside. It felt even more unfair on Mom that not only did I survive, but I had nothing to remember her by."

"I know, I remember."

"I tried to kill myself."

Annabel's grip slackened and she leaned back to look at him, hoping for a sign that it was just a sick joke or anything to show it wasn't true. But he looked back at her with cold, grey eyes.

"I had been suspended from school; I was in so much pain and I hated being a werewolf so much that I wanted to end it. For it all to just stop."

"But, but you didn't – you stopped yourself or Dr Cooper stopped you?"

Alex slowly shook his head.

"No, I did it ... I took a silver knife and slit my wrists. Bled all the way to the bathroom where I climbed into a hot bath and lay there saying my goodbyes."

The blood drained from Annabel's face.

"But nothing happened; it didn't work. I woke up when the doc found me. He freaked out, made me promise never to do anything like that again. I agreed, but it felt like my only option to escape had been taken away from me. I tried not to think about it because at that point the idea of being immortal sounded like the worst torture I could imagine." He looked down, his shoulders slumped forward. "Has it really been three months?"

There were short gasping breaths as he pushed all thoughts from his mind, all images, all memories, desperate for the courage to say the words. Annabel nodded her head and said quietly: "Yes."

"I was being burned alive ... over... and over, and over. I ... I don't know how many times I was thrown into the fire, only to wake up sometime later and be thrown right back in. I tried to fight the first time, and had my bones broken, my neck broken. I was powerless ... I... I couldn't fight, I couldn't die I couldn't escape. I can never escape ... at the mercy of being alive. I'm immortal." His voice cracked as he looked up into Annabel's eyes.

"And I don't know how I'm supposed to deal with that. I'm ... I am never, ever not going to be this. I'm going to watch everyone I know die, everyone ... and there is nothing I can do to stop it. I don't know how to live knowing that, and yet there is nothing I can do but live."

For an instant his mind flashed with the vision of a pack of were-wolves and then Edward's pained expression burst into view so clearly that he shoved away his sister and leapt backwards, away from her, and into the wall. Then he slumped onto the floor and wept.

Kyle and Dr Cooper appeared as if from nowhere and wrapped themselves around him while a rattled Annabel tried to compose herself. Time passed as they sat, Alex trying to summon the energy to form thoughts, to calm himself; then it dawned on him. He hadn't felt the threat of a transformation and he wondered whether Mork was as distressed and afraid as he was.

"What would you like to know?" he turned to the others, his tone flat and defeated.

"Nothing right now, what can we do for you?" Kyle placed a hand on his knee.

Alex's mind felt full of mist, and thinking was difficult, save for one small dot of light in the distance.

"I need a phone. Also, what's the time in the United States?"

Kyle smiled.

"She's phoned three times since the news broke."

Kyle pulled his phone from his pocket and handed it to Alex. Once they were out of the room, he tapped at it until he saw her name, hesitating only for a second before hitting dial. He knew he wanted to speak to her, hear her voice, but had no idea why or what he wanted to say. The phone rang once before it was answered.

"Mr Harris, hi. How's he doing?"

Alex smiled to himself at the sound of her voice.

"Hi, it's … uhmm, it's me."

He heard her catch her breath in her throat.

"Oh my God, Alex!" "I … we … We've all been so worried, so scared."

Alex could hear the tears in her voice and had to take a breath before he could speak himself.

"It's okay. I'm okay. I am home and safe and alive."

"I just remember thinking that one minute we were talking and the next I was being woken up by police, paramedics all around me. And you ... you were... just gone. I ... I thought that maybe you had woken first or something, and every time I asked whether you were okay no one seemed to know what I was talking about. I had to tell them that there was someone else with me. I thought I was going mad, I think they thought I'd gone mad, until Annabel showed up." She let out a long breath, determined to stay strong. "I'm so glad you're all right."

Alex nodded, forgetting for a moment that she couldn't see him.

"And how are you?"

The line was quiet for a few seconds.

"Still a bit scared, but okay, I think. I ... I decided to come home fairly quickly, and I'm sorry for that, but I felt so out of place there, and so alone, and I really needed to get to a place where I felt safe again."

"I understand – and that's all right. How's it going at home?"

"Okay. It was even weirder getting back the second time but I managed. I moved to Seattle and got a job at the university here, started last week."

Alex smiled to himself.

"So does that mean I can't convince you to come back to the Island?"

He'd tried to sound as though he was joking, but he knew he wanted her to say that he could. He wanted to see her, even though a part of him was afraid for her.

"Alex, I can't do that. I ... I can't live that life with you." Her voice was harsher than she meant it to be, while his was a whisper.

"I don't have to be a rock star."

Another long moment passed as he sat listening to her breath, hating himself for even trying.

"It's not that; it's the lying. The constant lying. I know why you do it but I just can't be that person. And I mean, honestly, it's been lie after lie every step of the way with me and you. First you lied to me in Norway, then the Island where I was part of a lie. I ... I fucking hate it."

It occurred to him that he'd never been broken up with before and he felt what little strength he had left begin to slip away.

"Oh my god, Alex, I didn't mean to have this conversation with you right here, right now. I'm sorry, I'm so, so happy you're safe. I really genuinely am; I just I don't want us carrying around a 'what if'. I'm sorry. It's not that I don't want to see you, I just—"

Goosebumps erupted on the base of Alex's neck and spread numbly over his whole body, his vision blurring for just a second, and he cut her off.

"It's all right. I understand. My life is insane at the best of times and recently it's been worse. But, look, I never wanted to ruin your life ..."

"You didn't ..."

"It's okay, Cassandra, I'm not kidding. I'm not just being nice, I really do understand. What I wanted to say though was, I hope you don't think we have to cut all ties. I'm here, or somewhere, most of the time. Call, text, whatever. The door is open. I never really knew what we were anyway, so maybe, hopefully, we can be friends. I will ... always ... be ... somewhere."

It occurred to him that his always and hers were two very different things and the idea pulled at him, dragging him down. He felt weak and tired, as though even the simplest thing would sap more strength and energy than he could imagine ever having had. The line fell silent save the occasional sniff from Cassandra and then finally a faint whisper.

"Fredrik would be so disappointed in us."

The name brought another smile to Alex's face.

"Him? Disappointed? No, he'll tell us that we're just going through normal stages of ridiculous couple bullshit and that we'll end up together at some point, and that everything's going to be just fine."

Cassandra let out a soft laugh, recognising Fredrik's voice in Alex's words.

"We ... we won't though."

Alex knew it was coming but still it made him wince.

"I know."

They sat silently on the phone together for a while, neither wanting to end the call, in case it was the last time they ever spoke, but knowing there was nothing more to say. Finally, Cassandra found the strength to say, "Well, it's 2 am here and I have work in the morning."

"Oh ... shit, sorry. Okay, I'm serious about being here if you need or want anything."

"I know, and thank you, and ... and, yeah. Me too, sort of."

"Well, good night, Cassandra."

"Good night, Alex. I'm so glad you're safe."

He smiled again and waited until he heard the beep that told him that the call had ended. Then he sat in the darkness, feeling more alone than he'd ever felt in his life. Confused and scared, he decided to just climb back into bed, close his eyes and quietly fall back into the fearful comfort of his favourite nightmares.

Chapter 23

When Alex next opened his eyes, Josh sat in view reading. Which seemed an odd choice, considering.

"What ... day is it?"

Josh looked up quickly.

"Holy shit."

He quickly moved closer to the bed and put a hand on Alex's shoulder.

"It's so good to have you back, man, and to see you. Fuck, dude ... I can't even..."

Alex pulled a hand free from the blankets and placed it on Josh's.

"What day is it?"

Josh thought for a second.

"Monday, I think. July, 20th."

Alex blinked a few times to clear his head.

"What phase is the moon in?"

Josh frowned.

"That's funny, I heard your dad and sister talking about that too. Apparently new moon tonight?" Alex smiled, remembering something he couldn't quite put his finger on. "How are you feeling, man?"

A fog had settled back over Alex, like a heavy damp and cold blanket.

"Tired ... hungry. How long have I been asleep?"

"Couple of days, in and out. You wake up, say a couple things, fall back to sleep. Doc's been in to check on you every few hours. Said you just needed time to reacclimatise, settle into your surroundings. Personally, I've never seen you go this long without food – or coffee, for that matter."

Alex's eyes drifted out of focus for a few seconds. He'd forgotten about coffee. Then he remembered the last morning at the house with Bastian and Cassandra, sipping on coffee, severely hungover. He closed his eyes and pushed the memory away, afraid of where it might lead. He then took a deep breath and his nostrils filled with the fear emanating from Josh. It took a force of will and effort but Alex pushed himself upright on the bed.

"I don't even remember what coffee tastes like."

Josh's face had turned pale, but he squared his shoulders.

"I think it's about time we remind you then."

"I'd like that."

A thin, slightly sad smile spread across Josh's face. It was clear that he was deeply worried, but just seeing him sparked a light in Alex.

"Yeah, man, yeah. You think you can make it to the kitchen? Need a hand up?"

Alex ran his mind over his body, really feeling how he felt for the first time in what could have been years.

"No, I think I've got this."

He flexed his hands, rolled his shoulders and pushed himself up to his feet, grunting like an old man as he did. Josh, on the other hand, jumped up excited, like a kid at Christmas, making Alex a little suspicious, but he also really wanted coffee so went with it. When they got to the kitchen they found the rest of the family and Dr Cooper, who all seemed so excited that he was finally out of bed. Again Alex thought about saying something, or asking what was going on, but they all seemed so happy and he wasn't going to be the one that popped that bubble, so decided to smile and stay quiet. As the thoughts washed over him, the world seemed to turn slightly greyer and a cold and familiar loneliness crept in.

Even with the overwhelming smells of the people around the table, and their heightened emotions, the coffee smelt particularly good. It felt safe and familiar. When he finally took a sip, it was hot and comforting. It tasted like mornings and, despite himself, a few tears rolled down his cheeks, killing the conversation around him, and the room filled with the unmistakable scent of fear.

"I ... I haven't had coffee in a really long time," he offered into dead silence.

The coffee and the familiar scene took him back to that last morning and, as hard as he tried, he couldn't shake it. His first impulse was to just go back to bed and hide in the dark. Go back to sleep. But he could feel all eyes on him, sensed their expectations, their relief that he was awake and back and Alex. Deep in the back of his mind he felt Mork, not pushing, but there, mirroring his fatigue. Then he did the only thing that seemed to make sense, given his situation. He stood, walked over to the cabinet and took out a bottle of vodka.

"Little early for that, son?"

Alex looked at his dad.

"I have absolutely no idea what time it is, but I'm fairly certain it's 5 pm somewhere."

Intentionally ignoring the worried looks making their way around the table, he put the bottle to his lips and started drinking.

Annabel made the second attempt.

"Is ... that really a good idea right now?"

Alex stopped but didn't look at any of them., "Who cares?"

"We do, Alex."

Annabel's voice was soft and worried and he couldn't help but wonder what she was really afraid of. Alcohol couldn't hurt him … nothing could really hurt him. A darker voice in his head whispered, "They're worried about themselves," and it sent a shiver down his spine.

"Why? What difference does it make?"

They stared at him in silence but he could feel their eyes like hands pulling him down and his voice came out hard. "Oh, come on, just a minute ago you were all so happy I was awake, so let's celebrate! Let's have a party! Let's get drunk, get high, get laid, fuck it. Live like rock stars for a bit. Let's have some fun! What the fuck do I have to be afraid of now anyway?"

The others cast worried glances at each other and Josh raised his eyebrows feeling annoyance rise up.

"Commitment?"

Alex barked out a laugh and took another swig of vodka.

"Give that man a medal. Also, neat vodka on a very empty stomach really does the trick. You should try it."

He held up the bottle, offering it around, but no one moved. Everyone just stared at him, and the pressure, the fear and the memories finally broke what little resolve he had left. The bottle flashed across the room and shattered against the far wall.

"Fine. Be like that," he growled and turned to go back to bed.

"Hey, come back here." His father's voice followed him. "Can we at least talk a bit, please?"

Without looking back he all but whispered, "No."

***

Kyle stared at the closed door at the end of the passage. For a moment he stirred in his chair, but Dr Cooper's hands fell gently on his shoulder.

"Thoughts, Doc?"

"That boy. No path is ever simple or easy with him." Dr Cooper's eyes turned to the others in the room. "It's going to be hard; it almost always is with him. But I truly believe we need to be patient. And forgiving. He's been through something terrible, something we cannot even begin to imagine. It would be foolish to presume he's just going to bounce back. Physically he might look fine, but we need to be wary of that. Alex only ever wears his scars on the inside. But that doesn't mean they're not there."

A hush fell over the room. He was right, of course, and if they really loved Alex they needed to be there for him, now more than ever. Josh nodded to himself, picked up his coffee and headed back to the room.

"My shift isn't over. I'll sit with him until Bastian gets home from school."

Annabel trotted up behind him, and pulled him into a kiss.

"Thank you."

Josh smirked and they rested their foreheads together. Meanwhile, Kyle picked up the bottle of vodka and put it back in the cupboard, trying not to think about how many times he'd had encounters like this with his mother after her accident.

Chapter 24

Although sleep came easily, Alex could feel the outside world pressing in on him. He felt restless, twisting and turning. At first, he could still make out the hum of voices in the kitchen down the passage, but couldn't be sure of whether it was a real conversation or fragments from yet another tortured nightmare.

When he next opened his eyes, Edward was seated on his chair in front of him. For a few seconds Alex just lay there.

"This is a dream."

"Well, yes," Edward smiled, "but thank you for not calling it a nightmare."

"Fuck off," Alex murmured and rolled over, turning his back on him, only to find Edward sitting on the other side of the bed.

"Language, young man, that's no way to speak to your grandfather."

Turning onto his back and closing his eyes, Alex breathed a sigh.

"Wake up, wake up, wake up …" he whispered to himself through gritted teeth.

"That doesn't work, you know."

Rubbing his face with his hands Alex pulled his legs in under himself and shot out of bed, at Edward, grabbing him by the collar and slamming him against a wall.

"What. Do. You. Want?"

Edward looked down at the hands holding him and smiled.

"You do know I'm not actually here, right? This is all in your head. I mean, probably. How much do you really know about your dreams?"

Frustrated, Alex let him go and started pacing the room.

"I've changed my mind. This is a nightmare. Now, what do you want?"

"I'm just here to tell you something you already know."

Alex stopped and raised his arms, exasperated: "Well?"

"It's time for you to move on. Time to go. You can't stay here any-more."

A cold shiver ran over Alex's body as he stood listening.

"What can you offer these people? It's like Cassandra said, you've turned them into liars. And how does that story end? You outlive them all and end up alone anyway. Are they really better with you here? Does it look like they suffered without you? Annabel is happier with Josh than she's ever been. To Bastian you appear and disappear, another father figure he doesn't know and can't rely on."

"Shut up ... Just, just shut up."

"Be honest with yourself, you want to stay here for you. Because you need them. How very noble. Selfishly lean on people who love you just to make yourself feel better."

Furious, Alex turned and swung a wild fist at Edward who leaned out of the way and then burst forward as the G'mork and Alex's eyes opened suddenly. Annabel and Josh were asleep in the bed opposite him with Bastian curled up between them. The image re-minded him of how he used to like crawling into bed with his parents when he was little. He sat dead still for a moment, checking whether he'd disturbed them, then slowly and quietly, he slipped out of bed and out of the room.

His dad was sitting up in the kitchen.

"Morning."

Alex looked around for a clock.

"Is it?"

"It's around 4 am."

"Why're you up?"

"In case you woke up. We've been taking shifts."

Alex's cheeks flushed and he looked down.

"Sit down, son, we have some leftover pizza. I want you to eat," said Kyle, getting up and heading over to the fridge "You haven't eaten in a few days."

Alex pulled up a chair and did as he was told, partly because of the serious tone of his father's voice, and partly because he didn't need to be reminded that he was starving. Kyle grabbed a few pizza boxes, a fresh mug of coffee and put them down in front of Alex, who instantly started stuffing his face. After a few big gulps and one near miss at choking, he looked up.

"Why's there so much pizza?"

"We always ordered a couple extra for you," Kyle smiled, "in case you woke."

"How ... When last was I wake?"

"About three days ago."

Alex bowed his head as he felt a pang of guilt.

"We're family, we look after each other. You used to know that."

"It's … been a weird, mostly, fairly shit … year?"

Kyle reached a hand across the table and squeezed Alex's wrist.

"But you're here now. Frank's on the case, and there are even more police watching the house than usual. You don't have to be afraid."

A small smile touched the corner of Alex's lips.

"What do I have to be afraid of anyway?"

Kyle frowned. "Why do you keep saying things like that?"

Alex looked up but his eyes lost focus, and his voice trailed.

"I'm … immortal."

"You're what? What do you mean? Since when? How—?"

Tears welled up in Alex's eyes and he looked down again, unable to force himself to look at his father.

"It … I've … had it proven to me."

A shiver ran over Kyle's body as an old terrible joke about, 'how do you prove you're immortal' came to mind. He tightened his grip on Alex's arm.

"Well, you're home now."

An urge to start smashing things washed over Alex, as the voice from his dream whispered that it was time to leave, that he was ruining his family's lives. He closed his eyes and started taking very deliberate breaths.

"Are you all right?"

"Not really … no."

Alex's voice came as a growl and his breathing started to speed up. He shot to his feet, lifting the table as he went. Letting out a yell of rage and tensing every muscle in his body, he snapped the table, sending splintered fragments flying across the room.

"I can't take this! I can't do this anymore! I don't want to be this … this Thing any… more!" Alex dropped to his knees, shaking with anger, his eyes burning bright green. Eventually, his voice dropped to a whisper. "And I'm going to be this way forever; I'm going to be alone … forever."

He looked up at his father standing motionless on the other side of the room. They locked eyes for a moment until Alex let out a final whimper of surrender and transformed.

Dr Cooper and Josh appeared in the doorway, fear filling the room after them. With the raised voices, and the noises coming from the kitchen, Josh was convinced that he'd be needed to break up a fight, or at least try to calm Alex in the middle of a breakdown. Looking around the room, his mind went to one place.

"Alex! Where's Alex?"

Dr Cooper and Kyle exchanged glances. Mork sighed and groaned, then he gestured towards Josh. Instinctively, Kyle shook his head. Josh watched still dazed from the rude awaking.

"Wait, Mork? What's going on?"

Mork nodded and then gestured to Josh. Kyle looked at Dr Cooper.

"It's probably long overdue," said Dr Cooper with a shrug.

Frustrated, and feeling spoken over, Josh blurted out, "What? What's long overdue? What are you talking about? What's going on?" His eyes scanned the kitchen, the debris and the wolf. "Who wrecked the place? Where'd Mork come from? And where the hell is Alex?"

Both men looked at each other, then pointed to Mork.

"Mork ate Alex!"

"What? No!" Kyle looked down at Mork anxiously pacing back and forth and then back at Josh. "Let's go sit down somewhere and talk."

Josh, clearly confused, questions bubbling up in his mind, nodded, knowing that the smart thing to do would be to wait for an explanation and then ask questions. While Dr Cooper fetched Annabel, Kyle led the way to the living room, Mork padding softly behind.

"You've known Alex and the family for a long time now," Kyle gestured Josh to sit.

"Yes?"

"And, over and above being an eccentric rock star, have you noticed anything particularly out of the ordinary about him? Anything strange? Something you couldn't explain?"

Josh thought for a moment then shook his head: "Where are we going with this?"

Kyle wrung his hands together.

"Okay, let me try this another way." He put his hand on Mork's head. "Have you ever noticed that Alex's dog Mork has stayed the exact same size and age for the eleven years you've known the family?"

Josh looked down at the animal, then back up at Kyle.

"Well, I … I just presumed you got a replacement at some point?"

"From where? You have any idea how difficult it would be to import an animal like this onto the Island?"

Josh opened his mouth and then closed it again, even more confused.

"Have you ever noticed that you've never seen Alex and Mork together, ever?"

"No, wait … What? Like, 'I'm not saying I'm Batman but have you ever seen me and Batman in the same place at the same time?' Are you trying to tell me that Alex is actually Mork in disguise?"

Josh looked down at Mork, back up at Kyle, then back at Mork.

Just then Annabel walked in with Dr Cooper.

"Oh, thank God, honey, your dad is trying to convince me that Alex and Mork are one and the same."

Annabel looked over at her dad, who shrugged then looked down at Mork who nodded.

"Wait ... did Mork just nod?"

Annabel moved across the room and took Josh's hands in hers, then looked back at Mork.

"Can you show him?"

Mork took a moment to quiet his mind and was hit by a surge of frustration, visions of fire, causing a deep growl to echo out of him as his eyes pulsed bright green light.

"Jesus Christ! The fuck was that!" Josh freed his hands and covered his face. "Okay. Okay, wait ... Let me get this straight." He dropped his hands and looked up at Annabel. "You're actually telling me that Mork and Alex are the same ... What? The same person? That Alex is actually, an honest-to-God werewolf?"

Annabel stared at him for a moment, making sure she was as placid and as matter-of- fact as possible.

"Yes, that is ... exactly what we're telling you."

Josh put his head back in his hands: "Well, I guess that would explain a lot, but, but that's also completely insane. I mean, that sort of thing isn't really ... real. Is it?" Josh looked over at Mork. "Really?"

Mork dipped his head to the side, sighed and nodded.

"Dude, that's so fucking creepy, and weird, and ..." He turned to Annabel again. "Since when?"

Annabel blushed.

"Oh, uhmmm, well ... since he was ten."

Josh turned to Mork.

"This whole time! I'm your best friend and you're only telling me this now?"

He then turned his attention to Annabel and paused, taking a moment to control his voice: "A lot of your dumber-sounding, I guess, blatant lies suddenly make sense."

Annabel blushed again, ashamed.

"I mean, I guess ..." Josh knelt to look into Mork's eyes. "I think I believe you. It does make sense in a really weird kinda way, in a world where things like that are real. You have always been a bit weirder than the rest of us, but, man, I think I understand why you didn't tell me or any of the guys ... But, dude, we love you, you could have. You totally could have."

The words washed over Mork and seeing the change in Josh and hearing the honesty in his voice brought a calm to the room. Mork closed his eyes and a shiver ran over his body, and to Josh's horror, transformed back into Alex. Josh stared wide-eyed at his friend, then quickly stood up, raised a hand pointedly and said, "I ... am going to throw up." He hurried from the room, hand over his mouth, Annabel scurrying after him.

Kyle wrapped a blanket around Alex and sat down next to him.

"What was that about? You've always been so against telling them about it. What changed?"

Alex closed his eyes and took a deep breath, feeling his energy slip away and the urge to go back to bed creeping in behind his eyes.

"Something Cassandra said, that being with me turned her into a liar, turned my whole family into liars. And I just ... I just don't want to be that person."

In Alex's head the sentence continued to, 'I don't want to be a person any more', but he managed to hold back in front of his father and Dr Cooper. As he sat there, he wondered whether thoughts of suicide really mattered if you could never die and it was only when his father wrapped his arms around him that Alex realised that he'd started to cry.

Chapter 25

Alex thought long and hard about what he was going to do, and how he was going to motivate himself to do it – whatever it turned out to be. He'd decided it didn't matter what it was, but it had to be something, anything. He couldn't spend the rest of everyone's life sleeping. His instinct was to find Nuria, but he was afraid Edward was watching, waiting to see what he'd do. Hoping he'd lead him to what he was looking for. And although a part of him wondered what difference it would actually make to reunite them, he simply couldn't face the idea of seeing Edward again, not so soon. Then as his mind started to flood with ever-more horrifying 'what ifs' he reached up and turned the water cold, then quickly stepped out of the shower. Josh sat waiting for him in his room.

"Beer?"

"Sure."

Josh had been holding a couple in anticipation and handed one over; they clinked bottles.

"I've got questions."

"Okay, but can I put on some clothes first?"

Josh smiled and shrugged.

"I mean, yes, but we've been in orgies together."

"We agreed we weren't going to talk about Stanford."

Josh frowned, thinking for a moment: "No, we didn't."

"I know, but I've always liked that line and so rarely get to use it."

Josh shook his head chuckling.

"Goddammit, man, I don't know … You are still you, right? Like, not everything was a lie, right?"

Alex looked at his friend and took a long deep breath.

"Of course not everything was a lie. Really. Only one thing was actually. And it wasn't so much a lie as a secret, one that created lies."

"You know how bad that is, right? I mean, I get it, but you could have told us, could've told me."

Alex dropped his head and searched for words. None came.

"So, you've always had this mystery illness. That's what you told us at the very beginning. Childhood illness. That was what? Werewolfism?"

"Lycanthropy, if you wanna use the Greek word, but yes."

Josh took a calming breath in and long sip of beer.

"And that's why you looked twenty-five at sixteen and haven't aged a day since? That's why you can sing the way you do? Party the way you do? Know when people are angry, sad, scared? It's why you're a lot stronger than you think we think you are."

Alex looked up sharply.

"What?"

"Oh, don't give me that! When we were kids you almost killed someone by kicking them across a room, and then slammed Rick the Dick through a table."

"He did kind of deserve it," Alex said plainly. "But, yes, to all of that, being a werewolf is behind all of that. But, Josh, man, everything we did, everything you know about me is still true."

"Is it? You're a mythical creature that up until an hour ago I didn't

279

believe existed. Everything is different! The car accident with your mom? Bastian's nightmares. His being saved by the family pet? You killed a bunch of people, dude."

Josh stared at him with a look somewhere between fear, anger and disappointment. A flood of emotion coursed through Alex's veins and he stood up fast, knocking his chair back as he did, and started pacing the room.

"What the fuck do you want from me? Yes, yes, yes, to everything. Yes, I've been lying for years; yes, I'm a fucking monster; yes, I saw my nephew in a pool of his own fucking blood and lost control. And yes! I just spent the last three months locked in a cage with a fucking psychopath who decided to prove to me that I couldn't die by repeatedly setting me on fire, because I'm a werewolf! But that's not who I am! It's what I am. Who I am is the same person you've always known."

Tears had once again started rolling down Alex's face and he felt as though his sanity was fraying.

"It's why I missed my mother's funeral, it's why I've chased away every relationship I've ever been in, it's why I know exactly how my mom looked moments before the truck crashed into my side of the car. It's the overwhelming driving force of my life, and that will never change, will never go away. Like, ever. I can't help what I am, or change what I've done. All I can do is change it going forward."

He lifted his chair back up and sat down. A few silent minutes passed with neither looking at the other.

"Are you going to tell the others?" said Josh finally.

Alex took a sip of the beer, mulling it over.

"I mean, just because I'm a werewolf doesn't change the fact that Brandon can't keep secrets."

Josh half smiled but seemed to stop himself.

"He can when it's important."

Alex took another sip of beer.

"I don't know, man, I ... I don't know a lot of things at the moment." He emptied the bottle. "It's always been something that's defined my life, but I'd always felt in control of it, but, but now ... I just don't know."

"What changed?"

"The dude who kidnapped me, he ... he was also a werewolf. Is also a werewolf. He told me things and then tortured me to prove them."

Alex's vision drifted as he thought back to the fire, the incessant flames.

"Jesus, man. That the only other one you've ever met?"

"No, I've found two others. It's actually why he took me, he wanted me to tell him how I found them."

"Did you?"

Alex looked up and shrugged.

"I don't know. I don't think so – I know I swore I would never ... but there are a lot of blank spots."

Josh moved closer and put his hands over Alex's.

"Dude, what do you think you want to do now? I mean, like, maybe if we just start trying things, we'll either hit on something that works or you'll be so distracted by the doing that it'll help, almost by accident."

"I don't know. Normal rock-star stuff, those distractions? Getting drunk and getting laid." Alex paused briefly. "Which reminds me. How's Brandon?"

Josh returned to his seat and threw back the last of his beer.

"He did all that stuff for a bit; we think he only actually banged one girl though and they're now kinda a couple. Which of course Bitch tried to use against him in the divorce, but your dad and sister helped out, making sure she gets absolutely nothing. Like, zero. She was soooo pissed."

Alex nodded approvingly.

"What's this new one like?"

"Nice, actually. Took her a bit to get over the groupie kind of excitement, which put Danny off right away, but now that she's calmed down, she's actually super sweet. And real kind. She did try setting Danny up with one of her girlfriends though."

Alex snorted.

"How did that go?"

Josh smiled.

"It was at a party and she turned up with this girl, also sweet and a bit shy, but smart too, and she clocked on real quick, thank God. I think they did end up hanging out for a bit after that."

"That's cool. Danny actually seeing anyone at the moment?"

Josh shrugged.

"Don't think so ... He'd probably have mentioned it if he was, but you know him, almost as secretive as you are."

A childlike smile spread across Josh's face and his eyes practically sparkled with excitement.

"You don't think he's also some kind of mythical creature, do you?"

Alex mirrored the smile, more relieved than he'd ever been.

"If you say unicorn, I'm telling."

"Dude! I didn't say that! Also, what just happened? You were the master of secrets ten minutes ago, now you're Brandon?"

They both threw their heads back and laughed, good clean honest laughter that cleared the air in the room, and it took a minute or two before they managed to pull themselves together.

"Can I put some clothes on now, please?"

For the first time since having been found, Alex felt okay again, safe even. It was only fleeting, but it provided the spark of hope that things could be good, life could be fun again.

Chapter 26

As Alex dressed, he considered his actions, his options, and his life. Seeing it now only as a fraction of a much, much longer journey, he realised something. He realised that his fears had been based on something that no longer exists, his own mortality, and to hide his findings from the only other person he really knew was in the same boat as him was a fear carried over from that other life, his past life, a life that no longer existed or, perhaps, never existed. To fear what Edward would do if he contacted Nuria was quite simply a waste of time, a waste of energy. It didn't matter. Edward couldn't kill either of them, so who cared whether he followed him or not. Nothing he did mattered.

The words hung on his shoulders like a weight but he felt that he was able to carry it, finally. He had made up his mind and immediately headed back into the kitchen to face his family, feeling for the first time both resolute and present. At last he felt as though he was out of the cage and back in the real world, and that freedom gave him strength, even if it also put distance between them and him.

Besides, he was also still incredibly hungry.

He smiled at his gathered family, their faces all turned to him with nervous apprehension. They hadn't noticed the change, and that was okay. From where they stood, he had gone from bad to worse all while he had been asleep. He smiled at them through the silence.

"So ... how about a giant pile of sushi?"

He knew what he was going to do, in many ways, he'd always known what he was going to do – but there was no need to jump the gun, to take that leap too soon. He needed to breathe on it, think on it, and most of all eat. He'd slept on it enough.

They called Brandon and Danny and arranged an impromptu party at their favourite sushi place.

In the taxi Alex caught Josh nervously eyeing Annabel and realised that his confession had caused problems, had become something of an issue.

"So?" said Josh when he noticed Alex watching them. "What have you decided about the others?"

"Yeah, I'm going to. Not at dinner, but yes, I think so. I have quite a lot of food to catch up on, but I ... feel better. More like myself. In fact, I feel more like me than I have in a really long time."

The car went quiet. The others looked him over and they believed him.

Brandon and Danny both threw themselves at him when they arrived at the restaurant and Josh, not to be left out, joined in for what turned into a two-minute tear-filled group hug. Once they all finally let go, Brandon's face lit up again as he took the hand of an attractive blonde in her late twenties. She, on the other hand, flushed crimson as she was all but dragged in front of Alex.

"This ..." Brandon announced with a flourish. "This is Ashley."

Ashley managed to pull herself together enough to at least conjure up a smile.

"Hello."

Alex cocked an eyebrow and smiled broadly.

"Hi."

Although she'd gotten used to the band, he was still Alex Harris, frontman and lead singer, and her blush deepened, which made him smile, until Danny put a hand on his shoulder.

"Hey," he said, "stop that. We like her, so be nice."

"That's great to hear," Alex laughed, conscious to not add "finally".

"And it's very nice to meet you, Ashley."

Still blushing a little, she reminded herself that she was, in fact, dating a rock star and that the lead singer was just another person. Alex proceeded to order rounds of drinks and bottles of expensive wine for the entire restaurant as an advanced apology for the night they were likely to have, and then promptly ordered three of everything on the menu.

He enjoyed watching his friends and family interacting and only really joined the conversation at key points. It reminded him of being behind the bar at The Sanctuary, watching everyone not paying attention to him. It made him feel like a normal everyday person – even if the table groaned under more food than most people ate in a week. Dr Cooper was the first to try to leave, confident that Alex was finally looking up and moving forward. Alex, however, stopped him.

"Hey, Doc, I have something planned, please don't leave."

"What kind of a thing?"

Dr Cooper's comment caught the attention of Kyle and suddenly a hush fell over the table as they all turned their eyes towards Alex. Dr Cooper cringed at the thought that he'd pre-empted something important. Fear rose in the room, but Alex still smiled.

"I … hi, everybody, it's … it's really great to see you all, and hear you all and laugh and drink and have fun, and relax. I know it's a cliché but I really can feel the love at this table. I can't think of a single thing any of us wouldn't do for one another and that's just amazing. It genuinely warms my heart."

Alex took a moment to look everyone over, to gauge their reactions, their expectations, and took a weird kind of comfort that the whole band, and his family, all seemed to know where it was going.

"I guess … I guess I'm not that subtle. But knowing how much we all love each other actually makes this easier. Because I know you're all safe." He stopped briefly to look inward, to make sure he was being honest with himself. "I'm going to leave again, and this time … this time I don't think I'm coming back."

Before he could continue Josh stood and cut him off.

"But you said you were feeling more like yourself, more like you. That mean that the real you wants to leave us? All of us?"

Alex looked at his friend and saw the pain and the fear in his eyes.

"It's not about want. I love you. All of you. And I know it doesn't make sense to you right now, but … I have to. It's part of who I am, part of what I am. I can't fully explain it, and I'm sorry for that – I know it hurts." Alex broke eye contact. "I have to go."

Josh sank back down and, as had happened so often in the past at times of ressure and pain, Danny spoke up.

"We will always be here for you, man. You can always come to us, you know that. I get, no, we get that you have to do some stuff alone, but you don't have to do it alone. But … I understand. And, in time, everyone else will understand too." He reached his hands out and took Brandon and Josh under his arms. "But you don't have to be alone, you don't have to leave. And you can always come back."

"See?" There was a tremor in Alex's voice. "Everything really is going to be fine. And I appreciate you all so much. But, but it's time. I'm … sorry." He raised his glass, wiping his sleeve across his face to dry his eyes. "To all of you, a better family doesn't exist."

He swallowed his drink in one, and just watched them watching him, allowing himself to be at the mercy of their gaze. After a few moments he put his glass down and grabbed his jacket from the back of his chair.

"Right … right, I love you, and goodbye."

Mouths opened in shock and voices failed as Alex nodded and turned towards the door. Outside he hailed a taxi and before he could climb in Annabel, finally able to pull herself together, appeared on the sidewalk beside him. Her voice sharp, pained.

"What do you think you're doing?"

He turned to face his furious and terrified sister.

"Exactly what I said I was doing."

"But, but now? Like right now?"

"Yes."

A shiver ran over her whole body as a mix of fear and pain washed over her. "What about Bastian? Not even going to say goodbye to him?"

"He's better off without me," Alex's voice was steady, calm and left no room to argue. "I have only ever been a chaotic force in his life, a temporary one, someone who came and went. Never constant, never reliable."

"But he loves you," Annabel's voice caught. "We all love you and we don't want you to leave."

Alex put his hands on her shoulders and rested his forehead against hers.

"I know."

They stood like that for a minute before he gently kissed her cheek, and climbed into the taxi.

Chapter 27

It took Alex two full days to get to the farm. He had had to take two flights, one across to the United States and then one up to Canada. He considered running from the airport but even though he knew he had the time, he was also impatient. So, as a final act of fame, he bought a sports car. Nuria was sitting on the steps outside the front door when he pulled into the drive.

"Expecting me?"

"Yes. Actually. Your family has been on the phone with your grandmother almost constantly. Everyone thinks you're coming here."

"Well, they're smart people."

From inside, Alex heard his grandmother call his name and then she appeared in the doorway.

"Alex, my boy, come here."

She held out her arms and he walked into them, wrapping his around her.

"Hi, Grandma."

"So this is your big plan, after everything you've been through you're finally going to come and run the farm? Just like we all originally thought way back when."

Alex was a little stunned for a second, then let out a laugh.

"You know, I hadn't thought about that, or how it might look. That's actually really funny." His laughter faded quickly as he relaxed his hug and stepped back. "But no, no – I'm here to steal your helper."

Behind him Nuria frowned.

"Pardon?" she said.

He turned to her: "Let's sit down and have some coffee, I think we need to talk."

The women nodded and exchanged glances.

"Now that sounds sensible," said Nuria.

As was always the case on the farm, coffee had either just been made or was about to be, so it didn't take long before they were all sitting quietly at the kitchen table that was the heart of his grandparents' home.

Alex let his mind go to places he hated and, despite himself, his eyes welled up.

"I met Edward."

Nuria gasped and spluttered her coffee.

"Where?"

"That's where I was when I was kidnapped. He ... took me."

Marie took a long, slow breath. She wasn't the one Alex had come to see, and she knew it wasn't the moment to start poking into the conversation.

Alex then proceeded to explain what had happened to him, to the Order, and finally immortality.

"But it can't be, it can't be," Nuria shook her head. "Vincent always insisted that it wasn't true."

"I think ... I think he did that to give you hope. But Edward... convinced me, the hard way."

Nuria lowered her head into her hands, breathing in everything he'd said, what it all meant. She sat up sharply. She sniffed the air, and turned as her eyes flashed green. Prompted, Alex mimicked her and stood when he realised what she had smelt. He reached out a hand and covered Nuria's.

"I ... I kinda knew this would happen."

"You lead him here? Why?"

"Technically, yes. But, also, it doesn't really matter."

Edward gently knocked on the doorframe.

"Hello, Nuria." There was no mistaking that smirk.

A shiver ran over her body.

"Edward."

Alex looked at them and then at his grandmother.

"Don't worry, everything's going to be just fine." He rose from his chair and turned to Edward. "I hate you," he said.

The flat honesty in his voice caused Edward's back to stiffen, his hackles to rise.

"I really, really, hate you," Alex breathed a sigh and shrugged. "That said, would you like some coffee?"

"Yes, thank you."

Edward took a seat at the table, and Alex poured more coffee.

"You want to tell us something, don't you, boy?" said Edward as Alex handed him a cup. "You brought us here for a reason."

Alex looked across at his grandmother.

"I'm ... I'm sorry, Grandma but ... but can ... can you leave?"

"What?"

"I ... I can't say what I need to say with you here. I love you, but I can't."

She looked at him a little hurt and a little worried, but smiled and nodded.

"I love you," she said, patting him on his hand. "I trust you, and I trust Nuria. I'll be in my room pretending to read if you need anything or want me back. Just don't leave without saying goodbye."

Alex rose with her and they hugged before she left the room. Still standing, he then turned to the others and was a little surprised to find that even Edward looked wary. Alex slumped into a chair as soon as he heard the bedroom door close. He looked visibly older.

"I ... I can't, and won't keep living like this." He looked up at Edward. "You took that away from me. You took away any hope or chance I ever had of living a normal life, a happy life with the people I love. Even if it was only ever temporary, you stole something very precious from me and I hate you for it ... But that's not the same as blaming you."

The words struck Edward and he rocked back in his chair as he felt the power behind them. There was nothing mystical about them but the weight of the honesty sank hooks into his shoulder and pulled him down.

"I'm ... I'm sorry. I hadn't thought about that. I haven't thought a lot of things through for a very long time."

Nuria's eyes darted from Alex to Edward, then back to Alex. "I don't think you would have told me if you didn't have some sort of plan, some idea," she said to Alex. "You aren't that man. Or I hope not."

Alex smiled.

"A part of me has always felt out of control and wild. I can always feel the wolf, pacing behind my eyes, waiting to burst out at a moment's notice." Three pairs of eyes shone green in the dimness of the kitchen. "But I could contain that feeling of recklessness, knowing I could always kill myself. If the horror movies ever came true I knew that I still had that control. It wasn't an active thought, I didn't think about it every day, but I think the idea was always there. Not that I ever wanted to, but that I could. There was that possibility, a way out. But now that I know that I can't, all I want to do is die. It's in my head, a constant whisper behind every thought."

Edward and Nuria both turned their gazes to him and he could feel the pressure of their thoughts on him, wordlessly willing him to explain more.

"I'm going to end Alex, by becoming Mork," he said. "I'm going to stop being a man who can become a wolf, and become a wolf who can become a man." He gestured at himself. "I'm not going to be this person anymore." He put a hand over his heart. "I'm going to embrace my other side. And I want you to join me."

They looked at him, and then at each other and then back at him.

"And then?" Edward asked. "What then?"

"And then we run, and we hunt, and we run and we never stop moving and we forget what it is to be human. And maybe we become reborn as wolves, or perhaps even other people later, but I have spent my life living one way and it's not working."

Nervously, Nuria shot a glance at Edward and almost whispered: "What's the longest you've ever stayed a wolf?"

Edward let his mind wander over painful memories.

"A week? Maybe. Time gets a little fuzzy when you have been immolated. You?"

"Around the same."

Alex took a breath and butted in.

"A couple of months." His words drew their attention back to him and he squared his shoulders. "But even after a few weeks I could feel the difference, and it's that difference that is guiding me, that feeling of forgetting what it is to be human. I think … I think, that sounds like death and it feels right."

Nuria thought about Alex's grandmother and looked at him through sympathetic eyes.

"But what about your family?"

Tears immediately started streaming down his face.

"I will not sit on the side of life and watch the people I love die, one by one. I cannot spend the next thousand years collecting tombstones." His whole body shuddered and every hair seemed to stand on end. "No … no, I won't, I can't do that. …"

Then a voice whispered through each of their minds, a calming familiar sound that got them all to stand as one.

"He's right," it said, and they spun around, desperate for the source, the person it belonged to. And there he was. Standing in the field behind the house. Jet-black hair down to his shoulders, a beard as thick as sheep's wool, eyes the colour of emeralds. Edward's knees began to shake, Nuria's hand to tremble.

Slowly, they all walked out to meet him, simultaneously empowered and terrified. They stopped in front of him and he smiled at them all, then focused on Alex.

"Boy, I am Vincent."

Alex swallowed.

Vincent nodded and turned to the others.

"My children, it's been a very long time."

Nuria looked down, Edward fighting an internal battle with himself. Part of him wanting to lunge for Vincent, scream accusations, vent pain, enact violence, and cry. But he also found peace in finally standing in front of him. Vincent raised a hand in acknowledgment.

"I know, and I understand, and I'm sorry."

Edward opened his mouth, hoping words would simply come out, but none did.

They stood in silence for a few more moments, the four of them, just soaking up each other's presence.

Finally, Alex turned to Vincent.

"I just need to go say goodbye to my grandmother."

The End.

MOSTLY HUMAN²

D.I. JOLLY

Photo: Ted Titus

A Guy, a Girl and a Voodoo Monkey Hand

A quirky tongue-in-cheek story about a detective with a difference and it's not his caffeine addiction or his strange collection of friends.

Through the course of three cases, Jones P.I. starts to discover that maybe he doesn't know that much about life, love and everything. Set on Syn Island a man-made enclave originally created as a maximum security prison but long since decommissioned and left for a few generations. It has now become one of the world's strongest economies, exporting brain power and work ethic. Changed it's become a city like any other filled with jazz, crime, mobsters, dark alleyways and more than a few night-time adventures.

Counting Sheep & Other Stories

From the acclaimed author of **A Guy, a Girl and a Voodoo Monkey Hand**. D.I. Jolly brings you this collection of Short stories.

Counting Sheep & Other Stories is written with the usual wit, irreverence and barbed comments that you expect from this modern writer.

Marvel as he takes you on a tour around the Sleep factories of a future world, immerses your imagination in the mythic cultures of mermaids, shows you the real side of a boy made from wood and much, much more.

This is a perfect introduction to this writer at a perfect price!

Mostly Human *Young Adult*

Alex Harris is a world famous rock star and lead singer of the Internationally acclaimed band The Waterdogs.

But Alex is no ordinary rocker, and has a secret that he and his family have painstakingly kept since he was ten years old. Whilst playing on his grandparents farm, Alex discovers what he presumes is a dead wolf. With a slip of the hand he realises it's not as dead as he thought, and come the first full moon, everyone realises it wasn't just a wolf.

What would you do if your son could never be normal again?

Berlin Poetry Club Volume 1 (Mature)

From the acclaimed author of **A Guy, a Girl and a Voodoo Monkey Hand**, **Counting Sheep & Other Stories** and **Mostly Human**. D.I. Jolly brings you this **Top Twenty Bestselling** collection of short stories.

Taking you deep into complex kaleidoscopic worlds inhabited by characters that reflect the darker and lighter sides of the human condition and it's psyche.

Presented in bite sized vignettes this collection of short stories takes its protagonists' and reader's on a physical, emotional and psychological journey.

Printed in Great Britain
by Amazon

86854419R00169